**Two brand-new stories in every volume...
twice a month!**

### Duets Vol. #57

Popular Jill Shalvis serves up a delightful duo—
the disaster-prone Anderson twins and the sexy men
they meet!—in a humorous special Double Duets!
*Rendezvous* says this author is "fast, fanciful
and funny. Get ready for laughs, passion
and toe-curling romance."

### Duets Vol. #58

Two talented new writers make their Duets debut
this month. Look for Candy Halliday's playful romp
about a bad boy who has a soft spot for his pooch—
and the gorgeous dog owner next door!
Then nurse-turned-writer Dianne Drake will tickle
your funny bone and send temperatures rising
with a fun story about a small-town medical practice.

**Be sure to pick up both Duets volumes today!**

## *"Cancel,"* Tanner whispered in her ear.

"Back off," Cami said. "You're making my knees weak."

"Really?" In an odd sort of male way, hearing that pleased Tanner greatly. "Just say you've come down with blind date-itis," he persisted. "Tell him you break out in hives in restaurants, that you drool when you eat."

Her shoulders went back. "I never drool."

"Then say you made a mistake and you already have a date tonight—first come, first served."

She looked at him, her eyes dark. "But I don't have another date."

He could drown in those eyes, if she wasn't such a pain in the rear. "I could take you out," he heard himself say.

"But you don't even like me that much."

"Yes, I do."

"Really? What do you like about me?"

"I..." Tanner liked the way she looked wet out of the shower without a towel, but he sincerely doubted that was the correct answer.

*For more, turn to page 9*

## *"Don't say the word sex."*

Dimi put a finger on his lips, but Mitch was able to ask, "Why not?"

"Because when you say it, it does something funny to my knees."

Mitch liked that. She was close, her mouth softly parted, her eyes slumberous. He liked that, too. "Kiss me, Dimi."

"Uh." She swallowed, hard. "That would be extremely unwise."

"Think of all the fire it will give the show today," he coaxed, but that was where he made his mistake. He knew it as soon as her eyes cooled and her mouth hardened.

"That's right," she said, pulling back from him. "The show. This is all for the show." She gave him a tight smile. "Let's just save it for the camera, then, shall we?"

Grabbing her purse off the counter, she walked away without another look at him, back to the serious, quiet, original Dimi—not a cooking sex kitten in sight.

"Note to self," Mitch muttered. "Next time you get Dimi in your arms, don't open your idiotic mouth."

*For more, turn to page 197*

HARLEQUIN DUETS

ISBN 0-373-44123-1

BLIND DATE DISASTERS
Copyright © 2001 by Jill Shalvis

EAT YOUR HEART OUT
Copyright © 2001 by Jill Shalvis

This edition published by arrangement with Harlequin Books S.A.

® and TM are trademarks of the publisher. Trademarks indicated with
® are registered in the United States Patent and Trademark Office, the
Canadian Trade Marks Office and in other countries.

Visit us at www.eHarlequin.com

Printed in U.S.A.

# Blind Date Disasters

## Jill Shalvis

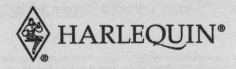

# HARLEQUIN®

TORONTO • NEW YORK • LONDON
AMSTERDAM • PARIS • SYDNEY • HAMBURG
STOCKHOLM • ATHENS • TOKYO • MILAN • MADRID
PRAGUE • WARSAW • BUDAPEST • AUCKLAND

Dear Reader,

I've never had quite so much fun torturing my characters as they navigate the tricky waters of love. Cami and Dimi, twins who are equally cursed in love, had decided to not even attempt it, but I managed to convince them otherwise. Cami, the more easygoing, whimsical twin, has a little problem with the word *no*. Which means she wears the proverbial doormat on her head that says "Oh please take advantage of me." This is how she ends up going on one blind date disaster after another, only to discover love has been right beneath her nose all along.

*Love* is a four-letter word in serious twin Dimi's mind. After all, it has never given her anything but grief. As host and chef of a cooking show, she decides food can be her life. That is, until her new producer walks onto her set and turns everything upside down, including her heart.

I hope you enjoy my special Double Duets.

Happy Reading!

*Jill Shalvis*

P.S. You can write to me at P.O, Box 3945, Truckee, CA 96160. And keep an eye out for my upcoming Temptation Heat, *Aftershock*, in September 2001!

# 1

THERE WAS NOTHING good to say about a Monday, especially a Monday *morning,* except maybe that the weekend was only five days away.

Cami Anderson hated Mondays with the same passion she loved Saturdays, so when the obnoxiously loud alarm clock on her nightstand went off for the third time, she nudged it gently.

Well, not so gently, since it flew right over the edge and crashed to the floor. But at least it went silent.

Sighing, she pressed farther into her soft, warm, comfy bed and tried to ignore the zealous morning sun spearing her in the face. She managed it, too, for one lovely moment, during which time she floated pleasantly in dreamland, which was filled with fattening food and gorgeous men. All the harsh realities of life, such as balancing her unbalanceable checkbook and pleasing her unpleasable mother, vanished.

But then something plopped on her head and

she was suffocating, blinded, held down and... choking on fur.

"Annabel!" Shoving free, Cami sat up, spitting out cat hair. "Yuck!"

Finding herself unceremoniously dumped to the floor, the tabby sniffed. Her tail whipped the air, and after a moment's reflection she leaped onto the bed.

"Meow." She butted her head against Cami's cheek.

"No, it's not time for food yet." Thinking she could catch a few more precious moments, Cami flipped over and buried her head beneath her pillow.

Mornings should be illegal. They needed a new law—the day should begin at a more godly hour. Say *noon.*

*Never going to catch a man lying in bed all day,* her mother always told her. Well, Cami was fairly certain one *could* catch a man doing exactly that—if a woman was any good at it, which apparently, given her marital status and lack of a single prospective date in the near future, Cami was not.

Annabel settled on her tush this time, fortunately a padded area, as she used her paws, claws extended, to knead the spot before settling.

"Ouch!"

"Mew."

"Later," Cami muttered, deliciously close to catching a few more Zs. She was past the checkbook, past her mother tsking, past everything and picturing herself on a beach.

A tropical beach.

A faraway tropical beach with really cute guys on it. Yeah, there was a picture. Bronzed and gloriously built. Naked, too, their hands filled with suntan oil, which they rubbed over her body and—

The doorbell rang, ruining that fantasy.

Cami groaned and tried to pretend she hadn't heard it. Doorbells should be illegal, too, she decided. Maybe she'd change her plans and become a politician, just so she could make some new laws.

"Naked guys," she murmured, hoping to coax her terrific dream back. "With lots of suntan oil—"

The doorbell rang again.

"Mew."

*Darn it!* "Yeah, yeah. I heard it." She couldn't be faulted for not being a morning person. It was a personality flaw and therefore beyond her control.

"Coming," she called weakly, staggering naked out of the bed, naked because, no big surprise, she'd once again neglected her laundry.

Who would be calling on her this early— *Oh, boy.* It was almost…she had to blink at the clock for a moment to be sure. *Eleven?* She shot a guilty look at Annabel, whose green, unblinking eyes stared right back, clearly vindicated.

"Okay, maybe it's time for food," she said, relenting.

"Mew." *Duh.*

Cami's head pounded. Her stomach quivered nervously. Strange, since she was usually healthy as an ox. "Thanks, Dimi," she muttered, cursing her evil twin sister, who thankfully no longer lived with her. It had been Dimi who encouraged Cami to drink the two little itsy bitsy glasses of champagne in celebration, when Cami was a known lightweight who rarely drank at all. "Come on, Cami, it won't hurt you," Cami said, perfectly mimicking her sister.

The doorbell shrieked again, and she grated her teeth as the sound reverberated through her head, jangling her brain and hurting her teeth. "Coming!" Tugging her blanket around her, nearly tripping over Annabel in the process, she reached for the door, prepared to blast the visitor to bits.

Assuming it was Dimi. But then again, it was always Dimi, because other than her twenty-six-year-old twin, Cami didn't have much of a life. Neither did Dimi. Sorry state of affairs *that* was for two former Truckee High School beauty queens.

It wasn't for lack of trying. Cami, the clown of the family, had always had a sweet spot for a man with a ready smile and a quick wit. Dimi, the serious twin, preferred a man with the ability to hold down a job. There weren't many to choose from, but they'd done their best.

Being single in today's world was horrible. No matter that they'd both given it the old college try—dating, searching, yearning for Mr. Right.

Neither of them had found him.

Instead, they commiserated with each other on the sad state of the single male population. There was something wrong with every one of them. There was something wrong with society. There was something wrong with life, but the blame couldn't lie with them.

Could it?

Deciding that it indeed could, they'd agreed to *get* lives.

*Separate* lives.

So Dimi had moved out of Cami's town house

and into her own...all the way on the other side of the small complex, which constituted an entire fifty-foot walk. Silly, maybe. But at least Cami no longer had to share her razors, and there were always potato chips in the cupboard when she needed them, which was often.

Cami hauled open the door. "Thanks a lot for the hangover—"

*Oops.*

Not Dimi.

Not even female.

Male. Oh, most definitely male. *Gorgeous* male. "I— You— Um..." Cami let out an unnerved smile and started over. "Hi."

"Hi," the magnificent male said, smiling into her confusion. He looked at Annabel, who was leaning on Cami, eyeing him as if he were breakfast. "Hi to you, too," he said in a voice that could have melted the Arctic.

Annabel, who hated everyone except Cami on sight, left her mistress without a word and rubbed against his legs. They were very fine legs, too, encased in denim. Above those fine legs, were lean hips around which lay a tool belt. Above that was the finest-looking torso she'd ever seen, covered in a blue T-shirt and an unbuttoned plaid work shirt. And that was only the beginning, because then there were wide shoulders, a strong, tanned neck…and his frowning face.

"Do I have the wrong day?" he inquired. "I thought you said Monday."

"Monday? *Oh!*" Cami gaped at him, then winced and held her head because thinking was a big mistake on a two-glasses-of-champagne hangover. "Oh, no." It was all coming back to her now. Today. Her life. What she and Dimi had been celebrating last night. "You…you're—?"

"Tanner James," he said, holding out his big, work-roughened hand.

Oh, God. How could she have forgotten, even for a second, that today was the first day of the rest of her life?

Somehow between the dinner celebration last night and the pounding in her head this morning, she'd managed to forget everything she'd ever wanted was about to come true. She'd truly done it, she'd graduated design school and was officially an interior designer.

At just the thought, she grinned widely. It hurt, because everything anywhere near her head hurt, but she couldn't contain herself. The clown, the screwup, the Anderson everyone was certain would never amount to anything but a good time, actually had a career right in front of her, a career she wanted with all her heart.

Even if she didn't have any clean underwear.

Now all she needed were clients. And since appearances were everything, she figured she'd start with her own town house, fix it up, make it her own personal showcase. It wasn't a bad place to start. The small complex, which consisted of only four town houses, was in the town of Truckee, right on Donner Lake, a place not only immensely rich in western history but California legend, as well. The structure had been built in the late 1800s, which meant she'd have to deal with the historical society, but that was a minor detail compared to the challenge posed by the browns, greens and hideous yellows of the early seventies that dominated the place.

Needing a master carpenter, she'd sent out plans, taken bids and picked a contractor. She'd figured on someone older, someone experienced.

She hadn't figured on one Tanner James, who wasn't old, but who was, with that come-get-me look, most undoubtedly experienced—in making women's knees weak.

Not good. She needed to stay focused here "Um…"

"You are Cami Anderson, right?"

"Yes."

"So I have the right place."

"Yes, but—"

"Good." He shifted his big body impatiently. "Why don't you show me what you've got?"

"*What?*" She pulled her blanket tighter around the body that had been a curse all her life. Too tall. Too curvy. Too everything. The everything part consisted of five pounds too much fat, which brought her back to the potato chip thing. Actually, it was also a chocolate chip thing. And an ice cream thing. And okay, it might have been *ten* pounds, but who was counting?

"Your town house? The work I bid on?" The man's brow furrowed as he studied her. "You still want it done, correct?"

"Yes." She let out a little laugh. She was an idiot, thinking he'd even noticed her as a woman. "Yes, of course. The work."

"Good, then." His face was carefully bland, as if he was afraid to upset the crazy lady. "Let's get started. I hate getting going this late in the day."

Alarm bells rang in her head—not good, given her already firmly in place headache. "Just out of curiosity, what would you consider a good start time?"

*Noon,* she willed him to say. She'd probably even hug him in gratitude.

"Six."

She nearly dropped her blanket. *"In the morning?"*

"Yep."

*Oh, Lord.* Not only was he damn distracting with all sun-kissed, light doe-colored hair and even more intense doe-colored eyes, but he was a morning person, too?

This was not going well, but she hadn't had any caffeine yet and couldn't cope.

So she led him into the foyer, beyond which was the living room, which had been sorely abused by the previous owner. The walls were puke green and the carpeting puke orange. The windows were in horrible shape, as well, and bare since she'd stripped down the obnoxious shades covering them the day she'd moved in.

And for some unknown reason, there were half walls in three places, turning what could have been a wonderful, huge, open, airy room into a monstrosity.

"Ugh," Tanner said behind her.

"Yeah. I moved in last year, but I've been swamped with school and work until now." Self-consciously she tugged at the blanket, making sure she was completely covered, not that he'd given her a second glance.

As they walked, she caught sight of herself in the tiled mirror hanging in her foyer…and nearly croaked on the spot.

Her hair stood straight up in spots, and yet was matted down in others, where she'd lain on it all night. The right side of her face had a lovely red spot smashed into it, obviously from her pillow. Her eyes were completely void of makeup, and puffy.

The only thing she had going for her was that she wasn't drooling. At the moment, anyway.

Some ex-beauty queen. "I'll…be back in a minute," she said, amazed he hadn't run from her screaming in horror.

"Take your time." Clearly distracted, he pulled out the plans she'd sent him when he'd made his bid. "This is far worse than I remembered."

"Excuse me?"

"Your town house." He lifted his clipboard, which had a sticker on it that said, Life Sucks, Wear a Hard Hat, and started making notes. "It's horrible."

Feeling defensive, she halted. "Nothing a little fixing up won't cure."

"Oh, I know. Beneath your tacky paint job and

ridiculous wall placement, this place has huge potential. Don't worry, I'll see to it."

"It's not *my* tacky paint job," she said, wanting to be clear on that, and also feeling a little... jealous at his confidence in his abilities.

"Uh-huh," he said, not looking up from where he was scribbling furiously on his clipboard.

"And those walls? I had nothing to do with them."

"Yep."

She was standing there, practically buck naked, trying to convince the man that she hadn't decorated the place this way, and he didn't care.

She had to laugh at herself. "At least you're honest," she said to his back.

He didn't appear to hear her, or if he did, didn't feel the need to respond. Hunkering down, he spread the plans on the floor, oblivious to the way his shirt stretched over all his interesting muscles and how his tool belt tugged at his jeans, exposing a good inch of sleek, taut, tanned skin across his lower back.

Contractors were supposed to have beer bellies and too much butt crack showing.

Tanner had neither.

And what was he doing as she ogled him? He appeared to have forgotten all about her.

Wasn't that just the crowning glory on her ego.

Sighing, Cami continued out of the room, thinking maybe it wasn't so bad being single, really. She didn't have to worry about bed head. Or clean clothes. She didn't have to worry about her extra ten pounds. Much.

Besides, if she ever got herself a man—and if her mother had anything to do with it, she would—then she wanted a really great one, who could both laugh *and* think, maybe even at the same time.

Ha! There wasn't any such man.

But if there were, and she did, it wouldn't be Mr. Not-Even-Notice-Her, no matter how sexy she'd just realized a tool belt could be.

# 2

CAMI REALLY NEEDED pain relief, coffee and a shower, and not necessarily in that order. Then, and only then, could she perk up and be truly ecstatic about her future.

But she didn't have time. She actually had a man waiting for her, not an everyday occurrence. Granted, he was her contractor, but he *was* waiting for her.

In her bedroom, she managed to pull on a blouse and socks. Then the phone rang. She continued searching for her pants, which had been on the floor the last time she'd checked, mostly because she never had an available hanger. What was that about, anyway? It ranked right up there as one of life's little mysteries, next to why her keys were never where she'd last put them.

"Mew."

"I know," Cami said, on her hands and knees now, peering beneath her bed. "You want food. Go tell your new lover boy."

Annabel shot her a snooty look as the phone continued to ring.

"Where's my Advil? *Hello?*" she said into the receiver, just as she found her pants, but naturally they had a stain on them. "Oh, damn."

"Young lady, what kind of language is *that?*"

Perfect. Her mother was half Italian and half Irish. They didn't come any more bossy, stubborn or domineering than Sara Lynn Anderson, who alternated between attempting to run Cami's life and praying for her daughter's soul to keep it safe from the devil.

"Sorry, Mom. I didn't know it was you." Because if she had, she wouldn't have picked it up.

"Never mind, darling. Look, I wanted to talk to you."

*Never mind?* Cami had used a swear word and her mother had said never mind? All Cami's problems vanished as she sank to the bed and clutched the phone.

Someone had to be sick.

Dying.

Or already dead. "What's the matter?" she demanded, just as bossy, stubborn and domineering as her mother. "Tell me. I can take it."

"Nothing."

"Mom!"

"I just have a little favor, that's all. Can't a mother call her own daughter for one little favor?"

Cami was so relieved she let her guard down. A bad mistake with her mother. "Well, of course you can."

"I need you to go out with—"

"Oh, no, you don't." It didn't take a rocket scientist to know where this was going. "Not another blind date."

Her mother had started this when Cami and her sister turned twenty-one and she hadn't wavered in her single, solitary mission to marry her daughters off in order to get grandchildren.

"It's just one little date, Cami. One little favor. Just one little short night out of your life."

"Too many littles."

Maybe deep, *deep* down Cami had the same happily-ever-after dream for herself that her mother did, but she wasn't going to admit it to the woman who had given her more blind dates from hell than any dating service ever could. Plus, truth told, Cami was terrified of finding Mr. Right. She didn't *believe* in Mr. Right. *"No."*

"Just because you think you've got it all together now that you've received your design degree doesn't mean your future is set."

"My future is fine."

"Really? Is your laundry done?"

Cami glanced guiltily at the pile of dirty clothes in the corner behind the door. "What does that have to do with anything!"

"So it's not."

"No to the date. Double no. *Triple* no."

"Oh, sure." Her mother's voice softened as she switched tactics, became vulnerable. Sad. "Turn me down in my time of need. I understand. I only spent twenty-four long, sweaty, torturous hours in labor with you and Dimi, and—"

"And we nearly killed you," Cami said in tune with her mother, who was really getting into the story now, and had even mustered tears in her voice. "I know, Mom," she said, rubbing her forehead and the ache that settled there every time she spoke with her mother. "I remember." How could she forget when her mother pulled this story out at every turn?

"I'm going to die soon, you know."

"Oh, no, you're not," Cami said with a laugh. "You're going to outlive us all."

"You never know."

*"Mom."*

"You'd really send me off to heaven, where you know I'm going to run into Aunt Bev and

Cici, both of whom had daughters who gave them *five* grandchildren? *Each?*''

"Mom—"

"All I'm asking for is one little bundle of love to treasure in my final days, one grandchild. But apparently even that's too much.''

Cami's headache increased in pressure so that she could see herself keeling over in nothing but her shirt, socks and panties, with Mr. Sexy Tool Belt the only one around to resuscitate her. "Look, Mom, you know I love you, but—"

"He's very handsome, too. I promise.''

"Who?''

"Your date! Keep up, Cami. He's Great-Aunt Lulu's cousin's brother-in-law, and she swears by him, which is good enough for me. I hear he makes a wonderful living doing those fancy dub-dub-dub thingies…what are they called again?''

"Web sites." Cami let out a soundless sigh, tipped her head back and stared at the ceiling. As if divine intervention could help when it came to her mother! No one could help, not even God, not when Sara Lynn Anderson had made up her mind.

"You sound busy." Her mother sniffed in that way all mothers have that insures guilt to the tenth degree. "Too busy for me, probably.''

It was pure bad fortune that Cami happened to

have the gene inside her that made it impossible to enjoy herself in life unless everyone around her was happy. Yes, that left her wearing the proverbial doormat on her head that said Take Advantage of Me Because I Can't Say No, but it happened to look good on her, if she did say so herself. "I'm not too busy for you, Mom, but—"

"Good, because he's the catch of the year, and—"

Cami tuned her out, her attention drawn by a noise coming from the living room. Her master carpenter. Her *gorgeous* master carpenter.

The man who hadn't given her a second look.

Was she, at twenty-six, losing all appeal? So maybe she carried a few extra pounds, but she hadn't had time for exercise since...since, well, she hated exercise.

But even if she had the time, which she didn't, and even if she worked out seven days a week, which she didn't, she'd *still* have too many darn curves.

So really, all she had going for her was her hair and her own teeth. That had to count for something.

"Lulu says he loves the Tahoe region and he's thinking of relocating here permanently, seeing that his stock portfolio is worth more than her retirement fund.''

Cami hadn't had a date in…well, forever. Sad state of affairs, really.

Even sadder was the fact she was sitting here, without pants, actually considering it.

It was just one night. With a computer geek, which meant he had to be at least semiintelligent. ''Mom—''

''And I bet he has all his hair.''

''Mom—''

''Because he's blond. It's really hard to pull off a blond toupee.''

''Mom, stop. I'll do it.''

''And he has all his— What? You will? You really will?''

''Yes, but this is the last time. The *real* last time. Got that?''

''Absolutely. Probably.''

Cami could only sigh. And hope he indeed had all his hair.

TANNER WAS STILL leaning over the set of plans when his new boss came racing through the back door. Strange, since he would have sworn she was still in the town house, but even stranger, her cat took one look at her and hissed.

She was already dressed, in a pale green business number that showed a set of legs well worth a double take. There was makeup on her face, and her hair had been taken care of, piled on her head in some artful manner.

Pretty quick for a female, especially one who looked as she did, all blond and buxomy and naturally tousled.

That kind of natural look took women forever in the bathroom to achieve. Tanner knew this because, one, his mother had been both blond and beautiful, and in his memory of her, she'd never taken less than a lifetime to get ready to go anywhere, and two, in his wayward youth, he'd worked his way through plenty of blondes of his own.

At thirty-two years old, he had higher standards now.

Usually.

Skidding to a halt between the kitchen and the living room, she stared at him, clearly shocked to find him still there. "Oh," she said, blinking huge chocolate eyes that suddenly seemed...different.

"Yep. Still here." He wondered what she'd done, exactly, because though a sexpot was a sexpot, it was almost as if she was a completely different person.

"Oh," she said again, ignoring her cat, who walked away from her, tail switching back and forth in annoyance.

Very strange.

"Did you forget I was here?" he asked, her reaction reinforcing his earlier thought—he was working for a woman missing a few marbles.

"I...yes. Yes, I guess I did forget." She bit her full lower lip and looked at him, as if she'd never seen him before.

She was sleepy-eyed and pouty-lipped and could have just bounced out of bed, if not for the fancy clothes. He had a feeling she always looked that way, that she knew how to get exactly what she wanted by showing off her tall, lush body to her advantage.

In his dubious maturity, the one that came with preferring steady income over a hot babe to look at, he took a big mental step backward.

First of all, he was finally at work doing a job he loved after a year from hell fraught with family tragedy. He needed the work.

Not to mention, Cami Anderson was living in a *great* fixer-upper that he badly wanted to get his hands on. In fact, he was practically salivating at the opportunity. This particular town house complex was over a century old, and though it had been sorely mistreated by age and neglect and the severe weather of the Sierras, it had the potential to be brought to its former glory.

With his help.

Running a hand over the scarred, original wood flooring, he smiled. Yeah, definitely, beneath the abused material was a foundation based on character and strength. Personality.

And he couldn't wait to dig in—with or without the nutty lady.

"Um…" She continued to gnaw on her lower lip. "Why are you here again exactly?"

Tanner laughed, but when she didn't so much as smile, his humor faded.

Ah, hell, she *had* lost a few marbles. "To work," he said carefully. "Remember?"

"Work." She nodded. "Well, if you'll excuse me a moment." And before he could so much as move, she took her made-up self down the hall. Toward what he knew to be the bedroom.

Again.

Was there another exit that hadn't been on the set of plans he'd studied and memorized? Or had she crawled out her window to come around?

"Nutty to the bone," he muttered, shaking his head and returning to the plans.

DIMI MOVED down the hall and barged into Cami's bedroom, her face serious and intent as always. "First," she said to Cami, who was still dressing.

Or attempting to.

"First, I need my lipstick back. Stop stealing it and buy your own."

Cami ignored her twin, who'd obviously let herself in—again—and tried to zip up the trousers she'd just found. Man, she really needed to stop eating doughnuts for breakfast.

Wincing, she lay flat on the bed and sucked in a breath. The pants closed, barely, though she wouldn't be able to so much as sneeze all day.

"And second..." Dimi let out a rare grin. "Oh, baby, *major* hunk alert in your living room."

Cami managed to find a shoe. Breathless, she looked up. *"What?"*

Dimi gestured down the hall. "Don't look now, but you've got a really amazing-looking guy out there. He's wearing a tool belt and a killer smile, to boot."

"Yeah." It wasn't something Cami thought about often, because it was stupid. But when it came to men, she was actually jealous of her sister. Dimi was her identical twin, but somehow she seemed far more put together than Cami could ever hope to be. Prettier.

More likely to get lucky.

As a result, Cami rarely told anyone, especially any date she might be lucky enough to get, that she was a twin. Didn't say a lot for her confidence in herself, but it was a fact. "Oh, damn."

"What?"

Cami held out her shoe, which had a suspicious-looking lump in it, one that smelled like... Craning her neck, she glared at Annabel.

From her perch on the dresser, the cat blinked innocently.

"Ugh," Dimi said, wrinkling her nose. "Dump the cat. But the guy, let's not dump him. Did you know that he thinks I'm you?"

Cami sighed. "Did you tell him you're not?"

"Now why would I do that and waste a perfectly good opportunity to mess with his head?"

"Don't you have work or something?"

"Yep." Eyeing Annabel warily, Dimi grabbed Cami's purse off the dresser, dumping it out onto the bed. Rifling through, she pounced on the tube of lipstick and pocketed it. "Don't you have work, too?"

Cami had made her way through college by sewing clothes. By using her own designs and materials obtained at cost through school, she made enough money for tuition, books, gas and her mortgage. Whatever was left over went into the redo-Cami's-town-house fund, which meant she ate lots of cheap soup, but she'd gotten used to it. "Less than usual now that I'm looking to get my designing going."

"Hmm. I'm trying to convince my boss to let you come redesign the studio."

Redecorating Dimi's kitchen studio for her cooking show would be nothing short of huge. "Really?"

"Really." She grunted when Cami threw herself at her and hugged her hard. "Jeez, wait till you get the job."

"Thank you!"

"Yeah." Dimi disentangled herself and headed toward the door.

"Wait. You've got my lipstick."

"You owe me. Hey, want to double date with me this weekend? The guy I met at the doughnut shop has a brother who needs a date."

"I already agreed to go out with Great-Aunt Lulu's cousin's brother-in-law."

"Mom caught you, huh?" Dimi looked superior, and not just because she was wearing a great-looking suit while Cami had managed stained slacks and a wrinkled blouse.

"How many times do I have to tell you, screen your calls."

"He doesn't sound that awful," Cami said in her defense. "He's got all his hair."

Dimi slanted her a look of sheer pity. "Have we forgotten who's setting you up? Mom has a terrible track record. You know this."

"It's not that bad."

"No? Remember Ed? He had all his hair, too."

Unfortunately most of that hair hadn't been on his head. The guy had been a virtual gorilla. Remembering that, and all her other recent pathetic dates, Cami sunk to her bed, mystified. "What do you think is wrong with us?"

"Nothing's wrong with me. But you? You're a case."

"Thanks."

Dimi pointed to the living room. "What about pretty boy? Why don't you go out with him?"

Humiliating as it was, Cami always told Dimi the truth, even when her sister didn't want to hear it. Like that time Dimi had gone out with a resident doctor and had come home dancing on air, baffled because her "perfect" date hadn't kissed her at the door.

Cami had been the one to break the news—the large piece of spinach stuck between Dimi's two front teeth, the result of the lovely Italian dish they'd had two hours earlier.

Dimi, queen of hygiene, had nearly died.

"What happened?" Dimi asked, already sensing something good. "Don't even say nothing. *Something* is all over your face."

"All right, fine. You want the horrifying scoop. I answered the door naked and pretty boy, as you call him didn't even notice."

"Didn't notice, or was being polite?"

"Dimi, I was *naked.* There's no polite when you're naked."

Dimi considered. "Define naked."

"I had a blanket, but it kept slipping."

Her twin shook her head. "Why are all the cute ones gay?"

"I don't know," Cami answered, miserable at the thought of all that magnificent maleness going to waste. "So I have to take the blind date. I have no other prospects in sight. None."

"Don't do it, Cam. Refuse. All you ever do these days is go on blind dates. You're just sabotaging yourself. Setting yourself up for failure."

"Am not."

"Are, too. You have this fear of commitment."

"Funny, last time I looked, you were a food-show host on cable television, not a damn psychiatrist."

"Your fear is fueled by Dad's seven marriages and Mom's inability to find a man for herself," Dimi continued. "Everyone knows this but you. Just give up on the blind dates, okay?"

"You're the one who just asked me to go on another one with your friend's brother!"

"That was for me, not you. Now face these stupid fears and find your own man."

"Spoken by the goddess of love, who herself hasn't had a decent boyfriend in two years."

"*One,*" Dimi said, miffed. "And I don't have your fears. I just haven't found Mr. Right yet."

"I don't have any damn fears!"

"Really? Then why are you always agreeing to go out with these guys, none of whom ever work out because they're from some other planet entirely?"

Because she really was pathetic. But she couldn't maintain any sort of self-righteous anger because she did have fears. Big time. "This is the last one."

"Yeah, right."

"Really."

"Just call Mom and cancel."

"Hell, no. I value my life, thank you very much."

"Fine," Dimi said, disgusted. "Suit yourself. But if he has buck teeth and a bad toupee, not to mention breath from the sewer plant, don't blame me."

"Fine."

"Fine! And stop stealing my lipstick."

"It's my lipstick," she called, but it was too late, Dimi had slammed the bedroom door.

"Love is the pits," she muttered, and slipped her foot into her shoe, too late remembering Annabel's "present" until it squished between her toes.

# 3

THEY SIGNED the contract, and because Tanner had reservations about his new client's mental capacity, he got a good chunk of his fee up front. He agreed to remodel in three shifts. First, the back half of the town house, consisting of the master bedroom and bathroom and the small spare bedroom.

Next, they'd do the living room, kitchen and second small bathroom. And finally, the back deck, which overlooked the lake. Old, rotting and rickety, the entire wooden structure needed to be redone before his client could get any serious sunbathing in without being terrified.

He figured she loved sunbathing. With her sexy body and come-hither looks, he imagined her in a red bikini. A skimpy, red bikini, one that was going to be the dominant feature in his sexual fantasies for the rest of the day.

Renovating the entire town house was slated to take approximately one and a half months, the first phase two weeks of that time. This meant, of course, that Tanner's new client was going to be sleeping on the couch for the foreseeable future.

She'd claimed not to mind that, or living in a construction zone, but he was sure she didn't have the slightest clue as to what she was getting herself into.

He'd found most people didn't, even the ones in the profession, as Cami now was. They simply wanted the work done. Yesterday. Which is why he often encouraged his clients to vacate for the duration, but Cami refused to go anywhere. She wanted to be involved, she'd said, each step of the way.

*Oh, joy.*

So at six o'clock on Thursday morning he let himself in with some trepidation, followed by a demo crew of four laborers. After all, he knew firsthand she wasn't exactly a morning person. "Let me make sure the back half is clear," he told his guys, leaving the mostly Spanish-speaking workers in the kitchen while he made his way down the hall.

As promised, Cami had boxed up the things in her bedroom and master bath and moved them out, except for the heaviest pieces of furniture, which he'd told her he would tarp and work around. He had no idea where she was. Maybe she'd heeded his advice and left, though he didn't really care. He wanted to start. Calling his workers, he did just that.

The noise was extensive as they stripped the walls down to the studs. But Cami had supposedly forewarned her neighbors, and since no one came to complain or arrest him, Tanner and his crew kept at it.

Working again, with the weight of his tools in his hands, the plans in his head, felt incredibly good. He'd been out of it for too long. Not that Tanner regretted taking the time off—nearly a year—to care for his father after his stroke. He didn't regret a moment of it. But he'd missed this.

That his father had improved enough to allow Tanner to resume his life was a huge relief. His checkbook was grateful, too, as were his mind and body. As much as he loved his father, he needed this.

Two hours into the demo, he headed into the kitchen for some desperately needed water. Leaning against the counter, he tipped back his water jug and spotted the client's cat sitting near his box of tools.

"Hello, kitty," he said, squatting to hold out a hand. Cami had told him Annabel hated everyone equally, except for her, of course, but the cat didn't look as if she hated him. Sniffing his fingers, she preened a bit and then started to purr.

That was when he caught sight of the mess at her feet. The mess that looked suspiciously like a chewed pouch. *His* chewed pouch.

"Hey." Tanner glared at Annabel, who sat on her haunches and appeared to smile at him. There was a piece of leather hung up on her front tooth. *Expensive* leather.

She'd eaten one of his pouches from his tool belt. "Foul play, cat."

Before he could do anything about it, the back door opened and Cami raced in. She wore a harassed, harried look. Not even glancing his way, she pushed past him and down the hallway toward the bedroom.

Her nearly demolished bedroom.

"Wait—"

But she was gone, her heels clicking on the wood, her voice chanting softly, "I'm late, I'm late, I'm late for a very important date. Need a rose lipstick, dammit."

Definitely, she was a little off, but he followed her anyway. "We've done the demo—"

"Ack!" She came to a skidding halt and smacked her forehead. "I forgot!" With that, she reversed her steps, rushed past him and out the kitchen door.

Without a word to him.

He shut the door behind her. "Nice owner you've got there," he told Annabel, who'd stretched out lazily by his lunch box. "Real friendly."

"Mew."

"Oh, stop nuzzling my lunch box. I don't feed cats who eat expensive pouches."

Insulted, she lifted her chin and ignored him.

Amused at himself for talking to a damn cat, and also for agreeing to work for a crazy lady, he strode out of the kitchen, intending to get back to work.

Annabel followed him, winding her way between his legs as he walked, tripping him in the hallway. "Go back," he told her. "No cats in the work zone."

Obviously not caring about the sacred work zone, the cat licked her chops and sat in the doorway of the destroyed bedroom.

"You can't stay," he told her. "You'll get dusty."

Annabel yawned, turned in a circle and lay down.

Sighing, a complete sucker for animals—even

ones who destroyed perfectly good leather pouches—Tanner went into the one good bathroom, grabbed a towel and set it on the floor. "There."

As if it were her due, Annabel settled on it and proceeded to bathe herself.

Tanner went back to work.

Fifteen minutes later came a very loud, very outraged, very female screech.

Tanner ran out of the bedroom and tripped over Annabel. *Again.* "Dammit," he said to her irritated growl. "I told you that was a bad spot." He raced into the living room. Empty.

Kitchen was empty, too.

The screech came again, and just as he turned toward the bathroom door, it slammed closed in his face.

"I'm naked!" came Cami's annoyed voice.

*Okaaaay.* He took a firm step away from the bathroom door and waved his curious workers to the bedroom. He'd seen a naked client once. Or clients, rather, as they'd been married and had been knocking it out in their linen closet when he'd inadvertently interrupted them. They'd been sixty-five, wrinkled and whiter than white, and he still had nightmares about it.

That Cami was alone—he hoped—and was

twenty-something, heart-stoppingly beautiful and had no obvious wrinkles didn't make him feel any better.

He didn't like naked clients.

"Where's my towel!"

Tanner looked at Annabel, who apparently lay on the towel in question. She yawned so widely he was certain her head was going to turn inside out.

*"I said, I'm naked and I don't have a towel and I just got out of the shower!"*

Tanner's vivid imagination went to town. He had no trouble picturing Cami on the other side of the closed door, wet and shiny and maybe a little chilly...hmm, maybe he could revise that no-naked-clients policy thing.

*"Who stole my towel?"*

*Oh. Oh, yeah, the towel.* Guiltily, Tanner kneeled by Annabel. The towel she lay on had been a lovely deep forest green, before he'd set it on the dusty floor and before she'd added myriad red, white and black cat hairs to it.

"Uh, Cami?" he said, eyeing the sleepy cat. "I appear to have your towel."

"You— Why?"

"It's a bit complicated. Is there another somewhere?"

"Sure. Shoved into boxes!"

"How do you feel about air drying?"

There came a thunk, the distinct sound of her head hitting the door. "Can't we renegotiate this whole morning thing?" came the muffled plea. "Like noon. Let's start work at noon."

"We'd never finish. And anyway, you were already up and dressed, moaning about your rose lipstick and being late. Why would you take a shower now?"

"Dammit, it's *my* lipstick!" she muttered. "Oh, never mind, just shove the towel in when I open the door. And keep your eyes closed!"

The door creaked open, and Tanner stuffed a corner of the towel in. "Really," he said to the crack in the door. 'Trust me, you're not going to want to use that—"

"Your eyes are open!"

"Well, yeah. I'm just trying to—" But he stopped, because one, he'd just gotten a peek of what it was she didn't want him to see, and oh man, she was better than his most wild fantasy.

And two, she'd slammed the door again, missing his nose by a millimeter.

"Go away," she demanded.

Gladly. Because while she had a bod that could make a grown man drool, she was still a loon.

CAMI HAD DONE some interior-design jobs in college and also part-time work for other designers in the area. Being so close to Tahoe and the pocket of incredibly wealthy people who lived there, she'd had plenty of experience. It was fascinating, satisfying, glorious work.

Unless one was trying to drum up that work solo.

The day after the towel incident, which also happened to be blind date night, thanks to Mom, Cami gathered her briefcase and files and sat at the kitchen table, intending to call her two prospective clients.

The table was covered with plans for her own town house remodel, though, and was a cluttered mess. Not too picky, she glanced at the floor, but it had tools scattered from here to there.

The living room wasn't in much better shape, as she was sleeping in it. "Note to self," she muttered. "Clean house before blind date."

The only usable area in the entire place was the hallway outside the one good bathroom. Dragging her phone—with a thankfully long cord—her laptop and her paperwork, she made herself at home right there on the floor.

She was counting on work to help keep her mind off her troubles, such as why she couldn't get her checkbook to balance or why she'd spent so much money at Amazon last month.

Or why she'd agreed to go out tonight.

And lastly, as a bonus, she could now obsess over the fact that her master carpenter had seen her naked as a jaybird.

*Definitely not gay,* she thought with a twist of her mouth. She'd have to tell Dimi. Tanner's eyes had nearly popped out, and that hadn't been the only thing.

But if he wasn't gay, and the sight of her naked body had created some…tension, which it definitely had, then why didn't he seem interested?

Not that *she* was interested. Nope. He was too know-it-all, too tell-it-like-it-is. Too calm, cool and collected.

Too…well, perfect.

Besides, other than the towel thing, he still hadn't noticed her as a woman. The unexpected blow to her ego reinforced her pathetic need for this date tonight. Sad as it was, she needed the affirmation that someone, anyone, as long as he was male, could be attracted to her.

Needing the distraction, she picked up the receiver, prepared to make her first business call, then caught sight of her contractor at the other end of the hall. He had his portable CD player tuned into some very loud rock music, but that wasn't what caught her attention.

He was on his hands and knees, facing away from her. His work boots were scuffed and broken in. So were his jeans and T-shirt. He had a great set of legs, long and powerful, flexing and straining against the denim. He had a great spine, too, and arms that made her want to sigh. Still, it was his butt that really caught her attention.

Her fingers actually itched to grab it.

Pathetic, staring at her contractor's behind, as if she were a sex-starved woman.

She *was* a sex-starved woman.

Damn, he was distracting. Just as he caught a glimpse of her, she dropped her gaze and concentrated on her phone. Wouldn't do to be caught gawking.

"That's not a great spot to be working," he said, coming up on his knees. The front of his blue T-shirt strained across his broad chest and flat belly. She wondered if he ever got too hot and took off his shirt.

"I don't have a choice," she said coolly. "I have a lot to get done before tonight."

"Tonight?"

She hadn't meant to say anything about her upcoming date, but if he worked late, as he had last night, then he'd find out soon enough, anyway. "I have a date."

"Ah."

The way his light brown eyes lit up with humor had her frowning. "What's so funny about a blind date?"

"A *blind* date." Now his smirk of amusement turned into a full-blown grin. "What's the matter with you that you have to go out on a blind date?"

"Well…" Why did he always put her on the defensive? "Nothing's the matter with me."

"It's probably your lack of a sense of humor," he decided.

"I have a great sense of humor!"

"Uh-huh."

"I was the class clown in high school," she informed him loftily, and his grin widened.

"Who set you up?"

"My mother," she admitted, and when he laughed out loud, she said through her teeth, "It's a favor."

"So you don't really want to go?"

"Not really."

"Then cancel," he said with a shrug.

Spoken like a man. A confident man who didn't give a rat's pattoodie about what his mother thought. "You don't know my mother," she said. Then, unable to help her own curiosity, she asked, "Are you telling me you've never been on a blind date?"

"I'm telling you I've never done anything I don't want to do."

Oh. Well, fine. He was strong-willed and strong-minded. Admirable traits, she supposed. Just not when compared to herself. "Not even for your mother?"

Only his eyes gave away a flicker of sadness. "My mother died when I was ten."

Great, now she was the jerk. "I'm sorry."

He stood up and turned his attention to the wall he'd been working on. "So am I."

"Do you have other family?" she asked his tall, proud back.

"My father."

"You're close?"

Another shrug. "Yeah. More so now, since his stroke."

Feeling two inches tall, she sighed. "I shouldn't have pried." But the truth was, she was brimming with questions about this man who said what he wanted without a thought for the consequence.

"He's recovered," Tanner said, facing her

again. "It took all year, but he's finally all the way back."

"*You* nursed him?"

"You seem shocked." He smiled. "I can be very useful."

She believed that.

"But neither my father, nor my mother if she was still alive, would set me up on a blind date."

"Why not?"

"I was raised to make up my own mind."

She narrowed her eyes at the insult. "I can make up my own mind."

"Good."

"Good," she repeated, lifting her chin and the phone. Tanner turned to his work, for which she was grateful, because his eyes saw too much. And because she enjoyed the view of his butt.

She dialed her first—she hoped her first—client. "Mrs. Brown?" she said into the phone. "Cami Anderson here, checking in with you. Have you had a chance to look over my designs with Mr. Brown?"

"No, not yet, dear. My son is in town from Seattle for the week."

"Ah." In Cami's experience with customers— which, granted, was limited—the longer they took to decide, the better the chance they'd back out.

"I was hoping you could take a look sooner than that, you see—"

"I suppose I could...." Mrs. Brown's voice turned crafty. "For a favor in return."

*Uh-oh.*

"My son, he just turned thirty yesterday, and being that he's down here, far away from his friends, he's...lonely."

*Double uh-oh.*

"I imagine if you were to...oh, I don't know...go out with him this evening, that would free me up."

"I'm busy tonight."

"Tomorrow then. Or the day after. Name the night. Just go out with Joshua, and I'll be ready to meet with you the next day."

From the corner of her eye she watched Tanner. As he worked, the tools hanging on his tool belt clanked together with a rhythmic sound. His hands were sure and confident. His face was steeped in concentration.

He'd forgotten all about her.

She'd just forget all about him. "I don't think that would be appropriate," she said to Mrs. Brown. "Dating a client's son."

"Just one date, dear. One harmless little date."

No doubt, the woman had to be a distant relative of her mother's. "Mrs. Brown—"

"I'll double your budget," she promised rashly.

What could be wrong with her son for double budget?

*"Triple."*

Wow. One could forgive a lot for triple. Even if he had three eyes and spit when he talked, it was only one evening, right? "Well..."

"Oh, good, you won't regret it!"

She bet she would. "Just one date," she clarified. "Tomorrow night."

At that, Tanner craned his neck to stare at her. Cami heard the ripping sound of material caught on a loose nail.

Twisting, Tanner stared at the back of himself and the huge, jagged rip through his T-shirt.

At the sight of a long length of smooth, sleek skin, Cami's mouth went desert dry.

"Come to the house the day after tomorrow then," Mrs. Brown said into her ear. "I'll serve us some tea and cheesecake and we can talk about the work. Do you like cheesecake?"

"I love beefcake," Cami said, then nearly choked when Tanner whipped toward her again, surprise lighting those interesting, see-all whis-key-colored eyes of his.

"*Cheesecake!* I meant I love cheesecake," she corrected frantically. "Yes, yes, I like it with tea, thank you." Feeling heat creep up her face, Cami found her gaze locked with Tanner's. He was very amused. "See you Sunday," she said to her client, and hung up.

"Tea with your cheesecake," Tanner murmured. "Good combo. But what do you like with your beefcake?"

"Very funny. Everyone makes a slip of the tongue once in awhile."

"Yeah." He pulled off his useless shirt. "Do you make yours on your blind dates?"

For some reason, she could hardly breathe, and told herself it was all the dust in the air. "I don't do much with my tongue on dates."

"No?"

"Not that it's any of your business," she said as coolly as she could while suddenly sweating like crazy.

His gaze slid over her slowly, and she got the feeling he knew exactly what he did to her.

"So you've got another blind date," he said. "What does a woman like you need them for?"

"I don't need them at all. Other people need me."

"And what about what *you* need? Does anyone think of that?"

"I—I don't think so, no," she said softly, never having viewed it that way before.

"Remember that," he said just as softly. "The next time you make a slip of the tongue."

Two MINUTES before Cami's date was scheduled to arrive, Tanner came into the kitchen. He was covered in dust from head to toe.

"Demo is a messy business," he said apologetically. "We've tried to keep the mess to the back portion of the place."

And he had. He'd used plastic and tarps, always careful not to track the dirt to the usable end of the house. As one who hated to clean, Cami appreciated it. "You've been great," she said, preening a little, wondering what he thought.

He wasn't even looking at her, darn him. He'd grabbed his water jug and was chugging from it, not noticing what she'd done with herself.

Ever since puberty, which had happened unfortunately young for Cami, men had been noticing her body first, her mind a far second. Not Tanner.

She didn't know why it mattered exactly, when she had already decided he wasn't her type, but she wanted him to look at her, wanted some sort of appreciation. She wore a sundress and strappy sandals, both of which managed, by some miracle, to hide the fact that her scale had groaned under her just that morning.

She knew she looked good. And for once, she *wanted* to be noticed—by Tanner.

Slowly he lowered the water jug. "You look..."

"Dressed?" she asked with a self-deprecatory smile, referring to the towel incident.

"Well, yes. Dressed." His brows were knit together in displeasure. "Why can't you just back out?"

"Well...I guess I seem to have a little trouble with the word no."

"Hmm." Tanner leaned against the counter and crossed his arms, studying her. She was a puzzle to him. One, she had trouble with no. That was interesting, especially since he'd seen her coax his workers to her slightest whim. He'd heard her on the phone with subcontractors, bulldozing her way through yards of red tape. And when it came to her opinions on paints, materials or colors, don't get her started. Two, she wasn't a meek woman, or a quiet, mousy one, so it was fascinating, and frustrating, to him that she let the people she cared about walk all over her. "That must be interesting," he said casually. "At the end of all these blind dates, not being able to say no."

As always when he baited her, her nose went to the sky. "I manage just fine then, thank you very much."

"If you manage just fine, why can't you—" He broke off when she suddenly let out a little cry and dropped to her hands and knees. "No, Annabel, *no!*"

On all fours, she chased her cat across the kitchen floor.

Tanner stared in amazement as she gathered dust and shimmied her very fine rear end from one side of the kitchen to the other. "What are you—"

"Oh, darn it!" Wriggle, wriggle. "She's going after a poor spider."

Annabel had made herself known as some sort of freak cannibal, loving to toy with insects. Tanner knew Cami couldn't stand it. He had watched cat and owner battle it out before.

"Annabel, stop!" She cornered the fat, greedy cat, who'd in turn cornered her prey with a joyful growl. Just before Annabel could paw the little spider, Cami cupped her hand over it.

"Move it," she told the cat. *"Honestly."*

Reaching up, she grabbed a cup, urged the spider into it and came to her feet, dust on her hands, knees and, for some reason, her chin. Gently, she shook the spider out the back door, nudging it along as if it were her baby, and was just dusting off her hands when she realized he was staring at her.

"What?" she asked self-consciously.

Before he could answer, the doorbell rang. She went a little pale. "He'd better have all his hair," she muttered.

"You can still say no."

"I promised."

He shook his head, but followed her to the front door, wondering at the woman who looked like a sexpot but wasn't. No sexpot saved spiders at the risk of her clothes and went out on dates with dust on her chin.

"I can answer it by myself," she said.

"What's his name?"

"Ted."

"Let's see if Ted has all his hair."

*"Tanner."*

He hated the look on her face, hated knowing

she didn't want to go. Hated that he cared. "Just open the door, Cami. Open the door and tell him you changed your mind."

"I can't."

"*I* can."

"No."

"Fine. But that doormat on your forehead? The one that says walk all over me?" He slid his thumb over her chin, removing the dust. "It doesn't look so good on you."

# 4

CAMI IGNORED HIM.

Tanner expected no less. But as she reached for the door, she hesitated.

"Cancel," he whispered in her ear.

"Back off," she said to the wood. "You're making my knees weak."

"Really?" In a sick sort of male way, hearing that pleased Tanner greatly.

Clearly, it didn't please her. "I promised to go," she said.

Tanner's mouth was only inches away from her nape. His chest nearly brushed her back. He caught the scent of her shampoo and the scent of her as a woman. Soft, sweet. Sexy.

Incredibly, his mouth watered with the need to nibble at her, and the urge to put his hands out and hold the front door closed became incredibly strong. He took a deep breath and let the air out slowly.

In response, she shivered.

Stunned by the unexpected sexual tension shimmering between them, he stared at the back of her head. He'd been out of the world for an entire year, caring for his dad. Still, he'd managed to have casual dates here and there. Not once had he felt this need to grab a woman and hold on, and he didn't think he liked it.

"I have to go," she whispered, just a little shakily, assuring him he wasn't alone in this insanity.

"Just say you've come down with date-itis," he said. "That you break out in hives at restaurants, that you drool when you eat."

Her shoulders went back. "I never drool."

He watched the strap of her sundress slide down her arm, and before he could stop himself, he straightened it, his fingers skimming over all that creamy skin.

She shivered again, and he nearly moaned. "Say you made a mistake, you already have a date for tonight, and first come, first served."

She looked at him, her eyes dark, so very dark. "But I don't have another date."

He could drown in those eyes, if she wasn't such a pain in the ass. "I could take you out," he heard himself say.

*"What?"*

He was crazy. That was the only explanation for what his mouth had just said without his brain's approval. "Well, I was here first," he told her.

"You don't mean it. You don't even like me that much."

"Yes, I do."

"Really? What do you like about me?"

"I..." He liked the way she looked wet out of the shower without a towel, but he doubted that was the correct answer that would win him the prize he wasn't even sure he wanted.

"That's what I thought." Again she reached for the door.

"Wait."

"I can't. I can't go out with you, even if you liked me, which you don't. We're too different."

"How?"

"You listen to obnoxiously loud music, for one."

"And you listen to music that makes my teeth hurt. I don't hold it against you."

"Okay, fine. You want a better reason? You're a morning person."

She said this as if he was a convicted criminal, which made him laugh. "I could teach you to like the mornings,'' he promised in a voice both teasing and seductive.

Her eyes darkened even more. ''Don't talk in that voice.''

''What voice?''

''The one that makes my knees weak.''

''I thought me standing too close made your knees weak.''

''Be quiet.'' She pulled open the door.

Her date smiled, showing teeth that did appear to be his own, Tanner noticed. And he definitely had hair. It was just a bad twist of karma that he looked like the Pillsbury dough boy.

Cami's furtive glance over her shoulder at Tanner seemed to dare him to point that fact out, but he smiled innocently.

No need to point out the obvious.

Cami introduced the men, and while they sized each other up, she excused herself to go get her purse.

Tanner followed her into the kitchen because it pleased him to have the run of the place while Ted had to stand politely at the door where Cami left him.

''Don't say a word,'' she warned him, grabbing the strap of her purse, which promptly snapped, spilling everything to the floor.

One lipstick, a brush and a set of keys rolled out.

Oh, and a condom.

Tanner picked it up and wondered at the strange tightening of his stomach. "Thought you knew how to say no at the end of a date," he said casually.

She snatched it out of his hand and shoved it into her purse. "These days a woman needs to be prepared."

The thought of her having sex tonight, with that sloppy guy at her front door—hell, with *any* guy—made him want to lock her in her bathroom. But that didn't make any sense at all. He didn't care who she went out with. Didn't care who she slept with. He only cared that she had a honey of a place he wanted to work on. *"Prepared?"*

"Yes, prepared. You might have heard of safe sex."

"Prepared would be more than one condom, Cami."

"That's a man for you."

He narrowed his gaze. "What does that mean?"

"Nothing, except for my sister was right. To men, having condoms in your wallet is a form of…bragging. To a woman, it's smart."

"It's smart for me, too. But one condom... now, that just seems a little pessimistic."

She snorted.

"Don't you like multiple orgasms?" He had no idea why he asked her that, but her reaction duly sidetracked him.

Her jaw dropped. A blush worked its way over her face. She didn't meet his gaze.

"Or didn't your sister ever mention those?" he wondered.

"That's quite personal," she managed to say. "Don't you think?"

"I think you're dodging the question. Sex is just a form of communication. You should be able to talk about it."

"Not everyone is as blunt as you."

"Nope. Nor as honest."

"Fine, you want honest?" She licked her lower lip. Then spoke in a whisper. "I've never *had* multiple orgasms."

Now he was the shocked one. She was beautiful. Really, earth-stoppingly beautiful. How was it she'd never—

"I'm not a virgin," she said quickly. "I just—"

"Cami?" This came from the foyer. Clearly

Ted had gotten antsy, probably wondering if she was escaping out the back door.

For a moment, she looked as if she might. "Look, I have no idea why I'm telling you all this," she whispered to Tanner. "Just…just good night. Lock up when you go."

And that quickly, she was gone, leaving him standing there dumbfounded in her wake.

"Mew." Annabel butted her head against his leg and started to purr.

"Well, if it isn't Ms. Cannibal," he said, still distracted by that multiple orgasm thing. "Did you find another spider to torture?"

The cat licked her chops, and with a groan, Tanner squatted, peering into the cat's face. "Dammit, you have leather in your whiskers!"

Swearing, he moved down the hallway, stopping short at the sight of his pouches, which he'd left on the floor.

Bad mistake. Annabel had gotten yet another one, chewing a hole that meant his stash of nails would fall out. "You," he said, pointing to the cat who'd followed him, who was at this very moment studying him with a cavalier attitude. "You are one very rude cat."

She merely lifted her chin.

And reminded him so much of Cami that he

had to laugh. "Stick to your own food, would you?"

She didn't even blink, which reminded him that he was speaking to a cat for God's sake. "I'm outta here," he mumbled. And purposely not thinking about Cami, the woman who couldn't say no, and what she might be not saying no to at this very moment, he started to clean up.

When his cell phone rang, his heart stopped out of habit. There was only one reason he'd get a call so long after hours.

When he read the digital screen of the incoming phone number, he didn't relax. "What's wrong?" he demanded instead of a normal greeting.

"Some hello."

"Dad." Tanner let out a careful breath. His father sounded...fine. "You okay?"

"Scared you, did I?" He gave a craggy laugh. "Good. Maybe you'll come by and bring me something."

"I'm not bringing you cigarettes or booze."

"Hey, I raised you better than that."

Relief filled Tanner. "You're ornery. That's a good sign. I'll bring you dinner."

"I'd rather have the cigarettes."

"Too bad."

"Tacos then, extra spicy sauce."

"Soup," Tanner said finally. "Take it or leave it."

"Double chocolate cake for dessert?"

"Pudding. Vanilla."

"Dammit, boy, you're the meanest son of a bitch I know."

Tanner laughed. How long had it been since he'd sparred with his father? Heard that joy of life in his voice? Too long, and more than relief filled him, along with a burst of warm affection. Tanner didn't have much, materially speaking, at this point, not after a year of spending every penny he had to get his father well. But he had this, and it was everything. "Love you, too, Dad. See you in an hour."

"Are you sure? Because if you had a hot date, I wouldn't want to interfere."

He thought of Cami. And multiple orgasms.

He could give her multiple orgasms. At the mere thought, his body leaped to attention.

"Tanner?"

"No date," he said, rolling his eyes at himself and his juvenile reaction.

"Why not?"

*"Dad."*

"Look, all I'm saying is, if you come across a

chance to get some instead of seeing me, well then, go get some."

"Some what?" Tanner asked warily.

"Sex, boy. Stay on the same page now."

Tanner groaned. "I'm hanging up."

"Okay, but just remember. Sex first. Then me."

THEY WENT all the way to Reno for dinner because Ted wanted to go to Denny's. In hindsight, that should have been Cami's first hint things weren't going to get better.

"They've got a great buffet," Ted said, huffing a little as he escorted her across the parking lot. They got to the front door at exactly the same moment, and Cami hesitated, thinking Ted might open it for her.

He opened the door, all right, and in his haste for food, pushed ahead of her.

And stomped on her toe.

"I love buffets," he said in lieu of an apology.

Cami grimaced at her throbbing toe and smudged sandal. "Gee, I hope there isn't a crowd."

"That's the beauty of this place," Ted answered earnestly. "It's never crowded."

Goodie.

"Dessert is included."

"Even better." This couldn't be happening to her, she decided, watching her date rush toward the buffet table. Her mother couldn't have really done this to her own daughter. Determined to believe it wasn't as bad as she thought, Cami pasted a smile on her face and tried really hard. "I heard you build Web sites."

"Look at that," he whispered reverently, pointing to a platter of biscuits, giving her a little nudge when she didn't move. "Take as many as you want."

"Great."

After dinner, during which Ted refused to talk because talking interrupted the eating process, which was apparently close to a religious experience for him, he offered to let her pay. Then offered to take her to the movies.

Dutch treat.

"It's not that I can't pay for you," he said quickly, walking with her to his car. "It's just that in today's day and age, I know how important it is for a woman to assert her independence. Plus, I find a lot of women take advantage, you know, and agree to go out with me just for a free night of entertainment."

"In the name of not taking advantage, let's just call it a night," she suggested.

"Oh, no." He looked scandalized. "That wouldn't be giving this thing between us a fair chance. Hey, I have an idea. We can do the drive-in theater."

"No, that's not necessary—"

"Shh," he said very politely, cranking up the radio and filling the car with what sounded like elevator music. "I love this song."

Cami clamped her mouth shut and actually wished for Tanner's far too loud rock music.

TED'S CAR DIED at precisely midnight, painfully reminding Cami that she was in no way, shape or form related to Cinderella, who'd at least had those cute little mice for company when it all went bad.

They were on a relatively untraveled stretch of road, because Ted had gotten off Highway 80 at least five miles from nowhere to see if he could locate the Big Dipper for her.

Now the car was dead and her cell phone had no signal.

Didn't get much better than this.

*Thanks, Mom.*

"Here comes a car," Ted said. "I'll see if I can flag it down."

Cami waited while he hopped out and wildly waved his hand, illuminated in the approaching headlights like a bouncing...dough boy. In the dark, Cami couldn't see what transpired, but a moment later, Ted came back.

"It's a woman," he said. "She's in a Porsche two-seater on her way to Auburn. She said she could take me into Truckee."

"Me?"

"No. *Me.*"

Cami frowned because Ted seemed...excited. Breathless, almost. Definitely more animated than she'd seen him all night. "You mean you're going to leave me here?"

"Just for a little while. I'll go get help."

"And come back for me?"

"Uh-huh." But he was craning his neck, staring dreamily at the other car. His demeanor had changed, he stood straighter and taller and looked happier even than when he'd been facing a twenty-foot spread of food.

"That must be some woman," she ventured.

"She's a Denny's fan."

"You found that out in two seconds?"

"Yeah. So listen, I'm going to get going."

Cami couldn't believe it. "Let me get this straight. *Your* car died and *you're* going to take the only ride, leaving me stranded out in the middle of nowhere by myself?"

"Don't be silly. You have my car."

"It doesn't run!"

"Yeah, about that. Don't turn on the radio while I'm gone, you'll waste the battery on top of everything else."

For a long moment after he'd left, Cami just sat there, rooted in…well, pissiness.

How had this happened to her?

Doormat. She wore one on her head.

*It doesn't look good on you,* Tanner had told her.

And he was right. Damn, she hated that, when other people were right. Sighing, she leaned back and realized for the first time just how alone she was.

There were no other headlights in sight, not in front, not behind her. In fact, with a pathetically low moon and some cloud cover, there was nothing in sight except the glow of the white buttons that ran down the front of her sundress.

She became aware of how noisy nighttime in the Sierras was. Trees rustled with the wind and seemed…possessed. From far, far away came the sound of a truck. Good, she hoped it was coming this way. She'd simply flag it down and...get her-self hijacked, kidnapped, raped and murdered.

Yikes.

Something very close by made a clicking sound. Probably a big, black ugly cricket. She quickly rolled up the window. Didn't stop the clicking, though.

If that big bug was in the car, she was going to have to scream. Loudly.

She wished for Annabel, who'd save her from the bug. She wished she'd never gotten mad at the cat for eating spiders. She wished for Dimi, who'd know what to do, even if she'd tease Cami to death over this ridiculous predicament. Hell, she wished she'd never answered her mother's phone call.

Setting her head to the dash, she closed her eyes and felt alone. Very alone.

*HIS HAND slid around her waist to the small of her back. He stood close enough for her to smell him, sandalwood, leather and...drywall dust.*

Stop. Rewind dream and try again, Cami told herself, jerking upright because she was abso-lutely not going to fantasize about that man, not Tanner James.

Slowly she drifted off again.

*He had her against his warm body. He smelled*

*like heaven, one hundred percent male. His broad chest and strong arms surrounded her.*

Yeah, that was better.

*He kissed her, softly at first, but with increasing heat and hunger, moaning her name in a voice that had shivers racing down her spine.*

*More,* she demanded of her dream.

*He lowered his hands to her bottom and cupped her in his palms, easing her closer, rubbing the heavy bulge at the fly of his jeans to the damp juncture between her thighs until she cried out his name.*

*Tanner.*

Dammit, not again!

Cami closed her eyes tighter and refused to look at the face of her fantasy man, forcing herself deeper into sleep.

*His hand skimmed up her spine, cupping her head. Tipping his to the side, he kissed her, deeper, wetter, using his tongue, his teeth, his touch to drive her close to the edge.*

She wanted that edge, she wanted *multiple* edges.

Which brought her back to Tanner, damn him, because it had been *him* who put that unbearably erotic thought in her head.

Hopelessly awake now, she straightened and blinked into the dark night that wasn't quite as dark anymore. According to her watch, she'd slept for five and a half hours, fantasizing about hot sex, which accounted for her hard-as-rock nipples and the ache between her legs.

It made her even grumpier.

Still no cars, but at least the sky was lightening. At five-thirty in the morning, the sun would be up soon enough. Grumbling, beyond fear, because she had to pee and was starving, she got out of the car. With her purse slung over her arm and cell phone in hand, she headed up the road, not intending to stop until she had a signal.

It only took about five minutes. She dialed Dimi's town house first, and got her machine. "Get up," she said unkindly into the phone. "I'm stuck out here in the middle of nowhere between Reno and Truckee and I need you to come get me." She gave the exact off-ramp and her approximate location in high hopes her sister would wake up and come rescue her.

In case Dimi didn't get her lazy butt out of bed, Cami tried her mother next. She didn't care about the time or waking up her mother, mostly because it was her mother's fault she was in this predicament in the first place.

But there was no answer there, either. "Okay, Mom, I'm stuck," she said to the machine. "Your dreamboat ditched me for a babe in a two-seater.

Who'd of figured, huh? I expect a ride pronto. Don't you dare stop to take out your curlers first or I'm never giving you a grandchild.''

Cami tipped her head back, studied the stars making their exit into the day sky and sighed.

*What now?*

Ted, the jerk, had clearly ditched her. That, or he'd gotten very lucky.

Either way, she was on her own. And she wasn't up for the walk, not without a bathroom, and there was no way she planned on squatting behind a tree, thank you very much.

On the off chance Dimi was at this very moment raiding Cami's bathroom for lipstick, or her kitchen for chips, she tried calling her own town house. Okay, yes, she knew there was no chance in hell Dimi would be up this early, but desperate times… Fact was, she needed to talk to someone, and if that someone was himself, so be it. When the machine picked up, she said, ''Dimi, get your paws off my stuff and come rescue me from the date from hell.''

Nothing.

''Okay, yes, I've got an attitude,'' Cami said, trying to be nice just in case, because it was very easy to annoy Dimi. ''And I'm sorry, but you would, too, if you'd had the night I had.''

Still nothing.

Cami stopped walking and leaned against a tree on the side of the road. "Fine, you want a good laugh? It all started last night, even before I left. First my contractor told me I have this doormat on my forehead that says *oh, please take advantage of me,* and maybe I do, but it wasn't very gentlemanly of him to point it out, you know? And then I had to go to Denny's for the all-you-can-eat buffet, which believe me sounds much more appetizing than it is. And now I'm stuck out here around Highway Eighty all by myself because my date went off with another woman. The car won't start and I have to pee. And I'm wondering why it's so hard to have a nice date? It shouldn't be that hard, women are easy enough. A cruise would be nice, yes, but not expected. I mean really, whatever happened to candles and moonlight and romance? Are you there? Are you listening? Annabel? *Anyone?*"

Cami sighed and felt the surge of self pity wash over her. "Oh, jeez. Not that I'll ever admit it to him, but Tanner was right. I should have just said no."

# 5

TANNER ARRIVED at the town house a few minutes early. He was tired, having stayed up too late with his father the night before. Still, early mornings were ingrained.

His dad looked good, and the fear of losing him, the fear that hadn't once eased in the entire year since his stroke, had faded somewhat.

According to the man himself, he planned on living the next few decades doing nothing but enjoying life. And maybe driving his only son crazy.

That sounded good to Tanner, who wasn't ready to lose the only family he had left.

He could have done without the overt probing into his sex life. His father had wanted to hear that he had a girlfriend who could possibly turn into a wife.

It didn't take a genius to realize his father wanted grandchildren.

Tanner thought maybe he wanted kids, too.

*Someday.* But in order to get kids, he needed a wife.

That's where he ran into trouble.

Truth was, he liked his women hot and bothered, fast and edgy, and he liked them that way because he could enjoy them and move on. No worries about one of them getting too involved, no stressing that she was busy writing their wedding vows or planning what color flowers they'd have in their garden.

He didn't have time for that, and it wasn't just his father's illness that tripped him up on that score. It was his business, which required more than just the hours he put in during the day rebuilding. There was the paperwork, the billing, the planning, the bidding. It went on and on, and he just didn't see a woman working happily into the equation.

He'd tried, several times in fact, but whenever he was so stupid to date a woman long enough for it to be considered a relationship, the same thing happened.

He got dumped because he didn't spend enough time with her.

*Sorry, Dad, you'll have to wait a little longer.*

He let himself into Cami's town house in time

to hear her say, "Not that I'll ever admit it to him, but Tanner was right."

He liked the sound of that.

"I should have just said *no*."

Grinning, Tanner pocketed the key she'd given him and entered the kitchen, wanting to hear details.

But the place was empty, except for Annabel, who pounced on his shoe.

"Meeoowww," she cried pitifully.

He glanced at her empty bowl. "I know damn well you inhale your food, so go try some other sucker."

She rubbed against his leg, purring, watching him from beneath lowered brow, purring some more. Then suddenly she bit his ankle.

"Ouch!"

"Mew."

"Yeah, yeah." Tanner was far more interested in hearing Cami say he was right again.

"I really hate it when I'm wrong," he heard her grumble.

Walking through the kitchen toward her voice, he stopped short in the hallway, staring at the small table by the front door.

Her answering machine was talking.

"Fine," she said. "So no one but Annabel is

listening to me. Great. Figures. Story of my life. I hope you're getting a kick out of this, cat.''

Why was Cami, a woman who'd rather cut off her own limb than get out of bed before ten in the morning, calling herself at... He glanced at his watch. It wasn't even six yet.

''For summer, it's pretty darn cold out here in this ridiculous summer dress.''

And why was she still in her summer dress? She hadn't actually used that condom with the nerd, had she?

''Of course, what do I expect for being in the Sierra wilderness all night long. You know, I thought this was all my fault, but really, upon reflection, it's not. It's my parents. Dad's had what? Six wives? No, wait, I'm forgetting the unforgettable Brandy.''

Tanner lifted a brow. *Brandy?*

''She made seven. Seven stepmothers, some of whom were younger and had bigger boobs than me. It's no wonder I only date guys once.'' Her sigh filled the room. ''And then there's Mom, the mistress of control. Really, when I think about it, it's a miracle I'm normal at all.'' A short silence. ''It's sure quiet out here. Hope some ax murderer doesn't find me, there's no one to hear me scream.

Although there *are* some very annoying birds circling over my head.''

At that, Tanner dove for the phone, but just as he picked it up, she disconnected.

The digital readout on her machine starting blinking the numeral one.

He hit play, and once again Cami's voice filled the room, from the beginning this time.

''Dimi, get your paws off my stuff and come rescue me from the date from hell,'' she said, clearly annoyed.

*Who was Dimi?*

But then Tanner got sidetracked by the rest of the message, and he listened in growing concern. Dammit, it wasn't a joke, he decided, listening past Cami's light voice to the panic just beneath the surface.

She really was stranded, alone, and had been all night.

Swearing, he left the town house and headed toward his truck, because good God, if anyone stopped for her, she'd annoy the hell out of them, maybe even goad them into killing her just to shut her up.

A BIG RIG lumbered right past Cami's raised thumb, and feeling decidedly unladylike, she sent him a hand gesture she'd never had the opportunity to use before.

It felt so good she gave it to the next truck that passed her, as well.

"Oh, that's the way to charm someone into a ride."

Whirling around, Cami faced Tanner, who'd pulled up behind her. She'd been so busy swearing and kicking dirt, she hadn't even noticed.

"*You,*" she said brilliantly.

"Yep. Me." He looked her over. "Are you all right?"

The nerve of him to look so good in the mornings, all big, sexy male. She didn't want to think about how she looked—rumpled and pathetic. "Of course I'm all right."

"Yeah? So what are you doing?"

"Nothing."

"Nothing?" He came closer and tucked his hands in his pockets. "That's funny, I could have sworn you were enticing truckers to pick you up by flipping them off. Which doesn't work, by the way. You have to give them some sugar." He lifted a suggestive brow. "And I'm not talking the granulated kind."

Wasn't this fun? Not only did she have to face his amusement over her misfortune, she had to face the fact that her entire body tingled in awareness of him simply because he'd played a small part in her dreams.

Okay, a big part. Even more reason to be grumpy. "Go away."

"So happy to see me." He put a hand to his broad chest. "I'm touched."

"This isn't happening," she said to the sky.

"Yep. It is." He tugged off his dark sunglasses and studied her carefully.

She studied him back. He wore Levi's that had clearly seen better days. They were clean, for now, but worn white at all the stress points, of which he had many. She knew she was gawking, but she couldn't help it. She was starving, sleep-deprived, and even worse, she was sleep-deprived because her fantasies had involved *him*. Heavily.

Shrugging out of his untucked plaid shirt, he handed it to her. Now he wore only a plain white T-shirt.

"I'm not cold."

"You're covered in goose bumps." He set the shirt on her shoulders.

Damn, it was warm and smelled like him. She hugged it closer to her body and glared at him.

He smiled. "You've had problems?"

"Nope."

"Hmm. You're just standing out here for your health, I suppose. Practicing hitchhiking for the day it might come in handy?"

Pride was a terrible thing. And it had been a long night. Nothing had happened to her, but still, all that *could* have suddenly ran though her head.

Tanner's smile faded. "What's going on, Cami?"

God, that voice. It was low and husky and so sexy that, all on its own, her body leaned toward his.

Definitely sleep-deprived. "Nothing."

*"Cami."*

"All right, fine. I survived the date from hell. There. Are you happy?"

"I know about the date," he said quietly. "About Ted's love of the buffet. About the drive-in. About the car and how the son of a bitch left you out here all night." He stepped closer, all sign of amusement long gone. "What I'm asking is, are you really all right?"

She swallowed hard. "You...listened to my machine."

"Be grateful. Or you'd be sticking out more than a thumb right now, trying to get a ride."

Oddly enough, she *was* grateful. In spite of herself, and the fact that her fingers itched to lift his T-shirt and see if his belly was as magnificent as it was in her fantasies, she *was* happy to see him.

So much so that she might have thrown herself against him and started crying in relief, except for her damn ego, which was definitely straining now. "What are you doing here?" She asked this casually, as if they'd run into each other at the grocery store instead of a stupid, deserted road where no one had given her a second glance all night.

"I think that's *my* question to you."

"Oh. Well, I just—"

"Admit it," he said, stepping even closer, staring into her face. "You need me."

"Of course I don't."

"So your message was a lie. Your date went fine. Is that it?"

"Well, fine is relative term—" She stopped abruptly when he set a finger to her lips. It was warm and work-roughened and smelled like soap.

"Let's skip all the crap," he suggested. "And get right to the part where you express your gratitude for my rescue."

She pushed his hand away from her mouth. Her lips tingled at the loss of his touch. "I most definitely do not need rescuing."

"Really? You're going to walk home then?"

She studied the sky with great intensity, hoping he'd just vanish because it was easier than swallowing pride.

"Have it your way," he said after a moment. "See you back at the lake. Whenever you get there. Did I mention it was twenty-two miles from here to there?" With that, he turned on his heel and started walking away.

"Wait!" she cried, then watched him stop and slowly turn to face her. "Okay, I need a ride to Truckee. But not a rescue. Let's be clear on that."

Leaning against his truck, he crossed his arms. "Oh, you'll have to do much better."

"Or what? You'll leave me out here? I don't think so."

A blast of wind hit her, raising the skirt on her dress. Before she managed to shove it down, a passing truck honked in appreciation. "Oh, sure, *now* people notice me standing here," she fumed, trying to keep her dress down and her hair out of her face at the same time.

"Maybe he could give you a ride," Tanner said, unmoved.

"A ride from *you* will do," she said between her teeth.

He didn't move.

"What are we waiting for?"

He just stood there.

"Tanner!"

"I was hoping you could ask me nicely. Maybe even lift your thumb and smile hopefully, like you did for that other guy before I pulled over."

She gaped at him.

His smile went positively wicked, making her stomach leap. "And if you wanted to wait for another breeze to lift your skirt again and show off those pretty pink panties you're wearing, I wouldn't mind one little bit."

"You're sick," she declared, storming around the side of his truck, slamming the door after she plopped into the passenger seat. "Really sick."

"Just a thought." He started the truck and took a quick look at her. *Better.* She had some color in her cheeks and she didn't look close to tears anymore. In fact, she looked downright furious.

She wouldn't thank him for that, but he was relieved. If she'd broken down and cried, he wouldn't have known what to do. Tears always baffled him, especially when he was the only one around to soothe them.

Not that holding her against his chest, running his hands up and down her slim back would have been a hardship. But he'd gotten quite the view of what she had beneath that skirt. Hips that begged for his hands to grip them. Creamy thighs meant for openmouthed kisses. And what those pink panties covered made his mouth water.

Holding her now would be a definite mistake. It would take her about one second to realize he had more in mind than mere comfort.

"Who's Dimi?" he asked.

"My…sister."

"You don't seem too certain."

She let out a tight smile. "She is. She's just…a lot like me," she finished lamely. "I don't like to talk about it."

Big surprise. "Did you really have seven step-mothers?"

She turned on him, horrified. "You listened to the entire conversation?"

"Your entire conversation with yourself, yes, I listened. Which is why I'm here right now."

"Oh." She sat back. "Yeah."

"So…do you?"

"Have seven stepmothers? No. I don't think Brandy, Lulu or Cherry qualify as stepmothers, as they're the same age as I am."

"And have bigger boobs."

She ignored that. "My dad lives in Europe, so I didn't see much of them, anyway."

He glanced at her and saw past the little smile

that was supposed to assure him she didn't care. He saw a woman who'd probably never had half the love and support from her father that he'd had. He wondered where he'd be without it, and figured maybe he'd be far worse off than having gone out on a stupid blind date. "I'm sorry."

"Don't you dare feel sorry for me," she growled. "I'm sure lots of people had pole-dancing stepmothers, and fathers who forgot their birthdays and mothers who set them up with dates from hell who ditch them in a broken-down car for the night."

"Cami—"

"Say one more word and I'll slug you."

The silence grew, except for the loud, pulsing rock on his radio. When the song ended, a commercial for one of the big phone companies came on. A soft, warm voice told everyone if they were under eighteen and wanted to call home, they could call collect. Free. They could mend fences, speak to a loved one, get help without cash.

The ad was purposely designed to tug at the heartstrings, to let everyone know how much this phone company cared to offer such a service. It was a bunch of baloney, in Tanner's humble opinion, because the only the thing they really cared about was their bottom line.

And yet from the passenger seat came a suspicious sniff.

Accusingly he turned his head and found to his horror that her eyes had filled.

"Oh, no," he said.

"Shut up."

"It was just a commercial!"

"I know." She sniffed again, swiped at her cheek and glared at him. "Don't you say a darn word. I'm just hungry and cold and...and I have to go to the bathroom!" With that, she burst into tears.

"Dammit!" He pulled over to the side of the road and stared at her. "I don't have any tissues."

She used the shirt he'd given her, *his* shirt, wiping both her eyes and her nose. "Just dr—drive."

Oh, sure. Just drive. He could no more do that than shoot off his own foot. "Come here," he said, resigned, and unhooking her seat belt, he pulled her against him.

She was as warm and soft as he'd feared. More. "I'm sorry about last night," he murmured into her hair, which tickled his nose. "If I'd have known sooner, I would have been there." To avoid hair up his nose, he shifted so they were cheek to cheek and tried not to notice how wonderful she smelled. "I can't believe he left you by yourself." He knew exactly what could have happened to her, and it turned his blood cold. "I think we should look good old Ted up so I can slug him."

He felt her watery smile. She burrowed closer, and his hands tightened on her back as he ordered them to stay still. What they really wanted was to do some roaming. Serious roaming.

"I'm not crying because of him."

*Whoa.* Having her talk against his skin, having her lips slide over his flesh... Not good. "Um, Cami?"

"And I'm not crying because I had to sleep in his car," she said, winding her arms around his neck and pressing closer to his body. "Which is really uncomfortable, by the way."

She was nearly in his lap, but she was still shivering, so he didn't have the heart to push her away. He suffered from the biggest erection he'd ever had in utter horny silence.

Then she lifted her huge, wet eyes to his. "It was the commercial," she admitted. "Those long-distance commercials always make me cry."

Her mouth was a fraction of an inch from his, and he found himself leaning toward it until what she said sunk in. Long-distance commercials made her cry.

She rescued spiders.

She wanted everyone around her to be happy, to the point of risking her own neck on a stupid blind date. She was sweet, whimsical and funny.

And she was his biggest nightmare, because not only was his body clearly attracted to her, she would be higher maintenance than any woman he'd ever met.

And any woman he'd ever met had complained about his maintenance habits.

# 6

CAMI TRIED to forget what happened.

Denny's. Being ditched by Ted. Then rescued by Tanner. How she'd mortified herself afterward by crying all over him.

And she might have managed, if she could have just forgotten how she'd felt in Tanner's arms. Amazing. Special. Cherished.

It left her speechless even now, a full day later. She was in bed—which was really the couch, smack in the middle of the living room—the blankets pulled over her head so she couldn't hear Tanner, who had the radio blaring and tools banging at the other end of the town house. It wasn't even eight in the morning.

The phone rang, and though she wanted to ignore it, a client might be calling, and clients couldn't be ignored. Neither of them. Not if she wanted to eat something that wasn't out of a can this month. Reaching from her perch on the couch, she fumbled around on the floor for the phone, grabbing it just as she stretched too far.

And fell to the floor.

Tangled in blankets, hair in her face, she decided against fighting like a beached whale and lay still. "Hello," she said into the phone, eyes still closed as she discovered the floor wasn't so uncomfortable.

"Cami. It's Ted."

Well, that ruined her tranquillity in nothing flat. "Cami?"

"Hold on, Ted, I'm deciding whether to hang up or yell at you."

"I'm sorry. I just wanted to—"

Before Cami could hear what he just wanted to do, the phone was yanked out of her hand. Blinking her bleary eyes open, she saw Tanner standing over her in jeans and that tool belt, grimly holding the phone to his ear. "Ted. This is Tanner James. You don't know me, but I'm Cami's—" His gaze dipped to Cami, and she would have sworn his eyes heated to sizzling before his lashes came down and shuttered them from her. "Business associate," he finally said. He listened politely for a long moment, during which time Cami didn't breathe.

She wondered what Ted could be saying, but then Tanner put her wondering to rest.

"So this is all a misunderstanding, you say? That you left a woman—your date—alone in a broken-down car on a deserted strip of highway in order to hitch a ride with another beautiful woman who offered... What was that she offered, Ted? Dessert? Even though you'd already had it?... Uh-huh, I see. You risked Cami's life for a slice of pumpkin pie. Nice move, Ted."

He listened again. "No, that pathetic apology won't work. You know what? Let's get to the point here. *My* point. Basically, you're slime. A real bottom feeder. And if you call here again, if you come here, if you even so much as think about her, I'm going to find you and beat the shit out of you. Do you understand, Ted?"

"Tanner!" Cami gasped, trying to sit up, but not only was a blanket wrapped around her as if she were a stuffed sausage, Tanner leaned over and casually stepped on the edge of it.

Surely he hadn't done that on purpose. She tugged.

In response, he set his other foot on the blanket, as well, and looked at her from beneath those lowered lashes.

"No," he said firmly into the phone. "You're

right. You must have gotten the wrong phone number. No problem, Ted." You could only call what he did then smiling, because he bared his teeth. "Goodbye." And with shocking politeness given what he'd just said, he clicked the phone off and tossed it to the couch.

"What was that about?" she demanded, struggling to free herself, to no avail.

"Oh, it's just some caveman technique a woman wouldn't care to understand." He hunkered down beside her, careful to leave a booted foot on her blanket so she was still wrapped tighter than a pretzel. He studied her for a long moment, making her aware of things, such as the fact she had on no makeup, and that her hair was undoubtedly out of control, and that she hadn't yet brushed her teeth.

"You okay?" he eventually asked.

"You're stepping on my blanket."

"I meant did you get enough sleep? You must have been tired after the night before."

Short of reading his mind, she had no idea what the hell he was thinking. His eyes were guarded, his expression neutral. But she could have sworn she heard genuine concern in that low voice of his. "Funny time to worry about how much sleep I got, you've been banging around for hours."

"But I've been banging with consideration," he said. A slight smile softened his features. Then his gaze dipped down and heated, leading her to believe he could see right through her blanket to the large T-shirt and men's boxers she'd worn to bed.

"I'm not naked under here," she said. "You know, just in case you were wondering."

"A guy can hope," he said huskily.

"What would you have said to Ted if *he'd* said that to me?"

Tanner had the good grace to laugh, and surged to his feet. "You still have that other stupid blind date tonight? With your client's son?"

The thought made her want to groan and cover her head again. "I *need* that client."

"Enough to go through another Ted?"

"There can't be another Ted."

"Honey, beneath our masks of civility, all of us males are Teds."

"You mean all men like buffets?"

"Of different types," he said cryptically.

"What does that mean?"

"Not all of us get excited over food, but we're all reduced to basic stupidity when it comes to our weaknesses. Ted's weakness just happened to be food."

"What's yours?"

"Ah, that would be telling."

With that, he walked away, leaving her to watch his long, long legs, the way his hammer slapped against his hip with each step.

*He has the most amazing tush,* she thought ridiculously, then had to laugh at herself. Seems men weren't the only ones wearing masks of civility.

The phone rang again, and before Tanner could come back and step on her blanket, she grabbed it. "Hello?"

"You sound breathless," said Dimi.

Breathless? She was. It hadn't been Ted to do that to her, and it certainly hadn't been a sexy dream, not with all that banging going on, so it must have been Tanner. *Oh, boy.* "Yeah, well. I'm recovering. Oh, and gee, thanks for calling me back in a timely fashion."

"I was busy. Working. You might not know that concept."

"Hey, I work. I work hard."

Dimi sighed. "Sorry. I know you work hard. And I know you're trying to get your business going. But mine is the pits at the moment. Literally. I just screwed up today's show. Somehow left a pit in one of the peaches we canned, so my guest host swallowed it and choked.''

"On the air? *Live?*"

"Well, yeah."

"Ouch."

"That's not the worst of it. When I gave her the Heimlich maneuver, she coughed up the pit and it beaned the camera man right between the eyes. Gave him a concussion.''

"Holy smokes."

"I might get a ratings boost out of it, though. If people think someone might do it again, they'll tune in.''

There was Dimi. Positive to the end.

"Now tell me about this date from hell you were muttering about on my answering machine.''

"It's old news."

"Good. So you're still going out tonight with Mrs. Brown's dateless son, right?''

"I'd rather have my impacted wisdom teeth removed, without drugs.''

"You can't back out now. Bring laughing gas.''

"Funny."

"Mom told me your contractor rescued you.''

"Tanner." From her position on the floor,

Cami lifted her head. She could see him down the hallway, kneeling before a large tool chest, rifling around. He had two nails in his mouth, a baseball cap on backward, a T-shirt that said Bite Me across the chest, and he was humming to Led Zeppelin on the radio.

Out of the corner of his eyes, he caught her staring at him. He sent her a slow wink and a smile that could only be classified as bad-to-the-bone wicked.

Her heart fluttered. "Damn," she whispered.

"Is that damn, *yes,* he rescued you?" Dimi wanted to know.

"Yes," Cami whispered, her gaze locked with Tanner's.

"Oh, man, that's a loaded yes. Are you doing your contractor, Cami? *Cami?*"

No, but suddenly she wanted to be. "I've got to go now."

"Remember, date tonight. Date means income. A good thing."

"I know."

"Take your eyes off your contractor."

She couldn't.

"*Cami.* Right now. He's not your type. Yes, he's a smartass like you, he's darkly gorgeous, which I know is tempting, not to mention he's right there beneath your nose, but listen to me. *He's not your type.*"

"How do you know?"

"Let's just say I think he needs a woman who has more...*needs* than you."

"You think I'm not sexual enough for him."

"Now don't be insulted. I wouldn't be, either. Face it, Cam, we're not exactly sexual creatures."

Cami thought maybe she could be, with a little practice.

"You're thinking too much, I can hear it," Dimi said. "Listen, I can see it in those heated, intense eyes of his. He'll want...things. Things you won't want to do. You couldn't keep a man like that happy."

"Are we talking about oral sex?" Cami whispered.

"Cami!"

"Well, really. This is the twenty-first century. I could certainly learn." *Wanted* to learn.

"I'm not listening to this."

"How hard could it be? I'm sure he'd be willing to teach me good...technique."

"Oh, my God. Look, you don't even know him all that well."

"Sure I do."

"Yeah? Have you told him about us? That you're a twin?"

"What does that have to do with anything?"

"You never tell any man about me." Dimi gentled her voice because they both knew why, that Cami always held a part of herself back on purpose, a very important part. She didn't trust love, didn't believe in it. "I'm using that as my gauge. Someday you're going to tell a man you're a twin, and I'll know you're serious about him."

"Not this man." Cami's heart hurt at that and she ignored it. "I don't want to go tonight." She wanted to stay home and think about the things Tanner would want from her, how maybe he'd coax them from her in that sexy voice of his.

"Think mortgage."

Cami thought about Tanner instead, thought about how he'd said she went through mental hoops for everyone's happiness but her own. She opened her mouth to say something of that nature to her sister, to maybe ask for advice, but Dimi was wise enough to hang up on her.

WHEN TANNER heard the shower turn on, he imagined Cami in there, stripping down, stepping under the spray of the water. Imagined her wet, sleek, perfect body gleaming as she ran soapy hands over her limbs...

And smashed his thumb with his hammer.

While he was dancing and swearing, his cell phone rang.

"Get lucky yet?" his father asked.

"I've been working too hard to get lucky, thank you very much." He sucked on his throbbing thumb.

"Love's more important than money."

"Can't live off sex," Tanner replied. Damn, that thumb was going to hurt all day.

"I said love, not sex."

"Well, I don't do love."

"I raised you better than that."

Tanner gave up on the conversation entirely, ignoring his father's musing that maybe his son was overlooking something really special right beneath his nose simply to preserve his precious bachelorhood out of habit. Bad habit.

It wasn't bad habit that kept Tanner single, but dedication and hard work. No woman would want to play second fiddle to a struggling business and long hours and...oh, hell.

He *was* ignoring something special—Cami—in order to preserve his bachelorhood, which meant his father was right.

He could live with that.

Tanner worked some more, and later watched Cami measure a customer for a spring wardrobe.

She'd already explained to him that sewing was how she made money until she got her design business going, and with that news he should have worried about his own paycheck.

Instead he watched her, fascinated. Watched her slim, capable hands spread material, saw her hunch over her plans and talk to herself as she stuck pins into paper and once into her finger.

When she brought that finger to her mouth and sucked, he actually got hard.

So he worked some more and told himself to stop watching her. Which lasted until much later, when she came into his view wearing yet another summer dress, looking nervous.

"Don't tell me." He tossed aside his tool belt and studied her. "You're going through with tonight's date even after the last fiasco."

"I promised."

He opened his mouth to tell her what he thought of her promises to do things she didn't want to do, but at the look of trepidation on her face he closed it again.

The doorbell rang. They both looked out the window. A shiny red Corvette was parked in front of her walkway. Every inch of the car had been well tended; the chrome was polished to a mirror shine.

"There won't be any car trouble tonight," she said, staring out the window.

Any guy who drove a red Corvette with polished chrome was slick, Tanner told himself, and grabbed Cami's purse off her shoulder.

"Tanner!"

He pawed through the mysterious mess that made up the contents of a woman's purse and didn't answer.

"What are you doing?"

Hell if he knew, except the thought of her with a slick, rich mama's boy just didn't sit right with him.

No way did he want them to have the convenience of a condom right in her purse. Of course the guy could be packing himself, and if he was smart, he was, but Tanner couldn't control that.

Aha! His fingers closed over the condom, and he withdrew it.

"Hey!"

He pocketed the little packet just as the doorbell rang again. "Don't drink and drive, and remember, call if you're going to be late."

She gaped at him, then lifted a finger and

pointed it in the region of his face. "You've lost it," she said, turning toward the door.

Her hair spun silkily, teasing him with its light scent. Her skirt whirled with her movement, brushing his legs. And her bare shoulders were such temptation he nearly bent and bit her.

Definitely, he'd lost it.

"Not too late to change your mind. Or to stand firm on your own wishes."

She went still, her hand on the door. "If you know me so well, what are those wishes?"

"Maybe your fantasy date."

"With who?"

"Maybe with me."

The doorbell startled them both, and with a soft curse, she pulled open the door.

Tanner decided he couldn't watch, so he left her alone and disappeared into the back half of the town house, where he had more than enough work waiting for him.

"Meow."

He looked into Annabel's face. She looked worried. Dammit, now he was really losing it. "She'll be fine. She has a cell phone."

*She had one last time, too, and look what happened.*

He bent for his tool belt, but the ridiculous image of Cami in that Corvette stuck with him. She wasn't out with another Ted, that was certain. And for all her talent and charm, he knew Cami wasn't especially...well, worldly. Not naive, exactly, but far too sweet to be on her own with a spoiled rich jerk.

He'd have to hurry or he'd lose them.

He dropped the tool belt and grabbed his keys, cursing himself the entire way to his truck.

"WHY ARE WE HERE?" Cami asked Joshua a few minutes later.

Her date turned off the engine, unhooked his seat belt and turned to her with a smile that made her nervous.

It wasn't him, she assured herself. He was very handsome, in a boyish sort of way. In fact, he reminded her of a schoolgirl's dream, the sort of guy who was captain of the football team, who wore a letter jacket and made every guy jealous and every girl swoon.

"Joshua?"

"I thought we'd have a backward date," he said smoothly, reaching across her to unhook her seat belt, too. He slid closer, his lips curved, his eyes intent.

Oh, boy.

They were at the top of Tahoe Donner, miles above the town of Truckee and miles from civilization. Far below, the lights around Donner Lake twinkled invitingly.

Around her was nothing but darkness, reminding her of last night.

Her heart started pounding, because here it wasn't Ted and his unreliable car. It was Joshua, who seemed to be famished for something, and since it obviously wasn't dinner, she leaned against the door and gave him a weak smile. "You know what? I'm not really fond of backward dates."

His hands closed over hers, squeezing once before traveling slowly up her arms. He licked his lips. "You're far more beautiful than I imagined you'd be. My mother doesn't usually have the greatest taste."

Since Cami made his mother's clothes and thought Mrs. Brown had excellent taste, she bristled. "Hey—"

"I'll have to thank her."

He was leaning close, far too close.

"You know what?" she asked on a shaky laugh. "I might have forgotten to mention—" Her back pressed into the door handle, hard. "I like my own space. You seem to be invading it."

"Funny, too," he murmured, his mouth unbearably close to hers. "I like funny."

"Back off," she warned, putting her hands to his chest.

"Ooh, and tough. Good. Get rough with me." When his mouth slid over her jaw, she gritted her teeth and shoved hard.

He didn't budge.

She'd tried to be nice. Given that, she had no compunction about waiting one more second, just as he pressed his body into hers, before she put all her weight behind it and drove her knee into his groin.

The air left him in a rush, and he collapsed over her so hard she couldn't breathe. Just as she would have shoved him off, the door supporting her flew open.

She immediately fell to the ground, with Joshua sprawled over top of her. The air whooshed out of her lungs, but she managed to blink her eyes open just in time to see Tanner haul Joshua off her.

*Tanner?*

She blinked again. Yep, it was him. No tool belt, but he looked intense and fierce and really mad. Madder than when he'd hammered his own thumb.

"Tanner—"

"Hush, Cami," he said. He pulled back his fist, but Joshua was groaning so loudly and had turned so green that Tanner dropped him to the ground in disgust.

"Well," he said, brushing off his hands, turning to Cami. "Excuse me. Seems you did your own rescuing this time."

THEY DIDN'T TALK on the ride home. Or rather, Tanner didn't. Whenever Cami tried, his hands fisted on the steering wheel and steam came out of his ears.

"That's really silly, don't you think?" she asked finally. "Not talking to me? Is it because I didn't need your help?"

He broke his silence at that. "Are you *kidding?* I'm thrilled you didn't need my help to knee that idiot in the family jewels."

"Then why are you so mad?"

He shook his head and let out a low laugh that held little humor in it. "Because you frustrate the hell out of me." He downshifted and glared at her. "And I guess it's because I want you to do something you're not capable of."

"What's that?"

"I don't know...how about stop pleasing others and please yourself."

She stared at him.

"What's the matter, Cami? I've never seen you without something to say before."

"Well, there's no reason to be rude."

"You know, I can't figure out if it's because you don't *know* your own mind, or if it's because you know it all too well and are afraid of it, but I can't stand watching you do this to yourself."

Stung to the quick, she looked straight ahead. "Never mind," she whispered. "I liked it better when you were giving me the silent treatment."

# 7

CAMI THOUGHT she'd have to be tricky to avoid Tanner, but since he avoided her first, she had no trouble at all.

He used loud tools, a loud crew and even louder rock music, and spent every moment doing just his job.

He even avoided Dimi, unknowingly, of course, when she came in after work the next afternoon to steal a snack.

"Not even a courtesy hello," Dimi whispered to Cami on her way out the door. "I'm late for a date with my mechanic or I'd stay and mess with him to see he paid for that. Do you realize he didn't even give me the customary you're-a-loon look?"

"He's mad at me."

"Why?"

"Because…well, it's complicated."

"Honey, with you it usually is."

Cami should have been able to explain the truth

to Dimi, but since she'd just come to it, and it wasn't exactly flattering, she held her tongue.

She understood Tanner's anger and frustration. She really did. And the worst part of it was, he was more right than he could know. Cami *did* let others railroad her into their wishes. She did it because she knew those wishes would never lead her heart to true happiness, so in a way, it meant she was always safe.

She had no intention of leading her heart to true happiness ever, because she didn't believe in it.

There. She'd thought it out loud, now she'd deal with it. And Tanner.

Somehow.

He was still ignoring her. No teasing, no hot looks, no discussions that were deep and uncomfortable and oddly exhilarating.

No nothing.

She missed him. Stupid, since she was the one who'd wanted to do the avoiding, dammit. But though she had come to terms with the fact she wouldn't go for love, ever, she didn't plan on giving up other joys.

Such as lust.

This was the age of the woman. She could want a man, physically, and have that be it. And though it made no sense whatsoever, she wanted Tanner.

His crew left a few moments before him. Her client—not Mrs. Brown, who'd dumped her like a bad habit after she'd unmanned her son—had left, as well.

Just music and tools to compete with, but Cami hadn't been a beauty queen in high school for nothing. She knew how to get a man's attention.

She just didn't know how to *keep* it.

Dressed for the part, she slipped out of the bathroom and pulled the plug on his portable CD player. The rock music died.

She also pulled the plug on the orange extension cord that ran down the hallway and disappeared into her bedroom.

Abruptly all was silent.

"What the—" she heard Tanner say, with some colorful words added on the end of that.

Raising her brow, she followed the extension cord and found him standing in the middle of the room, back to her, arms extended over his head, holding a nail gun.

"That's not funny, Juan," he said without looking. "Just because you have a hot date and have to leave early, some of us still have work left to do. Plug it back in."

"It's not Juan," Cami told him, fascinated by the play of muscles stretching his T-shirt taut across his back. His arms were pretty nice, too, all damp and tense and straining.

She thought he might have sworn again, softly this time, before slowly lowering the nail gun.

At the sight of her, his eyes flared with heat, stroking her destroyed ego just a bit.

"Hi," she said, running her hands down her sundress. She'd worn a sundress on both of her dates, but those had been relatively conservative. Sleeveless, but loose and flowing and flowery.

This sundress was siren red, short as sin and just as snug. So snug, in fact, she hoped there wasn't a fire or some other natural disaster because she wouldn't be able to run for help without hitching the skirt to her waist, which wouldn't be exactly ladylike. Not that she was going for lady-like at the moment.

"You weren't wearing that a few moments ago when you came prancing down the hallway with a bag of potato chips."

Damn, her sister had stolen her chips. Again!

Somehow she knew Tanner should be told about Dimi, and now would be a good time, but keeping that part of her life to herself was deeply ingrained.

"Don't tell me," he said in a low, rough,

nearly strangled voice. "You're going on another date in that."

"No, I wanted to talk to you."

"In that?"

"What's wrong with it?" She smoothed the bodice, which lifted her breasts up and out so far she didn't dare breathe or she'd pop out.

Definitely not ladylike.

Still, her body was demanding air—it was funny that way—and she couldn't hold her breath another moment, so she drew in the shortest one she could manage.

Tanner's eyes nearly bugged out of his head. "Don't do that," he said, lifting a hand as if to stop her.

"I have to," she said, dizzy with effort. "Or I'm going to pass out." And because suddenly she really felt her world fading, she put her hands to her knees and bent over.

Tanner swore again, far more vividly than before.

Definitely he was still mad at her.

She heard his nail gun hit the floor. Then, from her bent-over position, his feet appeared.

"Sit down," he commanded.

She thought about that. "Can't."

"Why?"

"My dress is too tight."

He was silent for a moment, then suddenly her world spun as he swung her up. One of his arms supported her back, the other was beneath her knees, leaving her no choice but to throw her arms around his neck. And because she'd been wondering what his strong shoulders would feel like beneath her head, she set it there. Then she sighed, because it felt heavenly. *He* felt heavenly.

"Cami."

Just that, just her name, in a voice so serrated and sexy she nearly sighed again. She felt his arm supporting her back, his fingers angled just beneath her breast. It tingled.

His other arm held her legs, which meant the fingers of that hand were on the bare skin of the back of her upper thigh.

Nice. She wished he wasn't still so mad at her, wished that she could explain herself better, that she was as good at talking about her feelings as he was, because maybe then she could make him understand that this attraction could be a beautiful thing. Temporary—since she couldn't think permanent—but beautiful.

Thinking that, and melting just a little, she sighed.

Then remembered she wasn't supposed to

breathe or she was going to pop right out of her dress. With an odd mix of dismay and anticipation, she glanced down. Yep, her nightmare had come true. Definitely that was half a breast straining free of the red material, including a nice peek-aboo shot of one rosy, hard-tipped nipple.

"Cami," Tanner said again, in a voice so low and tight her entire body shivered.

"I'm sorry," she whispered, pulling one hand from around his neck, covering her bared breast with her fingers.

"You're killing me," he said huskily.

"Does that mean you're not still mad at me?"

He let out a rough laugh that held no humor. "Look, you wanted to talk, and I'm trying to remember that, instead of doing what I want, which would be to press you against that wall there and taste what you've just offered me up."

Visions of that very thing danced in her head and made her bones melt.

"Listen, Cami, client or not, crazy or sane, for better or worse, you're making me so hot and bothered I can't think straight. Do you understand what I'm saying?"

"That you...want me?"

"I want you so bad I'm weak as a baby."

The sound that escaped her was far more like

a whimper of pleasure than of mortification, and his eyes practically smoldered. His chest rumbled with a groan and he closed his eyes to the sight she'd unwittingly planted on him. "Talk," he said through his teeth.

"I…forgot what I wanted to say."

"Why?" he asked the ceiling. "Why are you doing this to me?"

"I don't even know what 'this' you're talking about."

"Don't you?"

Then she was falling, as he'd dumped her on the couch. Standing over her, hands on his hips, his chest rising and falling harshly. "I tried to talk to you before you went on either of those ridiculous dates," he said. "You didn't want to."

"Yes, I did."

"No. You wanted surface stuff, like how's the weather and can you redo my town house kind of talk. I'm trying to stick to that, because I understand you don't want more, but in that dress, it's nearly impossible."

"I didn't mean to flash you," she whispered.

"What *did* you mean to do?"

"Make you notice me."

"Done."

"Make you hot."

"Done."

Nervous, she licked her lips, and he groaned again. "Maybe you don't realize the truth here, so let me spell it out. I want more from you than you can give. You're too busy giving to everyone else. You give them your all and leave nothing for yourself, and I can't stand it. I want a woman who knows her mind and isn't afraid to speak it. I want—"

"I know my mind and I was *trying* to give it to you," she said in her defense. "It's just that I couldn't hold my breath and talk at the same time, so I chose breathing and you saw what happened."

"Yeah, you nearly gave me heart failure!"

He wasn't talking to her, as she'd wanted. He wasn't even lusting at her at the moment, which would have been nice, too. But he *was* yelling at her, which was better than being ignored, but not quite as good as, say, getting a filling. "What did you mean, you want more from me?"

"I'm tired of sending you off on dates you don't even want, then having to rescue you. I'm tired of you saying yes to everyone but yourself. I'm tired of you dressing up for men too stupid to appreciate you. I'm tired of—"

He broke off and clamped his jaw shut. Then

he shoved his fingers through his already unruly hair and turned in a slow circle before facing her again, where she was still sprawled on the couch.

"Tired of what, Tanner?"

"Tired of fighting your wall." He sank to the coffee table next to her. "You have one, you know. Made of stone. It's probably from watching your father flit from relationship to relationship, or maybe it's from fighting your mother's strong will, I don't know. But whenever I try to get close to you, you add another layer, fill up your moat, and hide behind it."

Not only was that true, but he was the first person besides Dimi to know her so well.

He gentled both his voice and his gaze. "I'm good enough to fix your town house, good enough to give you a hand beating up your dates when they go bad. Probably even good enough to develop a passing friendship with, but that's all you'll allow."

She let out a disparaging sound, but didn't know what to say because it was the cold, hard truth.

"Am I close, Cami?"

He was so close she could see the specks of light dancing in his amazing eyes. She could see the fair stubble lining his jaw. She could see his genuine frustration, and the fact that he cared enough to feel frustrated in the first place put an unexpected lump in her throat.

And yes, he was close enough to the truth to have her closing her eyes to it.

"No, you don't," she heard him say, and felt his hands on her face, cupping her jaw, lifting it to him. He waited until she opened her eyes again. "Don't hide."

"It's a habit of mine," she admitted.

"Not with me. Don't do it with me."

"I don't have a choice. You won't go away like all the others."

A shadow of a smile flitted across his mouth. His very sexy mouth.

"I really don't want to like you," she said around that lump blocking her air passage.

Unexpectedly, his smile widened. "See? You're being honest with me." He nudged her. "Did it hurt?"

"Less than a tetanus shot." She had to return his smile. "And you should know I don't want to want you, either."

"But you do."

"But I do. It's making me do dumb things. Like wear this dress."

His eyes were on fire as they slowly, slowly, slid over her body. "That wasn't so dumb."

For a long moment she looked at him, and he looked right back. It was doing funny things to her body. Her skin felt too tight. Her insides had turned to liquid, which seemed to pool in a bunch of places she hadn't paid much attention to lately. "Tanner...what are we doing?"

"We're finding ourselves attracted."

"I don't want to be attracted. I just gave up on men."

"When?"

"Last night."

"Don't give up on all of us."

Slowly she shook her head.

"Go out with me," he said, having no idea where that command came from. "Let me show you we're not all jerks. You have needs, stop shelving them and pay attention to what they are." He thought about her never having had multiple orgasms, but that thought just made him quiver with the desire to show her what she was missing.

"Tanner—"

"Just one date, your fantasy date." He didn't add the multiple orgasm thing. He didn't want to scare her off. But he'd really lost it here. He wanted her, in a totally foreign, not purely physical way, though he was still hard as nails from seeing her perfect, rose-tipped, pebbled nipple. Just thinking about it made his mouth water again.

"How do you know about my fantasy date?"

"You told me. Well, you told you, when you were talking to yourself on your answering machine."

"Oh, God. How could I forget? You listened."

"Unabashedly."

She frowned. "And I'm not messing up all my dates to punish my father."

"No? Then go out with me."

"We wouldn't work together."

She was scared, her eyes huge. And suddenly his impatience with her faded. "Just one date," he said softly. "You've been out with some real losers, Cami. Just let me show you how it could be. How it should be."

"And then you'll stop this."

"Absolutely." Probably.

Maybe.

Okay, no, he wouldn't. But for Cami, this was on a need-to-know basis, and she didn't need to know that. So he smiled. "Want me to prove to you how much you want to try this?"

She let out a nervous laugh. "I don't think—"

He leaned over her and set his mouth to hers. He had no idea what he was doing. Just the thought of Cami was a threat to his string-free heart, but he'd never wanted a woman so much.

From the very first touch of their mouths, he knew he was in trouble. Heat spiraled through his chest, shooting a straight line of fire to his groin.

Pure lust, he reminded himself, that's what this was, and he whispered her name to remember that.

She parted those soft lips. She tasted like strawberry lip gloss and the promise of something even sweeter. Without thinking—which had become impossible with the draining of all his blood for parts south—he deepened the kiss, using his tongue to touch, swirl, caress and tease hers.

Without hesitation, she returned the favor, and within ten seconds he'd run out of air. Pulling back far enough to look at her, he slowly shook his head. "You're right." He ran a finger over her jaw, along her neck, his gaze dipping to the front of her dress, where her nipples were straining at the thin material, begging for attention that he was dying to give. "You obviously feel nothing for me."

"You don't get it," she whispered, her lips wet from his.

"Tell me."

"You were right about…the others. I went out with them, with all of them, because I knew I was safe. My heart was safe. I would never have given it to them. But with you…"

"With me what? You think I would hurt you?"

"Yes. No. I mean, with you I couldn't keep my heart safe."

"One date, Cami. That's all I'm asking."

"Then what?"

"Then you learn how to have a great date."

"That's all?"

"Sure."

She pushed up to a sitting position and tipped her head at him.

"Honest," he said.

"What do you get out of it?"

"You out of my system."

Her lips curved. "Ah, a man with a motive."

"We all have motives." And his was to make sure he kissed her again.

# 8

*He was an incredible lover.*

*Sensual. Giving. Demanding. And she gave him whatever he asked for in that rough, serrated, sexy voice. Everything. Anything.*

*Shocking herself.*

*"More," he commanded, sliding down her body, kissing every inch of her skin, bringing her up again, up to that jagged edge, holding her there, quivering, whimpering, begging...then flying as she came, again and again.*

"Multiple orgasms," she whispered in disbelief, and woke herself up. It was completely black when she blinked her eyes furiously, and she couldn't breathe.

Surging up, waving her arms wildly in sudden panic, she heard the hard thump and hiss, and just before she hit the floor, as well, she knew.

She'd been on the couch, buried beneath the covers, with Annabel on her head. She'd been dreaming, dreaming hot, sweaty sex fantasies about her contractor.

"Not my fault," she told the insulted cat as they lay on the floor, nose to nose. "It was his kiss. And you're a bed hog."

"Mew."

"Okay, a couch hog." Hauling off the tangled covers, she stared at her yellow polka-dot panties, which happened to be all she was wearing. Her hair was in her face, her skin hot and clammy, a reminder of what she'd been dreaming about. "I've got to do laundry," she told no one in particular.

"No kidding," Dimi said as she came down the hall and looked at her sister. She wore Cami's favorite sweater, and as she zipped it up with one hand, she pocketed Cami's mascara with the other. "I can't find a thing to wear in this mess."

"Try your own place," Cami grumbled. "Or go to Mom's, you moocher."

"Mom doesn't have near the same quality in makeup. And you might think about pulling those covers back over yourself. You have a man down that hallway, a tall, dark, sexy man who would probably fall at your feet right there on the floor if he came in here and saw you lying there like that, all rosy and glowing."

Cami looked at herself. Her skin was indeed glowing, and her nipples hard. "I'm not rosy and glowing, I'm cold," she muttered, but she burrowed beneath the covers. "And don't even think about stealing my last bag of chips. That's my lunch."

Dimi shrugged and headed toward the door. "While you were moaning in your sleep, a client called."

Cami straightened. "Somebody wants something sewed?"

"No, a real client. A design client. Seems Mrs. Brown's son got himself in trouble on another so-called blind date she'd set up for him, and that woman wasn't quite as forgiving as you. He's in jail, and she's furious with him. She wants to make it up to you by sending her very rich, very best friend over this afternoon. This friend needs her ten *thousand* square foot home redecorated."

Cami leaped to her feet. "Oh, my God. Really? You're not just saying that because you look really awful in my sweater?"

Dimi looked at herself. "I look great in this sweater."

"No, you look awful. Pale." She wanted that sweater. "Fat," she added with inspiration.

"Well, shit." Dimi took it off and threw it at

Cami, who slipped into it, wisely keeping her smile to herself.

"I really have a client?"

Dimi moved toward the door. "Looks like. Don't date her son, and you should be fine."

"Yeah." But nerves worked their way to Cami's tummy, and she sank back to the couch. Annabel immediately jumped on top of her.

"Mew."

"Oh, Annabel." She hugged the squirming cat. "I'm really on my way." Burrowing beneath the bushel of covers, she allowed herself to dream. It was almost too much to imagine. She'd wanted this for so long, had worked at it harder than anything she'd ever worked at before.

And now it might happen.

It *would* happen.

She was fixing up her place. And she had her first real client. Then sounds coming from down the hallway registered.

Tanner.

He was an enigma to her. Tall, dark and intense. Very attuned to his work. Passionate. Passionate about his work, his father, about everything in his life.

She thought of all that passion aimed at her and quivered.

Silly. Though she'd read about it in novels, it had never really happened to her before. Why it was happening now, with a man like Tanner, her virtual polar opposite, she didn't know.

He sang off-key, talked in bastardized Spanish to his laborers and swore like a sailor when he didn't know she was listening. He also spoke gently to her cat, even when Annabel continued to steal anything of value and chew it up.

Her dream came back to her, vividly. There'd been no doubt who had been making love to her. He'd been highly sensual, earthy and uninhibited, and in return, he'd made her that way, too. He'd done things to her, shown her things she'd never imagined before.

It was his voice. It sent shivers down her spine and made her want to please him. This need for him was awesome, she thought, sinking deeper in her covers. And terrifying.

Thank God it had all been just a dream.

TANNER FOUND HER like that an hour later, fast asleep beneath a pile of blankets. He'd come to work exceptionally early because he'd wanted to get a few things done before he did it.

Before he kidnapped Cami and took her on a fantasy date.

It made little sense, this need to show her a good time. But he'd rationalized it to her as needing to get her out of his system, and he'd go with that.

"It's time," he said, lifting her in his arms.

She slept like the dead. Murmuring his name, she set her head on his chest.

"I'm having the best dreams this morning," she told him groggily.

It was almost no longer morning, and she wasn't dreaming, but he grinned and kept his mouth shut.

"Hey. Wait." Suddenly wide awake, she lifted her head to pierce him with those dark, dark eyes.

From beneath the covers engulfing her, Annabel poked her head out, as well.

"What are we doing?" Cami asked him.

"Going on that date. Without your cat though. Scram, Annabel," he said.

"Mew," said the cat.

"No," said the woman.

Tanner sighed. "I thought we agreed to get each other out of our systems."

"No, *you* agreed." Cami shoved against his chest, and he put her on the ground. "I'm date cursed, remember?"

"I'm willing to take the risk."

"I'm not." Grappling with her blanket, which she had wrapped around her like a sarong, she flashed him a good amount of leg. He saw bare thigh and caught a glimpse of yellow polka-dot satin. He had to swallow hard. "You're not wearing very much."

"I need to do laundry. And you're changing the subject."

"Just come with me. This one time."

"Where?"

"It's a surprise."

"I don't like surprises."

"You'll like this one."

She stared at him for a long moment, then relented ungraciously. "Fine. If it gets you out of my dreams, let's just do it." She grimaced. "I meant *do it* as in go on this date, not *do it* as in…as in… Oh, you know."

He laughed. "So you have ulterior motives for this date, as well?"

"Absolutely."

"See, now *that's* the way to approach going out. On your own terms." He was proud of her for that. "Take what you want, Cami. Always take what you want."

Her eyes darkened all the more, and she looked

at his mouth. "I think I'm going to like this new me."

God help him. So was he. "Let's go."

CAMI STOOD on the banks of the Truckee River, dividing a look between the raft Tanner had dropped at her feet and the turquoise blue waters. "You're taking me *rafting?*"

"Not exactly a cruise, I know." Tanner handed her an oar. "But just as fun."

While he held it in place, she stepped gingerly into the gently rocking raft. "And we're doing this so we can stop thinking about each other, right?"

Tanner sat across from her and looked into her questioning eyes. He saw a good amount of apprehension and a fear he was only just beginning to fully understand. "I think you should tell me about these dreams," he teased, pushing off the shore with his oar and setting them in motion downstream. "Since you seem so adamant about getting rid of them."

She blushed. "They're no big deal."

Smiling, he steered them around a fallen log. "Uh-huh."

"They're not." She gripped the side of the raft. "This is a bad idea. I knew it would be. I only agreed because I was afraid you'd get upset with me and give me green walls or something equally tacky, and then where would I be?''

"Your place couldn't get any worse, believe me. And is that really the only reason you're here? It has nothing whatsoever to do with the fact that we've discovered this mutual attraction—''

"I've discovered nothing.''

"Which explains why I had you hot and bothered this morning.''

"I was not—'' She let out a loud breath. "I'm absolutely not going to do this with you.'' Closing her eyes, she leaned back in the raft, tilted her face to the sun and went still.

Lying there beneath the gorgeous sky, surrounded by the incomparable Sierras on the Truckee River, she looked like a goddess.

It occurred to him that he might be in serious trouble here. She wasn't leaving his system.

"This is nice,'' she admitted quietly, her eyes still closed. "I've lived here forever and I've never done this.''

"I've only been here a year, but I raft as often as I can. Or kayak.''

She opened her eyes and turned her head to study him. "You've only been here a year?''

"I moved my father here from Los Angeles. It was too hot for him there, that heat and smog were killing him. After he had his stroke, we came here for his recuperation, and neither of us ever left. He lives in Tahoe City now, in a small senior community, and is happier than he's ever been."

"You love him very much."

"Of course."

"Of course," she whispered, once again closing her eyes. "I wouldn't have moved for my father. Or given up a year of my life to nurse him back to health. What does that say about me?"

"It says you two aren't close. It happens."

"I hate his current wife. Does that happen, too?"

"Why do you hate her?"

"Because she looks better in a bikini than I do."

He ran his gaze down her body, wishing she was in a bikini right now. "I find that hard to believe."

She smiled and relaxed again. "This really is nice."

"Better than Denny's?"

"Definitely." She cocked an ear. "What's that sound?"

He listened, and at the unmistakable hissing of

air leaving the raft at an alarming speed, he swore. "Air."

She went utterly still, except for her eyes, which had turned into two huge saucers. "*Air? As in leaving-the-raft air?*"

"Yeah." He tossed her a life preserver. "Looks like you're still date cursed."

"You're kidding me."

"You know how to swim, right?"

"Let me repeat. You're. Kidding. Me."

"I'll kid you later, I promise."

"Oh, my God." She slipped into the life vest and eyed the water, which as luck would have it was so deep in this spot they couldn't see the bottom.

"There are no sharks," he promised.

"Well, that's more than I can say about my date with Joshua."

Tanner checked her life jacket. "I'm sorry I stole your condom."

That coaxed a smile out of her. "No, you're not."

"Okay, I'm not." He took her hand. "But I am sorry about the raft."

She eyed the cold water warily. "Don't worry. It's still the best date I've had in a while."

Which wasn't saying much, he knew. "So you'll give me another."

She laughed. "No way."

"Come on. A second fantasy date."

"Nope. This was just to get you out of my system. And you're out. All the way out."

"I'm going to make you prove that," he promised softly.

"With another kiss?" She looked hopeful and terrified at the same time. "I'm sure I'll be utterly unmoved."

"Hmm." Scooting closer so they were kneeling facing each other in the slowly sinking raft, he slid one hand to the small of her back, the other beneath her hair, skimming his fingers over her nape.

She shivered. Her eyes were half closed.

"Unmoved, right?" he teased softly.

"Absolutely." But she leaned toward him.

Between them, her nipples hardened against his chest, making him want to groan. His fingers skimmed the skin at the base of her spine, and she arched under his hand, letting out a soft little sound that raged at his gut and groin. Especially his groin.

Water swirled around their knees, but he couldn't pay attention to that, not when she'd dropped her head back just a little, pressing her body closer into his, her eyes closed to the warm sun.

She was beautiful, and whether or not the thought gave him hives, she was his.

His.

Bending, he put his mouth to her throat.

She practically purred. Her hands lifted, fisted in his hair, held him to her.

"Still unmoved?" he asked, dragging open-mouthed kisses down to her collarbone, where he stopped to feast on a fascinating stretch of bare skin.

"Absolutely." Her fingers tightened painfully in his hair. "But don't you dare stop."

"I won't," he promised, dipping his mouth down a little farther, to the enticing curve of a breast. "Just getting each other out of our systems, right?"

"Uh-huh. Now shut up and keep that mouth working."

"Gladly." His tongue nudged aside the material of her shirt, and he went for his goal, only to be thwarted by a bigger problem.

The leak had spread. The water weighted down the raft so that more gushed in over the sides.

The raft wobbled. Cami let out a shocked gasp

and dropped her grip on his hair to clutch the side of the raft, which started to collapse. "Tanner!"

"One more kiss," he said, leaning in.

Her mouth was warm and soft and tasted like soda. For an instant she melted to him, kissing him back, but then the water hit high on their thighs, and she pulled away, gasping. "So much for the perfect date."

It had been perfect to him. "Perfect's relative," he told her.

Then the water hit the sensitive-to-cold area directly above and between his thighs. "Now swim!" he said in a voice an octave higher than usual.

# 9

"GOODNESS," Cami's mother said after she'd listened to her daughter repeat the events from the river-rafting date. "What caused the leak?"

"Fate, I'm sure." Cami was on her cell phone, and as usual, her mother had caught her just as she was pulling into her town house complex. She'd been gone since the day after the rafting incident, traveling to San Francisco on a referral from Dimi, which had actually panned out.

After two days of talking carpets, colors and lines, Cami couldn't wait to dig in and start.

Also, in spite of herself, she couldn't wait to see Tanner again.

"What happened?" her mother demanded. "Don't leave me hanging."

Cami parked and got out, her cell phone caught between her shoulder and her ear, one arm carrying her overnight bag, the other full of work materials. Juggling everything, she headed toward her town house. "We swam for shore."

"And then?"

"And then nothing," she said as casually as she could to the woman who could sniff out a lie within two thousand miles.

"You're leaving something out," her mother said slowly, her radar apparently well and working. "I can smell it."

Cami made it to her front door and set her head against the wood. "Mom."

*"What next?"*

"We walked back to where we'd left his truck."

"It was running, I assume," her mother said. "Don't tell me it wouldn't start and he hitched a ride, deserting you."

"Oh, it started. The tow truck guy had no problem at all."

*"What?"*

Cami had to laugh, it was so ridiculous, and she was so incredibly date cursed. "He'd parked in a duck zone and got towed."

"A duck *what?*"

"Zone. No parking allowed because it's where the ducks gather their little ducklings. Don't you dare cackle like that, this entire mess is yours and Dad's fault respectively."

"Oh, do tell how you figure that!"

"Well, Dad is always dumping his wife for someone better. And then there's you."

"Me?"

"You're always turning men down, waiting for someone better. Do you realize I destroy every potential relationship by sabotaging the date, subliminally of course, so that I don't have to dump him down the road? Or *be* dumped, which actually is far more likely."

"No one would dump you."

"Yeah, and the moon is made of cheese." Cami held out her key, but the door was ajar. From the back end of the town house she could hear banging.

Tanner.

Her stomach jittered. Or it could be the five doughnuts she'd consumed, but probably not.

Always, she'd told herself she wanted a man but that there wasn't one available. Sadly, that wasn't the truth.

She didn't *allow* one to be available. She'd always been told that knowing your problem was more than half the battle, but that wasn't the case here.

She knew her problem, and it was *still* a problem.

She was afraid. More afraid than when she'd

been sleeping in Ted's stupid car. More afraid than when she'd been fending off an even more stupid Joshua.

She knew Tanner wouldn't like it that she feared him, but it was fact. Somehow he'd reached in past her wall of resistance and had taken a hold of her heart.

"Honey, I hesitate to say this—"

"You never hesitate to say anything."

"Hush. I'm not going to hound you about your laundry."

Good. Because at this moment Cami was so low on clothes she'd been forced to go commando—no panties. If her mother knew, she'd have a coronary.

"I have this neighbor. He's young and—"

Oh, my God. "Hold it right there." Cami laughed. She could do little else. "Try Dimi. I happen to know she's home, probably eating my food, the thief."

"Your sister is not a thief."

"Uh-huh, right. Look, I have to go. Love you, though."

"I love you, too. Now really, he's—"

"Bye, Mom." Gently she hung up and shook her head. Some things would never change.

Walking through the living room, she dumped first her phone, then the load in her arms.

"Cami."

At the sound of his voice, she shivered and sank to the arm of the couch. They hadn't seen each other much. She'd been working, and he'd...well, given the looks of him, he hadn't been.

He stood there, so gorgeous she would have sat, if she hadn't already done so. His hair shone in the light, nearly hitting his shoulders. His eyes gleamed with some inner knowledge and good humor, and she wondered if he planned on sharing the joke. Then there was that mouth of his, the one she'd dreamed of every single night.

And finally, his body. She'd never seen him dressed in anything but jeans and a T-shirt, but now he wore a long-sleeved, incredibly soft-looking black shirt, tucked into black pants. No shoes. She'd always imagined men's feet as incredibly...well, ugly.

Tanner's bare feet seemed nothing short of sexy.

"I took a shower," he said. "I hope you don't mind."

Mind? She just wished she'd known. It would

have given her mental images she could have used for a year's worth of fantasies.

"I have something for you," he said.

Her mind got stuck on that one.

"Come with me?"

Tanner held out a hand, and when she took it, he pulled her up and led her down the hallway, which sported beautiful hardwood floors and freshly painted walls. He'd installed new wiring, too, that would allow her to have a hall light and a bathroom light on at the same time without blowing a fuse. "This is so beautiful," she said, reaching out to feel the texture of the wall.

"Don't touch," he said, grabbing her hand. "Wet paint. And if it's beautiful, it's because you have great taste."

She stood there facing him, both her hands now captured in his, looking at his face, which was still lit with far too many mysteries. "What are you up to?"

"I have another date for you." His mouth curved slightly. "Me, again. But this time, no cruise."

"No," she whispered. God, no. She'd found him practically irresistible last time, even though it had been disastrous. She couldn't do it again.

"I thought we decided we were out of each other's systems."

"I lied."

"Well, I didn't," she said unconvincingly. She cleared her throat and tried again. "I washed you right out of my hair, along with all the river water."

"This time I'll get it right."

He already had it right, dammit. "Tanner—"

With a finger to her lips, he turned and led her down the hallway. And then opened her bedroom door.

He'd finished the room. Completely. Flooring down, oak baseboards in place, oak trim on the two large windows and window seats. The oak ceiling fan was on low, and he'd managed to find the exact pale mint green she'd wanted for the walls. He'd even brought in her bed, made up with the white fluffy lace comforter and the dozen pillows she loved so much.

It was the only furniture in the room.

Which wasn't what caught her attention. No, the hundreds of white candles he'd lit on the windowsills and around the edge of the room did that. Rock played at a surprisingly soft volume from his CD player, next to a large picnic basket filled to the brim with food.

With candlelight flickering over his face, Tanner turned to her, his gaze touchingly nervous. "This is your real fantasy date," he told her. "Good food, candles, music. We can eat, dance, talk. Anything you want, it can happen, right here in this room."

*Oh, boy.*

"So what do you want, Cami?" he asked softly.

What she wanted, quite suddenly and impatiently, was standing right in front of her. "The date is over when we leave this room?"

His gaze never left her face. She could have sworn she saw disappointment flicker over those strong, beautiful features, but it was gone so fast she knew she'd imagined it. "Yes. It's over when we leave this room."

Telling herself she could believe it, she tried to relax. "You went to so much trouble."

He bent to the picnic basket and came up with two glasses and a bottle of wine. He handed her one, and when she took it from him, his fingers brushed hers. The bolt of pure lust that shot through her shocked her into making a little gasp.

"Cami?"

She meant to take only a tiny sip of the wine, elegantly, with some amount of sophistication.

After all, she hadn't been born in a barn. She could show this man that she could have a hot, passionate affair—and she was fairly confident it would be hot and passionate—and then walk away. But God, she was so nervous. So nervous she gulped the wine. The unfortunately large sip went down the wrong pipe, and she began to sputter very unattractively.

And in the process, spilled half her glass down her front.

Tanner grabbed the glass while she continued to wheeze. Eyes watering, nose running, she coughed and coughed and finally managed to smile at him. "I'm okay."

"And wet," he said regretfully.

"Yeah." Only one way to get past this strained moment, she thought, and that was to get seduced. Heck, she was *already* seduced, and he hadn't even touched her yet, so before she could tell herself it was a stupid idea, she reached out and up-ended Tanner's wine, as well.

Since he'd just taken a sip, the glass was high enough that the wine spilled down his chin, his throat and all over his chest.

"Whoops," she said, biting her lower lip. "Now we're both wet. I'm so sorry. Let me—" Leaning close, she nipped at his chin.

Shock held him immobile.

She shifted closer and ran her mouth over his throat, lapping at the drops of wine she found there. "Mmm," she said. "Better than out of the glass."

When she nosed aside the material of his shirt to nuzzle at hollow of his throat, he moaned. "Cami..." His eyes were closed. "Let me set down my drink."

"Hold on." She unbuttoned his shirt and slipped her hands beneath the material, sighing at the feel of his warm—and wet—skin, his sleek, tight muscles. She slid his shirt over his shoulders so that it fell to his elbows, trapping him by the glass he held in each hand. Unable to help herself, she reached out and licked at the drops of wine over one impressive pec. "You taste so good, Tanner."

Swearing, he staggered back a step. Empowered by his naked reaction, she followed him and pressed her body close.

"Cami—"

She shut him up with her mouth. She had to because, one, she didn't want to hear anything he had to say. She knew this was temporary, and though her heart was already complaining, she couldn't think about that.

And two, she'd never been so hot in her entire life. Never had a man set out to please her, and the music and candles and food did please her, but mostly it was the effort he'd made.

He got into the kiss quickly, expertly, opening his mouth to hers. Making a sound of relief, she plastered herself against him. Since he was wet, and so was she, they stuck together, but she just kept on kissing him. She couldn't stop. His mouth reminded her of his voice, quiet yet demanding, though he didn't say a word.

The fear and uncertainty she'd felt only a few moments before vanished entirely, replaced by a heat and a hunger only he could assuage, so she gave herself up to it. "I want to make love," she whispered against his mouth. "Now? I know you really wanted to eat first, but—"

A rough laugh escaped him. "It's your fantasy date."

"Well..." She grinned, feeling wicked with him as she'd never felt with anyone else. "Honestly? My fantasy would be you in a tool belt with nothing else on."

She definitely shocked him with that. He just stood there.

"But we can start with the basics," she added.

"The basics." He sounded strained. "Can I set down the glasses first?"

Letting out a nervous laugh, she took his glass and set it on the floor. Before she straightened, he reached for her, pulling her against him, burying his face in her neck, feasting his mouth on her skin while his hands skimmed over her body.

The heat and hunger spread, and Tanner knew just where to touch her to make it worse. When he slipped off her blouse and unhooked her bra, tossing both over his shoulder to the floor, she nearly cried in relief. Then, when he cupped her bare breasts in his hands, plumped them up and brought his mouth to her aching nipples, she did cry out.

His shirt hit the floor. Then his pants. He was reaching for her slacks when she remembered. Before she could open her mouth, he'd skimmed the material down her hips and went utterly still.

"Cami." He seemed seriously oxygen challenged.

"Tanner."

His gaze was glued to the area her mother had told her never to let anyone look at. "Where's your underwear?" he asked hoarsely.

"Um...my underwear isn't going to play a part tonight." To prove it, she pressed her bare chest to his and lifted one equally bare leg to his hip so that she could rub herself shamelessly against him.

With a rough groan, he staggered back and encountered wall. "Wait—"

But she couldn't. She didn't want to ever wait again. She wrapped her arms around his neck and lifted both legs, hooking them around his waist.

He swore softly, or maybe it was a prayer, but the next thing Cami knew, he'd gripped her buttocks and entered her. Good thing he held her so tightly because at the long, hard, hot feel of him stretching her to the limit, she would have sunk to the floor.

His face was a tight mask of barely restrained control, and he held himself utterly still. She didn't want still, she wanted wild, fast, she wanted...out of control.

Now.

Using him as her lever, she surged up and sank down on him.

He let out a rough, dark sound, and his head thunked against the wall.

"You okay?" she managed to ask, doing it again as her mouth busied itself on his fabulous throat.

His fingers bit into her hips. "You're killing me."

She continued her assault.

And this time he met her thrust. And the next, and the next.

It was heaven. The fire that had pooled low in her belly when she'd first seen the room had spread within her. She'd never felt anything like the shooting shards of sensation that made her arch against him and had her letting out needy little whimpering sounds. "Don't stop," she commanded. "Don't stop."

"No." There were reasons to put a halt to this madness, but with her body draped over his, her eyes dazed and glowing, Tanner couldn't remember a single one. All he could think was that being buried inside Cami was the only place to be. He'd fallen for her, hard. He hadn't planned on it, but now that he knew, he could deal with it. He could let it happen, even if it meant changing the rules on her.

"Tanner..." Her body welcomed him, pulled him in deep as she began to shudder around him.

Watching her come for him was the most erotic experience of his life, and he couldn't have held back his own release if he'd tried.

Still gasping for breath, Cami lifted her head

and smiled a wobbly smile. "And to think you wanted to stop."

"No." He could still hardly breathe, but he managed to kiss her. "I just wanted to move away from the wall."

"Really? I enjoyed the wall."

"That's because you're not up against the wet paint."

# 10

UNLIKE HIS USUAL SELF, Tanner woke in small degrees, coming to consciousness slowly.

His hearing came first. Or lack of, since there was only silence.

Then came sensation. Warm and toasty. Good. He liked warm and toasty.

Sight came last, and as he blinked the lacy curtains and white down surrounding him into focus, he remembered.

Cami.

After their incredible wet-wall experience, they'd made their way to the dock out back, where they'd sat and talked beneath the twinkling stars. One thing had led to another, and they'd ended up without clothes again, making love to the sound of water slapping against the wood.

Then they'd hit the shower and had removed all the paint from Tanner's bare butt. All soaped up and slippery, they'd made good use of the shower. When they'd finally staggered to her bed, they'd turned to each other yet again.

He felt like some sort of superhero. And given the state of his body at the moment, which happened to be ready to rock and roll yet again, he grinned and rolled over, reaching for Cami, thinking of a million wicked ways he could wake her up.

"Mew."

He'd rolled over on a warm, sleepy female, all right. A warm, sleepy female *cat*.

No Cami.

Sitting up, he ignored the hopeful purr from Annabel and searched the room. There were still candles everywhere, so he hadn't imagined that. And yep, there on the wall, right there, was a spot suspiciously devoid of paint thanks to his backside.

And on the floor were Cami's clothes from the night before. Blouse, pants.

No panties.

A certain part of his anatomy twitched at that. He wanted Cami in bed, warm and willing and maybe even screaming his name, as she had just a few hours ago.

But even more than that, he wanted to tell her what he'd discovered. That despite his own personal belief that he wasn't made for a long-term relationship, despite never wanting one in his past, things had somehow changed.

"Sorry, Annabel," he said, shoving covers and cat aside to get out of the bed. Hmm. No sight of his clothes. In fact, the only thing he could find was his tool belt, which he'd jokingly brought in the night before, teasing Cami about her fantasy.

*Fantasy.*

Grinning, he slipped the belt on. Didn't cover much. Wearing nothing else except for a silly, hopeful grin, he strode out the door and down the hall, following the sounds coming from the kitchen.

Cami was at the kitchen sink, her back to him. Fully dressed in a rose-colored business suit he'd never seen before, sipping from a steaming mug and staring pensively out the window. Staring at his truck, which was still parked in front of the small yard.

She looked as if she wasn't quite certain whether seeing it sitting there was a good or a bad thing.

Slipping up behind her, he put his hands on her hips, but when she would have turned, he held her still. He needed a moment to get his heart out of his throat. "Morning," he said softly. "I have to tell you something, and I have to say it quick."

"Look—"

"No, wait. Please," he added with a gentle squeeze. "I just want to get it out. I wanted to tell you last night, but that got quickly out of hand."

She stiffened.

"I wasn't looking for you, Cami, that's for damn sure, but you've come into my life like a breath of fresh air, when I didn't know I needed one."

She let out a slow breath. "Tanner—"

"I love you, Cami. I know that wasn't part of the bargain, but—"

Jerking out of his grip, she whirled around. "Bargain? There was a bargain?"

Then she caught sight of his attire. Or lack thereof. Her eyes went huge. Her mouth opened, then closed, then went wide with a grin.

A grin wasn't quite the reaction he'd been hoping for.

"Cami!" she yelled, staring at the tool belt. "Better get out of the shower quick. I've got quite a sight for you."

Footsteps came racing down the hallway, skidded into the kitchen.

It was Cami.

Again.

Seeing double, Tanner staggered back and encountered cold tile at his butt. Yelping, he leaped forward, and stepped on Annabel, who yelped louder than he had.

Cami number two, wearing only a towel, put her hands to her mouth.

Cami number one continued to grin. Widely. "He says he loves you, honey. So take pity." Reaching for the kitchen towel on the counter, she tossed it to Tanner.

Tanner grabbed the towel—which was far too small—and blinked. Hard.

Yep. Still two Camis.

And neither of them seemed to be able to take her eyes off his tool belt, even as he fumbled to hold the towel in the correct place.

"Twins," he said brilliantly. Once again he backed into the counter. He could handle a cold butt, as long as it was covered. "You're twins."

"Bingo," said Cami number one, lifting a finger to her nose. "You're quick. He's quick, Sis."

"That's Dimi," the Cami by the door whispered. "My sister."

Tanner divided a startled look between them, trying to come to terms with this. "So all those mornings, when I thought you—'' he pointed to Cami ''—were in bed asleep, and yet you—'' he pointed to Dimi ''—would come dancing through the kitchen muttering about makeup and chips, that was…?'' His pointer finger floundered.

Dimi smiled and waved. ''Me.''

He couldn't stop looking back and forth between the two women who were so alike and yet so dissimilar. ''I thought you were half crazy,'' he said to Cami.

''Well, she is,'' Dimi confided. ''But we don't talk about it much.''

''Dimi,'' Cami warned.

Tanner had about a bazillion questions, leading off with why the hell she'd never told him that very important fact about herself, but he had a more pressing problem.

Even more pressing than his nudity.

More pressing than the fact he'd made an ass of himself by opening up to the wrong twin.

The *right* twin hadn't responded to either his tool belt gesture or the fact he'd told her he loved her.

''Okay, look,'' he said, holding the towel to his essentials and feeling more than a little ridiculous. ''I'm definitely at a disadvantage here.''

''Maybe you should go get dressed,'' suggested

Dimi, not moving from her spot, which meant in order to get past her and down the hall, he'd have to parade his back half in front of her. His naked back half.

He waited for her to move.

She didn't. Not until Cami came forward and gave her twin a sharp glance that obviously was some sort of silent communication. Dimi sighed loudly in response.

"Fine," she said, miffed. "Although since I've already seen everything, this seems a little unnecessary." But she covered her eyes.

Cami didn't, and yet when he moved toward her, she backed away, giving him room to pass.

"Cami—"

"You're probably wondering," she said, biting her lip.

"Gee, you think?"

She let out a little sound of regret.

"Cami, I told your sister because I thought she was you, but you should know what I said—"

"Are you going to tell her you love her again?" Dimi interrupted, her hands still over her eyes. "Because if you are, I'd kinda like to see it. Mostly because this is an utterly new and foreign thing for her, having a guy fall so hard as to humiliate himself this way. But also because I love her, too, and feel a little responsible for this morning's events.''

"Don't you dare look," Tanner told her.

Dimi tipped her head to the ceiling. "Oh, and looking was so much fun, too. Hey, Tool Belt Man, if you're going to do this right, let me give you a little hint. My sister here runs hard and fast from love, so I wouldn't open with that."

Tanner searched Cami's gaze and got not one iota of a clue as to her thoughts.

"She's afraid love doesn't exist," Dimi told him.

"Is that right?" Tanner asked Cami.

"And as for why I was such a big secret," Dimi confided. "She'll probably never admit this, but she's under the misguided impression that men like me better, and if they discover me, they'll ditch her."

"Dimi, shut up," Cami said, her cheeks red. "I don't—"

"Yes, you do," Dimi said. "And you're wrong. You've got Mr. Right standing here to prove it. Now I want you to listen to him, Cami. And listen hard. At least keep your mind open."

"Dimi—"

"I'm shutting up now," she said, mimicking

the motion of zipping her lips, her eyes still tightly closed. "Mute and blind, that's me."

"How about gone?" Tanner asked as kindly as he could.

Dimi's lips quirked, but she didn't speak. Didn't move, either, and Tanner sighed. But he couldn't get mad because Dimi had just given him some pretty incredible insight into Cami's thoughts, and any insight at this point was invaluable.

"I'm going to get dressed," he said to Cami. "And then we're going to talk. *Alone,*" he said over his shoulder for Dimi's benefit. "You'll wait," he said to Cami.

"I'll wait," she said.

It was the best Tanner could ask for. He hightailed it in his very limited attire down the hallway, painfully aware of the picture he made from the back.

And even more aware of Cami watching him.

"STRIP," Cami said to Dimi the moment Tanner left the room.

Dimi lowered her hands. "Excuse me?"

"You heard me." Cami unwound the towel she'd put around her head to keep her hair dry in the shower. Tossing the towel at Dimi, she straightened her other towel. "Hurry."

Understanding dawned in Dimi's eyes. "You want him to choose between us."

"I want to see if he can tell the difference."

"No, you want to see if he really knows you. Cami, honey, that's not fair." But she started to strip. "I realize you've never played fair before, and maybe I've even encouraged that, but the guy wore a tool belt for you. *Just* a tool belt. So really, it's time to trust him."

"I know it's time, but knowing it and doing it are two entirely different things."

"So why are we doing this, really? He's not going to be able to tell us apart. Nobody can."

Cami waited until Dimi had wrapped the towel around her body and faced her. To her, their differences were obvious. Dimi's eyes were cooler, her features slightly more refined. Cami's hair couldn't be tamed, and she rarely stood as straight and sure as Dimi.

"*Cami.*"

"Look, if he can tell us apart, then it was meant to be."

"And you'll admit that?"

Cami's heart flip-flopped. "I don't know. But

there's no reason to worry about it. He won't be able to tell.''

"All right, but I've got to tell you, I actually feel sorry for him.''

"No cheating,'' Cami whispered, as Tanner walked into the room.

He took a double take, which might have been comical if her entire heart hadn't been wadded in her throat.

"I hadn't forgotten,'' he said to them. "But jeez, the reality of this is a bit unnerving.''

Dimi gave him a little smile.

Cami's heart was in her throat. She knew her sister would help him in an instant if she could, so Cami spoke fast. "Can you tell us apart?''

Tanner looked back and forth between the two of them.

Cami held her breath.

Slowly, he walked around Dimi, looking her up and down.

Then Cami was treated to the same intense gaze.

"Chilly?'' he asked softly when goose bumps rose on her flesh.

She shook her head. She could do little else because he was looking at her with heat and need and hunger, and dammit, also such tenderness her throat closed up. How could he still be looking at her like that? It wasn't in the plan.

"If you can tell us apart," Dimi said, "you win."

"What's the prize?" he asked, never taking his eyes off Cami.

"Me, of course," Dimi said. "Or her." She smiled.

So did Tanner.

Cami couldn't do anything but swallow hard, because, just looking at him made her ache.

He loved her.

Her knees wobbled. Ruthlessly, she locked them.

"Maybe you should drop the towel," he suggested, laughing when both Dimi's and Cami's hands went to the knot between their breasts. "Don't worry. I already know who is who. I knew the moment I walked in the door."

His confidence staggered Cami—as not even their own mother could tell them apart. It might have warmed her, soothed away her chill, except for the very real fact that if he knew exactly who she was, through and through, he would be the first man to do it.

And that was terrifying in its own right.

Tanner walked around to face them. "I should

warn you both, I'm kissing the woman I think is mine.''

*His.* Cami's heart stuttered.

"I'm kissing her senseless. Then I'm going to carry her back to that bedroom so we can have the morning we were supposed to have. And after that, I'm going to remind her how much I love her, and I'm going to hope she feels the same way back.''

*Oh, my God.*

Dimi looked at Cami. Cami looked at Dimi.

"Ready?'' he asked sweetly.

Was she ready? Hell, no. She could hardly stand the tension over this ridiculous stupid game she'd set up, and she stood there on pins and needles, wondering if he could really pick her out.

If he really knew her.

"Ready," Dimi said softly, looking hopeful for that kiss, and Cami sent her a dirty look.

Tanner took a step closer, and Cami held her breath yet again.

# *11*

TANNER LOOKED at the women, one of whom had stolen his heart but good.

He knew Cami. He wasn't kidding when he'd told them he'd known her the moment he'd walked into the room, even if the tension shimmering off her in waves hadn't given her away.

*Poor baby,* he thought, biting back his grin. She was so terrified by the prospect of his love, and equally terrified of losing it.

Taking mercy, he took the last step, skimmed his hands up her arms and pulled her close. Bending his head, he stopped a breath away from kissing her only because she'd slapped a hand to his chest.

"I know it's you," he whispered, dipping down a little to look deep into her panicked eyes.

"Pretty sure of yourself," she said, her chest hitching with her breath.

"When it comes to knowing you, yeah."

"Oh, man." Dimi turned to Cami. "That was a ten on the ah factor."

"You don't have an ah factor. You hate the ah factor."

Dimi shook her head. "This is different. This is the real thing. Face it, honey, he's on to you." Dimi stroked her sister's arm in sympathy. "He knows you. He loves you. Now, if you don't mind, I'm outta here, because I have a feeling you're going to get naked."

Cami gripped her sister's hand, but Dimi shook her off. "Nothing personal, but I've already seen you both in that state, and I have some upside-down raspberry shortcake to whip up."

She headed toward the door, stopping to scoop up her clothes. "Take it easy on her," she said to Tanner. "She's really pathetic at this stuff. She might even try to run, but don't let her."

"Hey, I'm right here," Cami protested. "And I'm not running anywhere!"

"Then she'll try to ignore it," Dimi said directly to Tanner. "That's her second defense. Watch for it."

"I'm on guard," Tanner said solemnly, but he let out a grateful smile. "Thanks. I think I can take it from here."

And he was pretty sure he could, because nothing had ever meant more to him. Turning to Cami, he stroked his hands up her arms and cupped her face. "Alone at last."

"She gave it away, didn't she?"

He kept his hands on her, stroking her jaw, sinking his fingers in her hair. Her breathing changed, which gratified him, but her eyes remained fierce and intense, making him sigh. "She didn't give anything away, Cami. I knew you. I'll always know you."

"You didn't at first. Remember? You thought I was the bimbo beauty queen who didn't know her own mind."

"I never thought you were a bimbo, but you were a beauty queen, that's a fact. And as for not knowing your mind, we both know that isn't true. You always knew what you wanted, you just didn't always stand up for it."

"I'm standing up now, aren't I?"

"Well, that you are," he murmured, lifting a brow when she marched him back so that his thighs hit her kitchen table, which as usual was piled with stuff. "What exactly are we standing up for?"

"We." Her eyes misted. "You keep saying that, *we,* as if it's a done deal."

"Because it's my greatest wish." It was all he

got out before she went up on tiptoe and kissed him—hard. Kissed him hard and deep and wet. It rocked his world.

*Think,* his mind ordered his penis. *There's something important here she's avoiding. You can see the relief and hope in her eyes as she's...oh lord, she's dropping her towel.*

He swallowed hard and ignored his mind. With her breasts flattened to his chest and her smooth, white arms clinging to his neck, she slithered against him. He felt his eyes cross with lust.

Her hands worked his T-shirt up over his head, and he obliged her. "Cami—"

"Love me, Tanner."

Slipping his hands beneath her silky hair, he brought her face close. "I do," he said, and devoured her mouth with his, feeling all those soft curves glide over his hardened body, smelling the scent of her shampoo and soap, fresh and seductive as hell. Sliding his hands down her body, feeling all her warmth and softness quiver, he groaned deep in his throat.

"I'm sorry I missed the full effect of the tool belt," she whispered, her fingers dancing down his belly to the button fly of his jeans. "Maybe we could revisit that little fantasy."

"Later." She'd already backed him into the table. Leaning against it, he skimmed his hands down her spine until he held a sweet, warm, rounded cheek in each one. He hauled her up until her legs were clamped around his hips, and that hot, delightfully damp feminine place between her thighs cradled his erection in a way that made him groan again.

In response, she made a mewling sort of sound and tightened her grip. "Please," she whimpered, rocking against him. "Please, now."

As if he could turn her away. She had her hands in his hair, her tongue in his mouth, her breasts crushed to his chest, with two tight, scrumptious nipples boring holes into his skin. Not to mention she was wet and hot, and gliding that wet, hot spot over the biggest erection he'd ever had. Craning his neck, he studied the table behind him dubiously.

She wasn't so far gone she couldn't lift her head and let out a gasping laugh. "No, it won't hold us."

"The counter then." He'd barely turned and set her on it before she'd pulled his body between her sprawled legs, her hips moving, moving, moving, driving him to the very brink. The unrelenting heat threatened to burn him alive, and all the while her mouth was busy attacking his until he slipped his hands beneath her, holding her steady as he entered her.

Her eyes were wide on his so that he could watch pleasure chase hunger chase heat chase need across her face. "Oh, Tanner," she whispered on a thready sigh. Her head fell back, and she opened her legs a little wider, so he could sink into her even more deeply.

He figured he had about three seconds before he exploded helplessly, but still, she beat him. His gaze was firmly on her face when she hit her peak, moaning his name, shuddering, shuddering, shuddering. Seeing her, hearing her, *feeling* her, capped it off for him, and he exploded, too, collapsing against the counter and Cami's body.

Practically purring, she rubbed her cheek against his chest. He rubbed his cheek on her hair and stared uneasily at the cat who'd somehow, at some point, managed to leap up on the counter and perch herself directly behind Cami.

"Mew."

Which reminded him what he'd been trying to say before they'd knocked it out against the tile like a pair of bunnies. "Cami—"

"Don't tell me. It wasn't good for you?" She smiled, teasing, looking very satisfied, very feminine, very happy.

"It was off the scale. But—"

Her smile slowly faded. "Uh-oh. Nothing good ever follows a but. Not in that tone."

"This isn't a bad but."

"Are you sure? Because I have it on good authority, a but usually precedes a dumping of some kind."

"No." He drew in a sharp breath and narrowed his eyes. "Dammit, I'm trying to get to a point."

She smiled tremulously. "Sure you wouldn't rather kiss me again?" Her arms snaked around his neck. She slid her breasts against his chest.

His body shuddered in pleasure, and though it had been less than two minutes, he actually responded again. "I'd love to kiss you, but—"

"There's that but."

"But," he said, putting his forehead to hers. "Good as the sex is, it's not everything." Shakily, he pushed away from the counter and her incredible body. His knees trembled, dammit, proving that while sex wasn't everything, it came really, really close. "Cami, I l—"

"Wait!" she gasped quickly, panicking again.

SHE WASN'T READY for this. But—and there was that word again—if she came right out and told him how terrified it all made her feel, how she needed some time, what would happen?

A man like Tanner James didn't just sit around and wait for a woman to make up her mind.

Bending, he grabbed the towel she'd discarded and wrapped it around her. Gently, he pushed her into a chair. Then he opened his mouth, but before he could speak she covered it with her hand.

Patiently, he tugged her hand free. "Cami, I love you."

"I...have to sit."

"You are sitting. Cami, you should know, this is the for-keeps kind of love."

From behind the closed kitchen door came a distinct whoop.

Dimi's whoop.

"See?" she heard Dimi say. "Did you hear that? I told you I wasn't making it all up."

"It's a miracle."

Cami thunked her head on Tanner's chest and groaned. "That's my *mother*," she moaned.

She felt the shock reverberate through his system and knew why. Two minutes ago they'd been having some pretty wild, fairly noisy sex against the cabinet. No one could have missed it.

"Your mother? Right out there?" He looked pale. "That door isn't locked!"

Given his state of undress, she could understand his panic. "Grab your pants," she whispered, securing her towel.

Tanner shoved a leg in before he realized his jeans were inside out. Staggering against the counter, he tried again.

"It's too late," Cami said miserably. "She knows everything, she's psychic when it comes to Dimi and me, and your shirt is on backward."

Tanner stared at her in horror. "Your mother knows what we just did on this counter?"

"Oh, stop worrying about us and finish talking," the woman in question shouted into the kitchen. "Cami, tell him you love him back. Then get decent. I want to meet this new son-in-law of mine."

Tanner's eyes widened. He looked more than pale. He looked positively faint.

And Cami wanted to crawl into a hole and die. "Aren't you tired of ruining my life yet, Mom? Go work on Dimi for a change."

"She's next."

"*Go away.*"

"Are you kidding? And miss this?"

Tanner scrambled to fix his shirt but the tag stuck up in the back. His hair stuck up, too, but that was from Cami's fingers. He looked rumpled, frustrated, a little unnerved, not to mention sexy as hell. And just looking at him made Cami's heart tip on its side.

What did she do with such a huge, gorgeous, incredibly sensuous man who looked at her as if she was his entire world? "Tanner—"

"Just say yes," her mother said through the door. "And hurry up, would you? I drank too much tea and I have to hit the toilet, but I don't want to miss anything."

"I'm sorry," Cami whispered.

Tanner sent her a weak smile. "You did warn me about her being controlling."

"Hey!" Her mother's voice sounded in protest. "I'm on your side, Tanner— What's his last name?" she whispered to Dimi.

Wrapped in her towel, Cami sank to the floor and groaned in misery.

In front of her appeared two bare feet. Two bare, masculine feet. Then Tanner crouched down before her and pulled her hands from her face. "I'm guessing we'll have to finish this later."

"Did I mention I'm sorry?" she asked miserably.

"You mentioned." Reaching out, he stroked her cheek. "But you have to admit, you're more relieved than anything else."

"Relieved at my mother embarrassing me?"

"Relieved at her timing."

"Her timing is pretty off, thanks."

"Cami, be honest. You aren't ready to talk to me about this."

She looked deep into his warm, accepting eyes and had to do as he asked. Had to be honest. She cared about him, deeply, but the rest…simply terrifying. "Okay, I'm not quite ready," she whispered.

He nodded, and before he stood, he leaned in and kissed her.

For just a moment, she clung to his big, tough, beautiful body because she needed him. And it had nothing to do with the incredible sex. She just wanted to hold him and have him hold her.

But he pulled away. "Remember," he said softly. "No matter what your mother says, you know what you want. Don't be afraid to go for it. Or not, as the case may be."

God, he wasn't saying goodbye, was he? Just because she needed some more time to face… "Tanner?"

"Don't ever back off from what you want. Promise me."

"I promise," she whispered. "But—"

He put a finger to her lips. "No buts, remember?"

And then he was gone, bravely opening the kitchen door to face her mother.

He introduced himself to the dying-of-curiosity woman and smiled at Dimi before vanishing out the front door.

# 12

TANNER SPENT the weekend at home. He had things to do. His choices consisted of handling the paperwork coming out of his ears, going grocery shopping or watching the ball game. He chose none of the above.

Instead, he sat slouched on the couch watching the shadows dance over the ceiling. For the first time in his life he'd let someone in, except she didn't want in.

Did she think she was the only scared one?

Figuring he deserved at least a moment of self-pity, he closed his eyes and tortured himself with memories.

Cami opening the door to him that first day, wearing sleepy eyes, pouty lips and a blanket.

Cami diving after her cat to save a damn spider from becoming Annabel's next snack.

Cami indignant and furious after her dates from hell.

Cami, her gaze rich and warm and right on his as he made love to her.

"Women trouble."

Tanner nearly leaped off the couch. His father stood at his feet holding a tray. "What are you doing here?"

"You're so far gone you didn't even hear the door. I'm bearing food, so don't get all pissy on me." He sank to the couch and offered the tray, which was filled with hot tamales and icy beer. "So...let's hear it."

"Angels are getting their butts kicked."

"Not baseball, boy. I meant your women trouble. Or should I say *woman?*"

"I'm not having trouble."

"Which explains, of course, why you look like hell."

"I don't—" Tanner sighed and cleared his face of its scowl, then ate a tamale and chased it down with some beer. "I love her," he said finally.

His father's eyes misted. "I know."

"She isn't ready."

"Well, then. You have something in common, because up until very recently, you weren't ready, either."

"Yeah."

His father smiled at Tanner's glum expression. "Don't worry. She won't be able to resist the James charm for long. No woman can," he boasted with a wink. "Not even your mom."

"Mom loved you from the start."

His father laughed. "Try again."

"She didn't?"

"Well, maybe she did. I am, after all, utterly irresistible. But she had to come to the idea slowly. Had to decide to take on a fixer-upper like me rather than a brand-new model, so to speak."

"She fixed you up?" Tanner asked, confused.

"She thought she did." He grinned. "And the arrangement worked perfectly."

Tanner shook his head. "I want Cami to love me. Just the way I am."

"She already does."

"How do you know?"

"Because you're my son. Who wouldn't love you?"

TANNER WANTED to believe his dad, but when he went to work Monday morning, he didn't have much confidence in the matter.

The radio—his radio—was on low, playing his rock station.

Odd. Cami hated his station.

She was on the floor in the living room. She had the phone to her ear and was telling someone, "No, that won't work for me, not today. I have the most important meeting of my life, so it's got to be Tuesday or you're going to have to find another designer.''

What little was left of Tanner's confidence faded. She'd found her mind, all right. She'd learned how to speak it. And she was on a roll.

After hanging up the phone, she picked it right back up again before Tanner could warn her of his presence.

''Mom?'' she said into the receiver with unusual force. ''Yes, it's early. I got your message. I'm sorry you're mad at me because I didn't give you the spectacle you wanted the other day, but my life is my own. And from now on, the only thing I want to be set up with is food. Preferably junk food. No more men, do you understand?'' She cocked her head, listening. ''That's right, no more blind dates *ever*... No, Mom, I'm not changing sides, and I'm not suddenly gay, a miracle really, given how I was raised. Now be a good mother and go bother my sister. I've got to go. Today is the first day of the rest of my life.''

She clicked off and then back on again, dialing quickly. ''Dimi, I just told Mom and now I'm telling you, too, no more blind dates. No. No. No. Got it? Oh, and by the way, I sicced her on you, so there. Now I've got to run, I've got something very special planned in about ten minutes, if all goes well. Yes! I know it's early! I've discovered mornings. Sue me.'' With a smile, she disconnected and tossed the phone aside. "There," she said to herself. "That felt good."

Tanner had to agree. She felt good, she looked good, and dammit, she seemed so strong and happy and fulfilled in her new ability to say no.

No more doormat on this woman.

But with this new No kick Cami was on, it didn't take a genius to know what else she was going to say no to.

Him.

Deciding he definitely wasn't in the mood to hear it, he backed toward the door, but as luck would have it, he stepped on Annabel's tail.

She screeched.

He yelled.

And Cami nearly fell over. Hand to her chest, she whirled and stared at him.

"Hi," he said inanely.

"You're early."

"Not really."

"Ten minutes," she said, sounding shaken. "How long have you been standing there?"

Long enough to know he was in for a serious heartbreak. "Well I heard the new No kick."

"Oh." She let out a nervous smile, though he had no idea what she had to be nervous about. *He* was the one getting dumped. "I thought maybe you'd like it."

"I like you," he said simply.

HER SMILE wobbled a bit. "Good. Like. You like me. Well—" Shaken, she grabbed her leather portfolio, slipped into her sandals and headed for the door. She had no idea where she was going. She couldn't think, because the most amazing man she'd ever let into her life had apparently decided he only *liked* her.

"Where are you going?" he asked.

"To meet a client." And to put the pieces of her heart back together. But she made the mistake of looking at him, looking into the face she'd come to rely on as she'd never allowed herself to do before.

*Know your mind. Go after what you want.*

"Oh, hell." She dropped her portfolio. Kicked off her sandals.

And went after what she wanted. After what she'd spent all weekend planning. "Did you mean what you said?" she asked, holding her breath for his answer.

He appeared to carefully weigh the question. "I said a lot of things."

"You said sex wasn't everything."

"Yes."

"You said you wanted more."

"Yes."

"You said…you loved me."

"I remember," he said. "I thought you had a meeting."

"*You're* my meeting." Drawing in an unsteady breath, she turned up the radio just as a Van Halen classic ended.

"What are you doing?"

"Shh," she said as the DJ started talking. She bit her lip, staring at him, heart thundering.

The DJ's voice boomed. "And out in Truckee today, we have one of our most loyal listeners. Tanner James."

Surprise widened Tanner's eyes.

Cami's heart nearly galloped right out of her chest.

"He's going to want to sit down now. Tanner, are you sitting?"

Tanner sank to the couch, staring at Cami, who bit her lower lip to stop herself from giggling hysterically.

"Tanner, today is a rare day indeed. The woman in your life wants to say…are you ready for this? She says she was wrong. Yes, men everywhere, take note. You heard it here first. A woman has admitted she was wrong. She let him put his feelings out on the line and she ignored them. Ouch! That's got to hurt, huh? She's sorry for that, Tan Man.''

Tanner pointed to Cami with a lifted brow, and Cami nodded. "Me," she said softly.

"Tanner," the DJ continued. "She let you be the brave one. She let you tell her you love her and she didn't say it back. Well, she wants to say it now."

"I love you," Cami whispered.

"She loves you, man. And now…" The DJ let out a drum roll. "Take it away Cami."

"And I want to marry you," Cami said, coming close, sinking to her knees at his feet. "Because this is the forever kind of love. Will you be my husband?"

"Tanner, you lucky dog. Crank up the tunes, guys, because Tanner's about to get some luuuuuuv."

Music blared into the room. Cami smiled shakily.

Tanner shook his head, looking shell-shocked. "I thought you were going to dump me."

"I'm sorry."

"I thought I was going to leave here with half my heart and none of my pride."

"I'm so sorry."

"I had no idea…"

"Tanner, do you think you could answer the question?"

He looked up, baffled, and she had to laugh. "I asked you to marry me. You didn't answer."

Now he let out a slow grin. "Really? I didn't answer you? Hmm. Maybe I should let you sleep on it, or rather *not* sleep, and then—"

"Tanner," she begged, tugging him down so that they kneeled face to face. "You're killing me."

Softening, he stroked her jaw. "That makes us even, then." He kissed her. "The answer is yes. Yes, I love you. Yes, I want to be with you forever. Yes, God, yes, I want to marry you."

"Really?"

"Yeah. But Cami? Do you think we can elope?"

Her eyes narrowed even as she laughed. "You're afraid of my family."

"Hell, yes."

"Oh, Tanner, that's so sweet."

# Play **LUCKY HEARTS** for this..

*exciting FREE gift !*
**This surprise mystery gif
could be yours free**

# when you play **LUCKY HEARTS**
## ...then continue your lucky streak
## with a sweetheart of a deal!

1. Play Lucky Hearts as instructed on the opposite page.

2. Send back this card and you'll receive 2 brand-new Harlequin Duets™ novels. These books have a cover price of $5.99 each in the U.S. and $6.99 each in Canada, but th are yours to keep absolutely free.

3. There's no catch! You're under no obligation to buy anything. We charge nothing— ZERO—for your first shipment. And you don't have to make any minimum number of purchases—not even one!

4. The fact is thousands of readers enjoy receiving their books by mail from the Harlequ Reader Service®. They enjoy the convenience of home delivery...they like getting the best new novels at discount prices, BEFORE they're available in stores...and they love their *Heart to Heart* subscriber newsletter featuring author news, horoscopes, recipes, book reviews and much more!

5. We hope that after receiving your free books you'll want to remain a subscriber. But t choice is yours—to continue or cancel, any time at all! So why not take us up on ou invitation, with no risk of any kind. You'll be glad you did!

# Exciting Harlequin® romance novels—FREE!
## Plus an exciting mystery gift—FREE!
## No cost! No obligation to buy!

# YES!

I have scratched off the silver card. Please send me the 2 FREE books and gift for which I qualify.
I understand I am under no obligation to purchase any books, as explained on the back and on the opposite page.

With a coin, scratch off the silver card and check below to see what we have for you.

## HARLEQUIN'S

# LUCKY HEARTS GAME

**311 HDL C6QK**

**111 HDL C6QA**
(H-D-OS-08/01)

| | | | | | | | | | | | | | | | | | |
|---|---|---|---|---|---|---|---|---|---|---|---|---|---|---|---|---|---|

NAME                    (PLEASE PRINT CLEARLY)

| | | | | | | | | | | | | | | | | | |
|---|---|---|---|---|---|---|---|---|---|---|---|---|---|---|---|---|---|

ADDRESS

| | | | | | | | | | | | | | | | | | |
|---|---|---|---|---|---|---|---|---|---|---|---|---|---|---|---|---|---|

APT.#                    CITY

STATE/PROV.                    ZIP/POSTAL CODE

**Twenty-one gets you 2 free books, and a free mystery gift!**

**Twenty gets you 2 free books!**

**Nineteen gets you 1 free book!**

**Try Again!**

Offer limited to one per household and not valid to current Harlequin Duets™ subscribers. All orders subject to approval.

# The Harlequin Reader Service® — Here's how it works:

Accepting your 2 free books and gift places you under no obligation to buy anything. You may keep the books and gift and return the shipping statement marked "cancel." If you do not cancel, about a month later we'll send you 2 additional novel and bill you just $5.14 each in the U.S., or $6.14 each in Canada, plus 50¢ shipping & handling per book and applicable ta if any.* That's the complete price and — compared to cover prices of $5.99 each in the U.S. and $6.99 each in Canada — quite a bargain! You may cancel at any time, but if you choose to continue, every month we'll send you 2 more books, whi you may either purchase at the discount price or return to us and cancel your subscription.

*Terms and prices subject to change without notice. Sales tax applicable in N.Y. Canadian residents will be charged applic provincial taxes and GST.

# Eat Your Heart Out

## Jill Shalvis

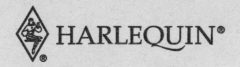

# HARLEQUIN®

TORONTO • NEW YORK • LONDON
AMSTERDAM • PARIS • SYDNEY • HAMBURG
STOCKHOLM • ATHENS • TOKYO • MILAN • MADRID
PRAGUE • WARSAW • BUDAPEST • AUCKLAND

# 1

"TWENTY-FIVE SECONDS until air time!"

Dimi ignored both that and the makeup woman powdering her face and concentrated on Suzie instead. "You think I haven't tried hard enough?"

Suzie consulted her clipboard, snapped her fingers at two people standing idle, both of whom leapt to attention and ran off, and then sighed at Dimi. "Look, babe. The truth hurts."

"But I *have* tried. I've tried everything!"

Suzie's expression was pure doubt. "Have you placed a personal ad?"

*"Twenty seconds!"*

Dimi didn't take her eyes off Suzie. "Only nutcases place personal ads. But I've tried everything else. Online dating services, in-person dating services, the grocery store, the zoo, everywhere. I've made dating a virtual spectator sport, and nothing." It was frustrating, this failure. She hated to fail. Maybe it was her father's seven divorces or her mother's controlling nature. Or maybe it was the fact that everyone she knew had someone to go home to except her, and she didn't know how to fix that.

Pathetic. "No Mr. Right anywhere."

*"Fifteen!"*

Suzie shook her head. "I've seen you at happy hour."

"So?"

"So you're far more concerned with the appetizers than the beefcakes at the bar."

Okay, she liked her food. A lot. "The beefcakes at the bar are only interested in one thing, anyway." Dimi stopped talking to purse her lips so the makeup woman could apply lip gloss.

"And so are you, after only one thing." Suzie adjusted the microphone on Dimi's collar. "After all, we are talking about getting laid, right?"

Dimi nearly swallowed her tongue.

The makeup woman let out a laugh.

*"Ten!"*

"Not exactly *laid,*" Dimi muttered, avoiding some interested sidelong glances from her eavesdropping crew.

The truth was, she wanted more, much more, than any physical release.

Although, in retrospect, that would be nice,

too. Embarrassing as it was to admit, especially for a single, relatively successful woman in the new millennium, Dimi wanted the minivan, the white picket fence, the two point four kids. She wanted to be held by warm, strong arms at night.

And yes, maybe she also wanted someone to take out the trash. So what? She wanted it all.

"If not sex, what then?" Suzie lifted a brow. "I know for a fact it's been years for you."

"Hey! Only two."

"*Years,*" Suzie repeated, as if Dimi had committed a crime. "Honey, a body like yours was made for hot, down-and-dirty sex."

Dimi tugged at her rather severe business suit, which had been the only thing to fit that morning without having to suck in her breath all day long. Not eating doughnuts for breakfast would help greatly, but that meant she needed to go grocery shopping, and that was worse than taking out the trash.

"Have you tried the Laundromat at about eight o'clock, any night of the week?"

Dimi blinked. "What does that have to do with anything?"

"It's a regular men buffet."

"The Laundromat? It's desperation city. No one goes there to pick up guys anymore."

"Wanna bet?" Suzie leaned close, inspecting Dimi's face. She tsked and pointed, and before Dimi could blink, she was getting her nose powdered. Again.

*"And five, four..."*

"I'm done trying," Dimi announced.

"You're far too serious." Suzie's eyes were kind but firm. "In both life and getting a man. Relax a little."

"Maybe I'm too serious, I'll give you that one, but I'm not changing my stance on this. No more losers. No more dates."

"Clear the set!"

The crew scrambled away. Everyone but Dimi's persistent assistant.

"You can't give up," Suzie protested.

"Watch me." Dimi straightened her chair. "I mean it, Suzie. No more men, not ever again," she vowed for once and all, at the exact moment Suzie finally backed off the set.

And just as the director punched a finger into the air, signaling they were live. The red light was on the camera. The camera pointed right at her.

The camera to which she'd just announced, on live television, no less, that she'd permanently sworn off men.

From just off the set, Suzie was shaking with

silent laughter. Oh, yeah. Funny. But Dimi Anderson, former high school beauty queen and homework aficionada for the football team, hadn't gotten to where she was today by giving in to public humiliation.

Host of the live cable cooking show *Food Time*, for the serious chef, Dimi forced a smile into the camera and said, "Just seeing if you're awake, folks." She cleared her throat and went resolutely ahead. "Welcome to today's show."

Off camera, but still in Dimi's line of vision, the determined Suzie held up her clipboard.

*A woman needs regular orgasms!* it said.

Dimi faltered but, always the ultimate professional, covered it up with an unfortunately stiff smile. "Today we're making—"

Suzie was busy scribbling, and she held up the clipboard again.

*And not from anything battery operated!*

Dimi choked, covered it with another smile, but she still had to repeat herself to get back on track. "Today we're making—"

*We're making sure you get some. In this millennium!*

"Carbonada Flamande and a lemon tart to die for," Dimi said firmly, refusing to look at Suzie again.

SOMEHOW Dimi managed to finish the show, in spite of Suzie's occasional very obscene clipboard suggestions. She'd created a new twist on the Carbonada Flamande and had made the lemon tart look interesting and challenging—she hoped. It tasted fabulous to her, anyway.

She should know, she'd put away three pieces of it, not a good thing. Not that any man would ever notice an extra few pounds on her hips, because she'd given up on men.

Things were fine. Really. She had a nice place to live and a job that let her eat all day long. What more could she want?

Plenty, apparently, given the odd sense of loneliness coursing through her as she drove home through the small historical town of Truckee toward Donner Lake and her town house. She could, as she always had, go to her twin sister's town house, just down the path. They could share an entire bag of barbecue potato chips, or maybe chocolate chip cookies. That is, if Cami had gone food shopping.

But even that wasn't the same anymore. Cami had Tanner now. He kept her happily fed, and given the constant expression of bliss on her sister's face, it wasn't with just food. It was a miracle, really, as Cami hadn't been any more lucky in love than Dimi had been until a series of blind dates from hell had changed the tide for her.

Dimi didn't begrudge her sister's newfound happiness. She didn't. She just wanted some for herself. Not likely, not now.

Oh, well. She had Brownie, her hamster. She also had the leftover tart.

Because she hadn't yet bought furniture after having moved out of Cami's place several months before, Dimi sat on the floor in her bare kitchen, the tart tin in her lap. Ready for her very own invitation-only pity party, she grabbed a fork.

Stuffing her face, she turned her head and looked into Brownie's cage, which sat on the floor next to her. "You should know, I gave up men today. No daddy for you."

The white and brown hamster poked her nose out of her little wooden hut and stared curiously at Dimi.

"On live television, no less. Should have seen it. Emmy-winning performance, no doubt."

Brownie's nose wriggled, and her dark eyes darted to the pie tin in Dimi's lap. "Ah, the important stuff. Smart girl." Dimi took a tiny piece of crust and offered it.

Nabbing it, Brownie quickly vanished into her hut.

"Not even a hamster wants my company," Dimi said to no one in particular, wondering in her sugar-induced stupor where on earth she'd gone so wrong. What exactly was missing from her life?

But she knew the answer to that.

Love. True, heart-stopping love. That's what was missing.

She polished off every last crumb of the tart, all the while telling herself she couldn't miss what she'd never had.

HAVING GIVEN UP her dream of wedded bliss in front of the entire world actually had a benefit, Dimi discovered. She couldn't have been lonely that evening if she'd tried, since everyone she knew called her.

First her friends, one by one, all of whom thought her little proclamation was hysterical.

Oh, yeah, just hysterical.

Then her sister. "Way to go," Cami said. "Way to ruin any prospective relationship you might have had."

"There was no prospective relationship,"

Dimi reminded her. "Now go back to your fiancé." She took some joy in hanging up soundly.

No peace, though; the phone immediately rang again.

"Oh, my God, you've given up men," her mother wailed. "How could you?"

"Mom...you watched."

"Well, of course I watched. I always watch."

That was so unexpectedly sweet, Dimi was speechless.

"I watch during Debbie Dee's commercials."

Dimi's competition. The *Debbie Dee Trash Talk Show.* Dimi put her head to her knees. "Gee, thanks, Mom."

"What's this about no more men? I want grandchildren, Dimi!"

"Mom—"

"Your sister is such a good girl, falling in love. Why can't you do that?"

Desperate times called for desperate measures. So she simulated static through her teeth. "Gosh, would you listen to that? Bad connection on the cell, Mom! Gotta go."

"Dimi Anderson, you don't have a cell phone in your town house!"

"Hey, did you hear that? It's my doorbell." But just as Dimi disconnected, her mother sighed.

"You can't fool me," she grumbled. "I know you don't have a doorbell, either."

WHEN DIMI ARRIVED at the studio the next morning, she found her staff huddled in the parking lot, unusually solemn.

"Hey, guys. Cheer up. Just because I gave up men—"

"For once, men are taking a back seat," Suzie informed her.

"Wow, really?" She studied the quiet faces. "It must be bad then."

"Ratings are down," Ted the cameraman told her. "Down, down, down."

"How can that be?" Dimi thought of all the calls she'd taken over yesterday's show. "Everyone I know watched."

"What?" Ted asked. "All of two people?"

"Hey, I know more than two people," Dimi said, insulted.

Grace, their cooking consultant, was wringing her hands. "You giving up men is the least of our problems. It's rumored heads are going to roll. *Today.*"

"It's fact, Dimi," Ted agreed. "We're in bad shape."

She didn't waste her breath wondering why everyone always knew these things before she did. The gossip mill in show business was in a league all its own, and being five hundred miles away from Hollywood only made it worse.

Everyone looked to Dimi, as if being host made her their leader. "Well, that's what happens when they pitch us against the *Debbie Dee Show*," she said, bemused. "Yesterday her show was How My Brother Married My Sister and Gave Birth to Puppies. We can't compete with that."

"Yeah. And today it's How Making Porn Videos Rejuvenated Our Marriage." Suzie shook her head mournfully. "We're going to lose to that for sure, unless..." She eyed Dimi speculatively. "Got any more exciting announcements?"

"No!"

From somewhere behind them came a roar like thunder, as if the heavens were agreeing with the dismal outlook of their beloved show.

But not a cloud marred the sky. Just bright, optimistic sunshine.

That's when the Harley came into view,

rounding the corner. The rider, leather-clad and broad-shouldered, cut the engine and coasted into a parking spot some distance away.

Silence fell again, and the staff stared morosely at each other.

"Maybe we can change the tone of the show," Leo, their set designer, suggested. "You know, go with something more…" A small, unusually pretty man, he gestured with his hands as he spoke. "I don't know. *Adventurous.*"

"No," Dimi said quickly. "People depend on a serious cooking show from us." And plus, she liked serious. She *was* serious.

"Come on," Ted cajoled, warming to the cause. "How does this sound? *Food Time* goes new age! Cook with us in the nude today!" He grinned lecherously at Suzie, who rolled her eyes.

"Just don't fry bacon. Not in the nude." This from Leo, ever safety conscious. "Bad plan."

"It's not the *tone* of the show dropping our ratings," Dimi protested. "It's the brass forcing us to make those frothy, fattening, decadent meals that have only a total of four bites to them, when what our viewers *really* want to see are low-fat, healthy, simple but fabulous-tasting cuisine they can easily whip up after a long day at work."

This was a huge pet peeve, and Dimi wondered when the powers that be would get a clue. Probably after the show was canceled. Damn them. Didn't they know that since she'd given up men, all she had left was the show?

"Ritchie isn't here yet." Suzie lowered her voice, looking over her shoulder to make sure no one of importance could overhear her. "They say he's been...*fired.*"

There was a collective gasp.

"They said," Suzie continued, "that we're getting a new producer."

*"Who?"* everyone asked together, in the same reverent tone.

"Mitchell Knight."

Everyone but Dimi, who hadn't heard of him, groaned.

"Ooh, he's wicked," Grace whispered.

"He's *gorgeous,*" Leo murmured, fanning himself.

"Gorgeous, but mean. *Real* mean." Ted looked terrified. "He likes to fire people, man."

"He's a troubleshooter type," Suzie explained to clueless Dimi. "Called in by our parent company when a show is on its last legs. He axes everyone, then starts from scratch."

"Yeah." Leo fanned his face. "He's bad, baby. Bad to the bone."

"He's a holy terror, is what he is," Suzie corrected. "And they say he's coming here. Today."

"That would be correct."

The very male voice came from behind their huddled group, and when they all turned, there stood the Harley rider. He was built in a way that suggested maybe he beat up cooking show crews for a living, all big and rugged and edgy. His dark wind-mussed hair fell to his shoulders, and a diamond stud winked at them from his ear. His aviator sunglasses gleamed back their own startled reflections. Beneath his open leather bomber jacket he wore a black shirt and even blacker pants. As a package, and definitely as a producer—*their* producer—he seemed...dangerous.

Dimi couldn't speak for the others, but looking at this man gave her a funny feeling deep down, like maybe she was sinking.

Fast.

At their utter lack of response, Mr. Harley Rider lifted a hand and waggled his fingers at them. "Anyone awake?"

Everyone but Dimi took several steps back, then separated, as if they'd never been talking to one another. Guilty expressions abounded.

The man nodded at Dimi, since she alone stood there, like Bambi caught in the headlights.

Dimi wished *she* was wearing reflector sunglasses, because she felt the need to hide the fact that her eyes had all but devoured him. She couldn't seem to help herself. His jacket spread across wide shoulders. His pants, dark and soft looking, covered what appeared to be very not-so-soft, powerful, long legs. Despite his motorcycle ride, there wasn't a spec of dirt on that body, not anywhere.

She looked.

Everything about him screamed attitude. Confidence. Danger. Funny, but she'd never really gone for the I'm-a-rebel look, and yet she was going for it now.

Or at least her hormones were.

Bad timing, since she'd given up on the male species as a whole, but she consoled herself with Suzie's mantra—most gorgeous men were poor lovers, anyway.

Then he slowly tugged off the sunglasses. Dark eyes stared right at her. His face was lean, tanned. Lived-in. Gorgeous.

And he didn't so much as crack a smile.

"Mitch Knight," he said. "Your new producer." He glanced at Ted. "I liked the nude show idea. Probably wouldn't fly with the FCC, though."

Ted beamed.

Dimi fumed. This was not a joke!

"Keep trying," Mitch suggested.

"What happened to Ritchie?" Dimi asked bluntly.

He cocked his head at her and still didn't smile. "Do you really want to know?"

*Probably not,* she decided. Ritchie had yelled a lot and thrown his weight around—which at two hundred plus pounds on a five-foot frame had been considerable—but at least what you saw with Ritchie was what you got.

Her new producer slipped his sunglasses into his chest pocket. He stood there with legs spread wide, hands on his hips, looking like he owned the world.

And he did. *Her* world.

"I don't suppose you're interested in low-fat California cuisine?" she asked hopefully.

"I'm interested in ratings." His voice was low and direct and full of authority. "What do you know about getting good ratings?"

"Apparently not much." She sent daggers to her so-called staff, who were slinking off like worms, every last one of them.

"Well, then, we have a lot to discuss. The show needs some serious spicing up."

She turned her attention back to Mr. Producer. "Spicing?"

"I thought we'd try humor, among other things."

"I don't do humor."

"You did yesterday when you announced your impending shriveled-up-old-maid status."

Dimi felt the blush creep up her face. "You said humor 'among other things.' What things?"

"Sex."

She felt her eyes bug out of her head. *"Excuse me?"*

"Humor and sex. That's what you need."

Dimi didn't gape often, but she did now. "That's what *I* need?"

"On the show," he clarified, his mouth quirking slightly.

The bastard.

He glanced at his watch. "See you in my office in, say, five?"

As if he was really asking her! Nope, this was a definite demand. A subtle one, but a demand nevertheless. "Are you going to fire me?"

He lifted a brow. "I don't usually discuss business in the parking lot."

Oh, definitely. She was toast. Burnt toast.

# 2

MITCH WALKED down the hall of the busy television studio toward his newly assigned office, ignoring the stares he received from every corner high and low. He was familiar with being the outsider. His job called for it, as well as for instilling a good amount of fear in his subordinates.

He knew that it wasn't exactly politically correct, terrifying the people who worked for him, but he'd found fear an incredible motivator.

He wasn't going to make friends, that was a foregone conclusion, and quite honestly, no big deal. Friends had always been rare, given that he'd come from a military family who'd moved around at the drop of a hat. Besides, until two years ago he hadn't needed friends. He'd had his brother.

He didn't have Daniel now. But friends were out of the question. He was temporary here. All he had to do was turn *Food Time* into the success the owners knew it could be. Once he did that, and accepted his large bonus for doing so, he could return to southern California.

Or wherever suited him.

"He's scary," he heard one clerk whisper to another as he strode down the hall.

"Yeah, but so sexy." The reply was hushed.

Mitch bit back a grin. Scary and sexy. Not bad for his first day. He'd been called worse, much worse.

Shame that he only had one minute before his scheduled meeting with Ms. Anderson, so he couldn't loiter and scare some more people into actually doing their jobs. Because if he knew Dimi's type— Ah, yes, there she was, standing in front of his office, staring at the door as if she were his sacrificial lamb, poor baby. Early, too. Being late would go against the grain for a serious workaholic such as her.

So intense. Obviously she hadn't learned what he had, to live each day—hell, each *moment* as if it were his last.

Work wasn't everything, not even close, and he'd learned that the hard way, after Daniel had died. As a result, he'd vowed to never work harder than he played, but he did play pretty hard. And yet, he believed in being the best, and that meant concentrating on *Food Time*, at least for now.

Which also meant he needed to decide if he was going to fire the far-too-serious chef in order to get the direction for the show he wanted.

Dimi still stood before his closed office door, hand raised as if to knock, staring at the wood. Her full bottom lip was being tortured by her teeth, indecision dancing across her beautiful face.

And she *was* beautiful, stunningly so. Tall, blond and curvy. Serious pinup status. Most men would be rendered stupid by just looking at her, unless of course a man was one who'd spent much of his life surrounded by the Hollywood starlet type.

But Dimi was no typical blond bombshell willing to sleep with him for a scrap of a part. Not even close. He'd caught her show. She had the basic looks, all right, but not the humor or natural grace with which to pull the entire package off.

Not to mention, despite that incredible, mouthwatering body, she was the antithesis of sexy. Take her outfit, for example—a full-blown navy power suit that barely showed her calves and covered every other inch of her except her face.

She definitely needed work.

Fortunately, Mitch specialized in such work. He could fix the show, and her, if he so chose. The question was, did he so choose?

In what appeared to be a sudden panic, Dimi dropped her hand to her side.

"God, what if he fires me?" she muttered, then, just as suddenly, she thrust her chin up. "Well then, I'll get another job, that's what." She brought up her hand again, then made a disparaging sound and dropped her head to the door. "So all you can do is cook," she told the wood. "There's plenty of opportunities out there. A restaurant, for one."

Fascinated by this picture of misery, and greatly amused, Mitch settled against the opposite wall to watch.

"Or I could become a wife," she said, resigned.

"But then you'd have to retract your whole giving-up-men thing," he noted.

Letting out a little squeal, she whirled around, hand to her chest. When she saw him, her eyes narrowed and she pointed. "You were eavesdropping."

"On the conversation you were having with yourself?" When she blushed, he pushed away from the wall. "You know, my office door works better if you actually open it."

She didn't so much as crack a smile, and he sighed. Just as he'd thought—no sense of humor. That was going to have to change if she wanted to stay.

"I was going to knock," she said.

"Before or after you finished talking to yourself?"

"Look, if you're going to fire me, I'd like to know right now."

"Right this second?"

Some of her resolve faltered, and she swallowed. "Y-yes."

"Out here in the hallway, where no less than five different crew members are lingering, waiting for the word on what happens to you?"

Dimi's gaze darted to the plants that lined the hallway, giving away her workmates. Not that he hadn't noticed hot pink go-go boots behind the giant creeping charlie, or neon green vinyl pants behind the miniature palm, and since the hibiscus was currently shaking like crazy, he knew damn well there were at least three more people hidden behind that, too.

Odd, since not one of them had appeared to give Richard a second thought. They obviously cared about Dimi, though, on whom he turned to give another long look.

She was still all bombshell body and blond hair and incredible expression. It'd be a shame to let her go. If she'd lose half her clothing, at least, and maybe try smiling, she'd bowl people over.

Instead, she squared her shoulders and regarded him seriously. "They're hiding because they're worried. They're not used to a producer like you."

"Like me?"

"Let's just say Ritchie had a different technique."

"I hope so."

"No, I mean..." Her gaze ran down the front of him, and he had to figure he only imagined that flare of awareness in her eyes, because he was pretty sure he knew what she thought of him.

"Ritchie wore jeans," she said. "Every day. His idea of dressing up was to tuck in his T-shirt. He never once wore leather, and since he fainted if he had to so much as trim his nails, I'm quite positive he had nothing pierced."

"It's just an earring."

She gave him a long look, and nothing about it was flattering, which made him want to laugh because women usually found him fairly irresistible. He leaned past her, past the soft, silky blond hair, past the oddly intoxicating scent of her shampoo, past the body so tall she could almost look at him eye to eye.

Hell of a time to realize how arousing *that* could be.

Opening the office door, he gestured her inside. "You get to go first. The plants, and the crew in them, can have the next meeting."

"First to the guillotine, what an honor. Thanks."

He widened his eyes in mock surprise. "Was that wit I just heard?"

He grinned at her back as she stalked into his office. "Hey, wait a minute. Tell another joke. Maybe there's a chance for the show, after all."

She whirled around, hope lighting her eyes…until she realized he was still teasing her. Then her face once again became carefully measured.

Oddly enough, he felt like a jerk.

Interesting. He'd done much worse than tease a woman with absolutely no remorse, so why did he suddenly feel like apologizing? "Please," he said, indicating a chair. "Sit."

She lowered herself to one of the two chairs in front of his big desk. Good. He sat in the other, noticing that her mouth tightened at his choice of being right next to her, rather than behind his desk. "Okay, let's be up-front," he said briskly. "We have two problems. Well, three if you count yourself."

Her eyes flashed him death wishes, but she said nothing.

Control. He liked that. He respected that. But he still had his doubts. "First, the show is too uptight. As I mentioned, we need humor. We need sex, Dimi."

"Can you stop saying it like that?"

"Like what?" he asked innocently.

"Look, it's a cooking show." She grated the words out. "Humor and—and…"

"Sex?" he offered helpfully. "Is that the word you're having trouble with?"

She folded her hands and managed, despite her come-hither good looks, to look like a prim schoolteacher. "Neither have any place on a cooking show. For that, they could turn to Debra Dee's station."

"But I don't want them to do that," he replied

reasonably. "I want them to tune in to you. Hence the good humor and sexiness."

She leapt to her feet and walked to his window.

"Why is this such a problem?"

Her back to him, she sighed and said, "Because I don't know how to be funny or sexy."

"So you'll learn."

That had her turning around to face him. "How?"

"Well, that's the beauty of it. I'll teach you."

"You'll— Oh, my God." She sank to a chair, his own, in fact, but he didn't point that out, mostly because she looked so utterly distressed and so utterly adorable.

"We'll have lessons," he told her. "You'll learn in no time, as I happen to be one excellent teacher."

Tipping her head back, she stared at the ceiling. "Terrific. Now I'm so pathetic I need help to turn me into a real woman."

His gaze took a tour down that lush body, and he slowly shook his head. "I never said you weren't a real woman, Dimi." His voice was a little lower, a little rougher, than he intended.

Her eyes narrowed. "Are you flirting with me?"

"I don't flirt with people who work for me." Never. Mixing business and pleasure was a bad mistake, one he didn't intend to make. "Are you open to my help or not?"

"And if I said no? You'll fire me?"

He had to shake his head. "You're into this firing stuff, aren't you." She only stared at him steadily, making him sigh. "Honestly? It'd be a damn shame to lose you. You're a fabulous chef, have an amazing voice, and beneath all those clothes have exactly the look I want for the show." He received such a scandalized glare, he nearly laughed. "All you need is the drive."

"The drive."

"Shoot for the moon, Dimi. With your outer package, you can have it all."

Her mouth opened, then carefully closed.

"I want fast banter, *live.* I want lots of warm, loving smiles, *live.* I want you bubbly and laughing—"

"Live," she said tersely. "I get it."

Not quite, she didn't. "And hot. *Hot,* Dimi. Do you know what I'm saying? I want skin, and yes, go ahead, roll your eyes and groan. Fine. But skin sells. I want some body language, too. Try it when you're walking from the refrigerator to the counter to the oven."

"Body language."

"Yeah. Good old-fashioned body language. Swing your ass once in awhile. You walk like a wooden doll."

"Swing my—" She shook her head. "This is insane. I don't swing when I walk."

"I know. But you need to."

"And I don't intend to show *anyone* skin." When he lifted a brow, she hoisted that chin so far he thought she was going to fall over. "And even if I did agree to this insanity, it's a moot point. I gave up men. Live. Remember?"

"You're going to have to recant that."

"Why? It's not like I have anyone to banter with."

"Well, here's the beauty of this whole tutoring thing." He grinned. "Meet your new on-air assistant. Your *bantering* partner."

When he bowed before her, she stared at him. "You're kidding me."

"Nope."

"I don't need an assistant."

"Ah, but you do."

"And if I refuse?"

He just looked at her.

"Your way or the highway, huh?"

At her look of hurt dismay, he actually felt a

twinge of conscience, which disturbed him. This was a job. Fix the show. Move on. Leave behind no regrets and no broken promises. "My way or the highway," he agreed quietly.

DIMI EXITED the meeting in shock. So much so that she forgot to check the plants for Suzie.

*Swing her ass. Show skin.*

Oh. My. God.

She'd never hyperventilated before, but she was close now. Needing fresh air, she headed toward the side exit of the studio and found herself in the parking lot, aimlessly walking the aisles of cars.

"Psst."

Dimi looked around and saw nothing but vehicles.

"Over here!"

She whirled, and there, in the back of Leo's cherry-red Ford pickup, sat her entire crew, huddled, looking terrified.

Sighing, she headed toward them. Ted handed her a mug. Leo filled it with coffee from a thermos. Gracie dumped a sugar packet into it. Suzie took one look at Dimi's face and added two more packets.

Everyone waited with bated breath while she sipped and got a good zap of caffeine and sugar.

"Well?" Leo finally demanded. "What happened in there? You took so long I thought maybe his leather jacket and amazing gray eyes finally got to you and you'd attacked him or something."

"Did you somehow miss the show where I gave up men?" Dimi held up her hand when they all started to speak at once, and took the time to swallow several more desperately needed sips of coffee. She wished she was home so she could raid her sister's kitchen for potato chips. Barbecue, high on the fat, because she needed a junk food run in the worst way. "It's...bad."

"He fired you?" Suzie whispered. "Oh, God. Unemployment, here we come."

"Worse." Dimi took another sip, then faced her crew bravely. "He wants to change the tone of the show. Wants to make it..."

"What?" Suzie demanded in unison with the others.

"Funny."

"We know that. It's no big deal, right?"

"Not just funny. He wants a little more..."

"*What?*" Suzie cried. "Spit it out!"

"Sex," Dimi muttered into the mug. "Dammit, he wants me to smile and laugh and probably coo disgusting sentiments while I'm at it."

"That's all?" Leo asked. "That's not so bad."

"Sounds easy enough," Ted agreed.

"No, it's not. He wants me to show skin and swing my—" Dimi blushed. "Well, let's just say I need to walk differently, too."

Everyone gaped at her, then suddenly broke into collective, relieved laughter. Suzie hooted the loudest, practically falling out of the truck bed.

Dimi folded her arms and bore the moment. "I don't see the humor in this, not one bit. None of you are going to have to—to..."

"Swing?" Suzie slapped her knee and started laughing all over again. "Oh, this is good," she finally said with a sniff.

"Yeah?" Dimi glared at her. "You haven't heard the worst of it. *He's* going to be the one to make sure I'm sexy and funny enough, and if you think I'm going to enjoy lessons from one Mitchell Knight, then think again."

"Are you kidding?" Gracie stopped laughing. "The sexiest, toughest, coolest man on the planet is going to give you lessons in being sexy? Oh, man. *Oh, man!*" She fanned herself, then turned a speculative eye on Dimi. "Hey, maybe we can switch jobs. *What?*" she demanded of the laughing Ted and Leo. "I wouldn't mind getting lessons from the likes of him."

"I thought he was the biggest, baddest producer and you were terrified of him," Dimi reminded her.

"Yeah, but that's in the work sense. This would be...pleasure. Oh, come on! He's all big and built and rugged, not to mention gorgeous. And those eyes...whew. Talk about dark, edgy intensity." She shivered. "He's quite the package, if you don't have to work for him."

"Which I do," Dimi said glumly.

Suzie shook her head thoughtfully. "Gracie's right. You gave up on men too easily. You could make this work for you."

"How?"

"Look, he's of at least average intelligence, right? And he's got a job. That's a big plus, Dimi. Think about it. It means he can afford not to live with his mother."

"I made a no-dating rule," Dimi said firmly. "I'm sticking to it."

"Did I mention he's heart-stopping to look at?"

He was that. "But I promised myself," she said weakly. "I really promised."

"He's going to teach you things," Gracie said wistfully. "Things that make my knees weak to even think about. Do you suppose he likes sex as much as he likes torturing people at work?"

"See, now that's a valid question," Suzie decided. "You can find out for us. And you can ask him if he's going to give us all a raise if you learn how to swing your hips."

"And maybe ask him if he's got any equally magnificent friends from Hollywood for me," Leo added hopefully.

"Oh, sure," Dimi said. "And why don't I just ask him if he knows that his entire crew is insane?"

"Okay." That low, husky, all too familiar voice was right behind her. "Ask away."

Dammit. *Dammit!* Slowly, already mentally slapping her forehead, she turned.

Mitch stood there, all big and tough and cool, leaning against a van. "Is this where you usually meet to discuss the new boss?"

"You're our first newbie in awhile," Leo said, scrambling out of the truck with the others. "Um…gotta run." He flashed Dimi a look of apology, but still hurried away like a terrified mouse with the rest of the crew.

One by one, they deserted her. Again.

Mitch looked at her, his eyes dark and full of secrets. "The answers are yes, no and yes."

"What?"

"Yes, if we succeed, your crew will get a raise. No, I don't have any gay friends that are single for Leo. And yes, I realize my entire crew is insane." He pushed away from the van and came toward her, until they stood only an inch apart. A light wind rustled her hair, and a blond strand escaped to slide over his face, clinging to the slight stubble there.

With one callused finger, he stroked her cheek and tucked the strand behind her ear. "And yes, absolutely yes," he said softly. "I enjoy sex as much as I enjoy torturing people at work."

She felt her saliva glands kick in.

"That look on your face," he said, still speaking in a low voice that made her tummy flutter. "That's the look I want you to wear on the show, starting tomorrow. You look a little ruffled, a little rosy. A little...needy. Even hopeful. Like you *really* need your lover to satisfy you."

Good Lord.

She'd publicly given up men. So what was

she supposed to do with the wildly sexy man standing in front of her, looking at her as if she were good enough to eat? "I can't do this."

"Yes, you can."

Having already humiliated herself, both in front of Mitch and also on live television, Dimi was not going to grovel. She straightened her weak knees and backed up a step. "Fine." She wanted her job. She wanted the job more than anything. It was her life. "I'll help you save the show."

"Good. But, if you don't mind my asking, how?"

"I'll...smile."

"Beautiful as that smile probably is—I wouldn't know, you understand, as you've not yet shown it to me—it's not quite enough."

She wanted to slug him. "I'll do the rest, too."

"What rest?"

He was going to make her say it, the jerk. "I'll get...sexy." Dammit. "But let's get one thing straight. Only on the air."

He just smiled.

"The rest of the time I'm going to be me."

His smile widened. "I'd expect no less from you."

Not only was she going to stick to her word, but she was going to ignore this infuriating man whenever and however possible. Starting now. "I have no earthly idea what's so funny."

"I know. Just keep looking at me like that during the show, and we'll do great."

"Keep looking at you like what?"

"Like you need me to take you right here and now."

# 3

THE NEXT MORNING, Dimi was in her dressing room, pretending not to be nervous, reading over her notes for the show, when Cami walked in. Her twin sister took one look at Dimi's teal blouse—buttoned to her chin—and shook her head.

"You told me you had to be sexy," she said, reaching out and unbuttoning the top button. "There. That's slightly better. Stand up."

"I've got to study these notes. We're going over barbecue techniques today and—"

"Stand up."

Dimi sighed and stood because there would be no getting rid of Cami until she had her say, whatever that might be.

Cami looked her over. "Lose the flats. You need heels."

"Heels are uncomfortable."

"Heels will help you swing your ass." Cami grinned and started rifling through the closet.

"Still can't believe you're going through with this."

"Yeah, well, I've developed a fondness for little things like eating."

"Here." From the floor of the closet came a pair of spiked heels. "These will do nicely. Just don't break your ankle. Now where's this new guy?"

Dimi recognized that matchmaking light in her sister's eye. "No. No way am I letting you meet him."

"Makeup," yelled Suzie from the other side of the closed dressing room door, and she entered the room with the makeup woman in tow. "Go for the slutty look today," she told Lucy. "Red lipstick and dark eyeliner. Ooh, nice shoe choice," she told Dimi.

"See? Told ya." Cami gloated.

Dimi sighed. Then slapped at Suzie's hand when she reached out and undid the second button on her blouse. But she sat obediently for makeup, her heart starting a slow, heavy drumming.

Nerves, she realized in surprise. She was nervous.

Because of Mitch.

Pressing a hand to her chest, she concentrated on breathing. And Lucy's tsk. "What now?"

Lucy undid button number three.

"Better," Suzie declared, pulling Dimi out of her chair. "Now what was that I was supposed to tell you?" She pondered this, then grinned widely. "Oh, yeah. Go swing some ass, girl."

DIMI DEBATED the button issue as she walked from her dressing room, down three different hallways, all the way to the kitchen set.

One undone button seemed okay. Two buttons...well, she supposed it could be construed as sexy.

But three, coupled with the come-do-me heels and the red lipstick... Yikes.

A low, appreciative whistle sounded as she entered the soundstage. And then another. And then another, as one by one, the crew noticed her new look and stood to salute her as she passed.

"Stop it," she grumbled, walking by all of them to stand beneath the bright lights on the set. Lucy followed her with the ever-ready powder puff. So did Suzie, with the clipboard that was more a part of her than her own limbs. The two of them were preening and accepting applause for Dimi's current look, as if it had been all their doing.

Which of course it had.

Dimi tried to concentrate on her notes instead of the attention she was getting. So when another hand reached out for her buttons, she slapped it away without looking up.

A big, warm, very masculine hand grabbed hers, and her gaze jerked to the dark, amused one of Mitchell Knight.

"You should know I've really had it with people putting their hands all over my cleavage," she warned him, jaw tight. "So if you don't mind—"

"I just—"

"Look, I'm wearing the lipstick, see?" She rubbed her lips together and ignored the heat that flared in his gaze. Kicking out a leg, she tapped his booted foot with her high-heeled one. "And the pumps, too, though if I fall and break my ankle, I'm going to sue you, whoever is in charge of you, and the entire crew on top of it all for thinking this whole darn thing is so amusing. So lay off with the buttons, I've done absolutely everything you've asked of me."

"Not yet, you haven't."

His eyes were a very dark gray. This close,

she could see flecks of blue in there, as well, dancing beneath all the bright lights. And he had the longest, thickest lashes, the sort a woman would kill for, which were totally wasted on a man. "What else, then?" she demanded, and not very graciously. "What other torture have you come up with that's worse than these shoes?"

One corner of his mouth quirked. "Torture, huh? Poor baby, turning every man's head like that."

"I don't like it," she said through her teeth.

"Which brings us back to the one thing you haven't tried yet, not once." His hands came up and, very gently for such a big man, he cupped her jaw. His thumb slid over her lower lip, urging it to curve. "Smile. I haven't seen you try that."

She sent him a smile, made such only because she bared her teeth.

He sighed. "You might want to keep working on that."

"Fine." Could she have possibly gotten off that easy? Maybe he'd changed his mind about going on the air with her! "We're set, then."

"Well…" His gaze ran down the length of her, scorching her skin everywhere it touched.

"Not really. But it's a decent start. Tomorrow, though, tomorrow *I* choose the outfit."

"But—"

His finger waggled in her face. "You've lost the smile already. Warm. Happy. Bubbly. Remember?"

She was going to grind her teeth down to nothing, and if she did, some sexpot-by-the-refrigerator she'd be. "I remember."

"Good girl," he said as if she were an obedient puppy. "Let's roll, people," he called, coming around the counter to stand next to her. He snapped his fingers at the assistant director, who snapped her fingers at her assistant, and she came running out to clip a mike on Mitch's shirt.

Apparently, he was staying.

Then he took her hand and pulled her around to the front of the counter to join him.

"But I always start behind the counter, I just dive right into the cooking part—"

"Too serious," he said, tugging her toward her new mark. "Right there. And remember..."

She bared her teeth into another semblance of a smile.

He rolled his eyes heavenward. "Close enough," he muttered, just as the director started the countdown.

"Ten seconds!"

"Oh, and about those buttons." Mitch moved a hand toward her, and she gave him her best I'm-going-to-smack-you look. In surrender, he lifted the hand away. "I was trying to tell you before—"

"Save it."

"Five!"

"Dimi."

She lifted her hands to her ears. Not very mature, but there it was.

"And three, two…you're on!"

Dimi's opening had been the same for the entire two years she'd been doing the show. "Hello, everyone, welcome to *Food Time.* I'm Dimi Anderson, and today we're going to—" She stopped abruptly at Suzie's widened eyes, where she stood just off set. Her assistant pointed to her cleavage.

Dimi glanced down at herself.

And nearly fell off her heels, as she was flashing the entire world—correction, all three viewers—her belly button.

"Tried to tell you," Mitch offered in a helpful whisper.

No use slugging him on live television, she thought, putting a hand to her heart and covering the view. She wondered how long she could keep her hand there and not look like an idiot. "We're going to learn some new barbecue techniques today."

"But first we're going to make a delicious cherry pie." Mitch broke in smoothly with a gracious, welcoming smile, distracting their viewers while Dimi raced to button up.

Then what he said sank in. "What?" She stared at him for one full second before she realized she was live—and gawking. Dammit! She managed a smile. "Well, that's a surprise."

"Yep." He slipped his hands into his pockets and stood there with utter confidence, looking one-hundred-percent male in a one-hundred-percent woman's domain. His angelic expression and sinner's looks charmed the camera to stay right on him. "Hi," he said into it. "I'm Mitch Knight. Dessert extraordinaire. I'm also Dimi's new assistant. Not that she needed one for cooking, but..." He grinned unabashedly, in a way that invited all their viewers to grin with him. "After yesterday's no-men proclamation, I couldn't resist coming on and seeing if she meant it. Did you, Dimi?" He batted those long, lush eyelashes. "No more men? Ever?"

Dimi ground her teeth and realized for the first

time exactly how appealing he was going to be to their audience. He should have looked ridiculous in a kitchen. He was so big, so...full of presence. But his dark hair gleamed under the bright lights, and so did his eyes. The diamond stud in his ear twinkled. His dark gray trousers fit him in a way that would make any red-blooded woman need a bib to catch the drool. His shirt, a light gray, clung to his broad shoulders and impressive chest. And then there was the clincher. His warm smile was just wicked enough to coax a nun into lusthood.

"Back to that cherry pie," she said in a voice that came out a little breathless, adding insult to injury. Ruthlessly, she cleared her throat. "I assume you have a recipe handy?"

"Always prepared," he quipped with a wink. "I guess you're going to ignore the man question, then."

"This is a cooking show, not a *man* show."

"But I'm a man. And I'm here."

"So let's cook, then." She remembered to smile, barely.

Mitch didn't have such a problem. He nodded in the direction of the refrigerator. She followed his masculine strut, watching his—

Oh, my God. She was staring at his butt.

On television.

She jerked her eyes up, only to find him grinning at her over his shoulder. *Swing it, too, baby,* his eyes seemed to say.

In her ridiculous heels, she didn't have much choice.

Finally, mercifully, they were at the refrigerator. Mitch talked the entire time, about the weather, about the Giants, about everything and anything, and she tried to keep up with him, but he kept looking at her with that look, the one she imagined making all the viewers swoon, and oddly enough, she felt a little dizzy herself.

*Ignore him,* she reminded herself. *Just do your job.*

"Now for the ingredients," he was saying to the camera in that silky voice. "First, cherries."

He handed a bowl of them to Dimi, who looked at the red succulent fruit.

"Now, no fair wasting time trying to tie any cherry stems with your teeth," he told the camera. "No one can beat my record." He reached into the bowl of cherries with his long fingers and grabbed the stem off one, his eyes directly on Dimi's. Popping the stem into his mouth, and still holding Dimi's gaze prisoner, he worked the strong muscles in his jaw back and forth. After about five seconds, he stuck out his tongue.

On it was the stem...tied into a neat little knot.

Dimi lost all ability to think, much less talk. Her skin went hot and itchy, and she knew she must have gone red as a beet. She was deathly afraid she recognized her ailment, and it was the very unwelcome emotion called lust.

Darn him! She'd given up men and she meant it, no matter how talented his tongue was.

"Now," he said calmly, as if he hadn't caused every single woman watching him to get rubbery knees. "We need the other ingredients." He rattled them off as he handed them one by one to Dimi, who was still standing there with too much cleavage, in heels that made her indeed swing her ass, stunned to the depths by what he was doing to her on live television.

"Here you go," he said, passing the sugar. "Is that about the right amount?" he asked, walking around her. As he did, he casually and lightly stroked a hand over the small of her back.

Just a barely there touch, and her entire body jerked to attention, including her nipples, which were pressing against the material of her blouse.

Glaring at him would do nothing but egg him on, she decided, but she was sorely tempted. Luckily, a commercial break was called.

"What do you think you're doing?" she demanded, so frustrated, so ruffled, so... Well, she wasn't sure what else she was, but certainly anger topped the list. "You're taking over the show!"

"Feel free to talk more instead of standing there with your tongue hanging out as you moon at me."

When she gaped at him, he laughed. "Yeah, that's the look I love so much. Oh, come on, this is fun. Let's go check the phone lines."

"No one ever calls during the show."

"No?" He didn't sound concerned.

They hadn't made it off the set before Suzie came running up to them, her eyes lit with excitement. "Every phone in the place is ringing off the hook." She turned to Mitch. "Keep baiting her, they love it. They love how she's trying to be sexy and is failing completely."

"What?" Dimi asked, faintly. "I'm...failing?"

"They love that when you look at her, she blushes." Suzie laughed, gripped her clipboard to her chest and turned to Dimi. "And they especially loved the belly button flash."

Dimi groaned. "This can't go on. I need a sweater, pronto."

"Why?" Mitch asked.

"Because maybe I'm getting cold."

He looked directly into her eyes. "It's not getting cold that worries you."

Bastard. "Get me a sweater, Suzie."

"Sorry." She grinned. "We're fresh out."

Before Dimi could kill her assistant, Gracie came running up to them. "The phones are wild. Whatever you're doing, don't stop."

"Twenty seconds, everyone! Take your places!"

Mitch offered Dimi his arm, which, much to his amusement, she flatly refused. Sauntering ahead of him, she took two steps on her four-inch pumps and promptly tripped. Muttering something obscene about the absurdity of heels, she kept going.

He worked hard to keep his grin to himself, but it was difficult. This was a personal record for him, starting a show's turnaround in less than two days.

There'd been a time in his life when he'd expected perfection from himself and all those around him, when he'd worked sixteen-hour days, living and breathing his job. There'd been a time when he'd been too busy for any pleasure, such as spending time with his beloved brother.

Well, Daniel was gone now. Too late, Mitch had learned all work was no way to live. Work had a place, yes.

But so did fun. Unexpectedly, this job could be both, and maybe even more fun than work.

"Five seconds!"

He got into position next to his still-fuming co-host and smiled at her. She didn't return it. "Ah, ah. Remember—"

"I'll remember!"

"Three, two, and…" The director punched a finger at them, and off Mitch went, slowly and precisely measuring out ingredients while making sure to touch Dimi whenever possible, which kept a nice color to her cheeks and fire in her gaze.

Perfect.

Then it was time to pull out his baked pie from the oven. He pulled on a mitt, noticing that Dimi very intently watched everything he did with a sort of helplessly fascinated expression.

He liked that in a way that had nothing to do with work.

"And now…" He went to the refrigerator and

took out the whipped cream, wriggling his eyebrows suggestively for the camera.

Dimi, who'd just stuck a finger in the leftover cherry mixture, telling their audience how good it was, glanced at him and at what he was holding.

And choked.

Mitch took a step toward her, and she backed up.

He smiled slowly.

"What are you doing with that?" she demanded.

He didn't answer.

She took another step back, looking every bit as ruffled and wildly sexy as he'd imagined she could.

She could have no idea how easily she was falling into his vision for the show, because certainly if she did, she wouldn't be nearly as cooperative, unintentionally or otherwise.

Knowing the audience was eating this up, he sent her his naughtiest grin.

"Mitch."

"Yep, that's my name." He thoroughly and methodically shook the can of whipped cream.

"The whipped cream," she said, staring at it. *"What are you doing with that?"*

"What do you want to do with it?"

She sputtered for a moment, then finally seemed to come to her senses. "It's for the pie."

"Well, of course it is." He set it on the counter. "Whatever did you think it was for? And remember, this show is G-rated."

She didn't say a word, but her eyes smoldered, and he knew she was going to light into him after the show.

In a sick way, he was looking forward to it.

# 4

DIMI DIDN'T calm down until she'd driven out
of the studio and past the small downtown area
of Truckee, winding her way around Donner
Lake toward her town house. Just the sight of
the pristine blue water, dotted with whitecaps
from the early evening wind, went a long way
toward cooling the steam coming out of her ears.

Her small building was right on the water,
converted from a century-old hotel the rich and
famous had frequented in the early 1900's.

Normally, she'd hit Cami's town house first,
raiding it for food or maybe some new makeup.
Any excuse not to go home and be alone. She
didn't do alone very well, which is why she'd
lived with Cami until they'd decided they'd gotten too dependent on each other. That's when
Dimi had bought a place down the path, and then
proceeded to spend all her time at Cami's, anyway.

Some independence.

But last month Cami had gone and done the unthinkable. She'd fallen in love. And now her twin believed love was for everyone. She'd been on Dimi's case to try it.

But Dimi had been trying to do just that for so long it left a bad taste in her mouth. She was no longer interested.

Mostly not, anyway.

Since Cami and Tanner were no doubt right this minute displaying some disgusting amount of affection for each other, she skipped Cami's place entirely and headed toward her own. She opened her door, kicked off her shoes because her feet were killing her from the stupid heels, and wished she'd remembered to go food shopping.

Standing in front of the kitchen window, she stared at the lake, letting out a long, shaky breath, realizing she was still wound up tighter than a drum.

Mitch's fault, of course.

She'd weathered the belly button flash fairly well. And then the sashaying across the set for the sake of any potential male viewers. Not to mention the legions of phone calls begging for more Mitch.

But the whipped cream. He'd really gotten her with the whipped cream.

It was his face, she decided. Those piercing eyes that saw everything, his sexy mouth. And that heart-stopping grin. He'd shot it at her while holding that can of cream, and her mind had just...shut down.

Sensory overload.

And he'd known it, damn him. He'd known it and it had amused him.

She flipped on the light, determined to figure out some sort of dinner that would include one food group and one food group only—major fat grams.

Brownie poked her head out.

"Hungry?" Dimi poured some pellets into the hamster's bowl. "Here you go."

Brownie sniffed at them, then looked at her.

"I didn't steal any potato chips from Cami today, sorry."

Brownie seemed to sigh, then waddled into her little wooden hut.

"Hey, the guy at the pet store promised me you'd like those."

There came a rustling from within the hut, but no Brownie.

"I can take you back, you know."

"Oh, nice, threatening a helpless little hamster." Cami shook her head and came into the room.

Dimi decided not to yell at her sister for scaring her to death, because one, Dimi always entered Cami's place uninvited, and two, Cami was holding up a bag of barbecue potato chips. "Thank God," was all Dimi said. She took two sodas out of the refrigerator and grabbed a bowl from the cupboard.

They poured the entire bag into it and took a seat—on the floor.

"You ever going to buy furniture?" Cami wondered around a mouthful.

Too busy eating, Dimi lifted a shoulder.

"Pretty sad state of affairs. A chef with an empty kitchen. You should really let me decorate." Cami licked the salt off her fingers one at a time. "It's ridiculous, you making all that money and not having anyplace to sit."

"You know I don't make all that much money. And anyway, I might be fired soon."

"No way." Cami's eyes gleamed speculatively. "Enjoyed the show today, by the way. Mitchell Knight is one hot guy, you know."

"What does Tanner think of you drooling over another man?"

"He's not threatened." Cami grinned. "I make sure of it." Then her expression went serious.

Uh-oh, thought Dimi.

"About Mitch," Cami started.

"No."

"You have no idea what I was about to say."

"Doesn't matter. The answer is still no."

"You're the one who gave me the love lecture only a few weeks ago," Cami said, exasperated. "'Give Tanner a fair shot, Cami,'" she mimicked. "Then you started in on how I always sabotage all my relationships to make sure I never fell in love. You said I was using Dad's seven marriages and Mom's control freakness to destroy my chance at happiness."

"Yeah, well, that was you," Dimi said, shoving some more potato chips into her mouth.

"It was me, and it worked." Cami's eyes glowed softly. "I fell in love, and it's wonderful."

"Love isn't for everyone."

"Okay, forget the wedded bliss, just go for sexual bliss."

Dimi laughed. "Tempting as that sounds, I gave up men, remember?"

"That's not the answer, Dimi. How about

Mitch? He could be your Mr. Right, and he's right under your nose.''

Dimi, who'd just taken a sip of soda, nearly spewed it across the room. ''No. No way is Mitch my Mr. Right.''

''Why not?''

''Why not? Because he…because…'' Well, heck if she could put her finger on it.

''Dimi, he can tie a cherry stem with his tongue.'' Cami shivered in imagined thrill. ''*Hello.* What more do you need from a man?''

Dimi wasn't quite sure.

''Just kiss him.''

''*What?*''

''Just once.''

''I am *not* going to kiss him.''

Cami looked majorly disappointed.

''Besides, I don't think I can handle him,'' she admitted. ''He's—''

''Sexy.''

''Too sexy.''

''Are you *kidding?* There's no such thing as too sexy!''

''No, I mean it,'' Dimi said firmly. ''If I'm ever insane enough to revoke my no-men rule, which I'm not, then I'm going to do it for a nice, comfortable, easy man who doesn't curl my toes, thank you very much.''

Cami grinned. ''He curls your toes?''

''Stop it.''

''You've got to go for it.''

''And you've got to get back to Tanner. Go.''

Cami rose, but at the door, she hesitated. ''Just one little kiss. No more, no less. Just try not being so serious for a change. How hard could that be?''

Pretty damn hard, actually.

''Think about it, okay?'' Cami waited. ''Dimi? Okay?''

As if she could do anything but. ''Yeah.''

MITCH DREAMED about cherry pie. Dreamed about scooping it across a woman's bare torso, over her softly rounded belly, her ribs, her breasts, then bending his head to nibble it off. Dreamed about moving down that warm body, slowly exploring every inch of it, then shifting up to look into her face before giving her a kiss she'd never forget.

Only it was *him* who would never forget. The chocolate-brown eyes gazing up at him, dazed and opaque with desire, were Dimi's.

That woke him right up.

He had no idea why he was dreaming about her, but apparently she wasn't the only one he'd rendered full of lust with the whipped cream yesterday. And now he was awake and it was only five in the morning. Awake and fully aroused and all alone.

His own doing, he reminded himself, and got up to take a cold shower.

As the icy water pummeled him, Daniel's voice came into his head. *Don't forget to live, man. Enjoy life. Seek it out and do it right.*

Yeah, well, he'd like to do it right. Do Dimi right. But that was out of the question.

He'd have to settle for finding his pleasure in work. As he dressed, he wondered if Dimi would be nearly as much fun to goad today as she'd been yesterday.

His anticipatory grin slowly faded as he remembered how ticked off she'd been. He'd expected her to skin him alive, but instead she'd simply vanished.

What if she didn't show today?

Damn, the more he thought about it, the more likely it seemed. He went for the phone, intending to call the studio and have them send a car for her.

Then he remembered. He wasn't in Hollywood anymore. The people of Truckee didn't send cars.

Sighing, he checked his computer personnel files and pulled up Dimi's address. Whether Dimi Anderson liked it or not, she was about to be escorted to work.

By him.

He had to admit to some surprise when he drove out to her place some time later. It was sitting right on Donner Lake, surrounded by glassy water and high Sierra peaks, and he thought he'd never seen a more idyllic, peaceful, beautiful setting. Given that, Dimi should have been the most relaxed person he knew.

Not the most uptight.

No one answered his knock, but he could hear music blaring from within, so he walked around to the unfenced back, counting to make sure he got the right town house. Her back door was ajar, so he pushed it open and peered into her kitchen. "Dimi?"

No answer, but he could hear her singing, loudly and off-key, which made him grin.

His serious chef wailing at the top of her lungs?

Interestingly enough, her kitchen had all the appliances and no furniture, only a cage on the floor opposite the refrigerator. "Dimi?" he called again, going down to his knees to tap lightly on the cage.

A hamster poked its head out. Solemn black eyes studied him. He whistled softly, and the animal toddled out of its small house and stared at him. He kept whistling as he reached into the cage and stroked a finger down its back. The little thing closed its eyes in ecstasy.

From behind him, the singing got louder as Dimi moved closer, and suddenly she was in the doorway, eyes wide and on him.

"Oh!"

Mitch rose to his feet. "I'm sorry. I knocked and called out. You didn't answer."

She had a hand to her chest, but she no longer looked frightened. More like intrigued, which amused him.

"You could have knocked again," she said.

"Could have, but you were singing pretty loud."

She shrugged. "Secret rock-star fantasy."

Yesterday she'd done everything in her power to stay away from him. Now, surprisingly, she stepped closer, smiling easily. *Easily*. Not Dimi's usual tactic. "Aren't you going to ask me why I'm here?" he asked.

"Okay. I'll play." She looked him over with sleepy, inviting eyes. "Why are you here?"

It wasn't until she had him in the corner, her hands on either side of him against the counter, that he realized the truth, that there was a very good reason that she'd been singing so loudly without a care, that she was smiling so unlike Dimi, but he decided to play, too. "I'm here to make sure my chef gets to the studio."

Cami narrowed her eyes and studied him for a long moment, during which it took all his control not to laugh and blow her cover.

Then, after that long stare, she leaned in close, lips slightly parted.

She obviously wanted him to kiss her.

"How far are you going to take this?" he wondered, his mouth a breath from hers.

Those expressive eyes blinked, but before she could do anything else, another voice came from the doorway.

*"Cami!"*

The woman in front of Mitch jerked back, turned red as a beet and whirled to face…a horrified Dimi.

*"What are you doing?"* Dimi demanded.

Cami wrung her hands, then must have decided to tough it out, because she shot Mitch an embarrassed glance and shrugged. "I figured if he thought you wanted to kiss him, he might make the first move so you wouldn't have to."

"Oh, my God." Dimi covered her eyes. "This isn't happening. You aren't making a move on my producer."

"Hey, I didn't actually kiss him!" Cami complained. "You don't have anything to be mad at."

Dimi dropped her hand. "I'm telling Mom on you. And then Tanner! My God, what would Tanner think?"

"Fine. Go right ahead and tattle, just like always." Cami hightailed it to the kitchen door. "Get me in trouble just because I was trying to help you get a little lucky." Turning to Mitch, she gave a self-deprecating smile. "I'm sorry I had to use you for that, but surely you can see I was just trying to help things along."

Mitch bit back his grin. "I understand."

"See?" Cami spoke to Dimi. "He understands." She stepped out and slammed the door behind her, but in a flash the door was flung open again. Cami stormed in and grabbed the bowl of chips off the counter.

"Hey," Dimi protested, gaze glued to those chips.

Without another word, Cami slammed out. Again.

The silence was deafening. "I suppose I should apologize for that," Dimi finally said.

"No."

"No?"

Mitch didn't want her apology, he wanted the kiss he'd almost gotten, and he wanted it from the real Dimi. He wanted it with a sudden, shocking yearning that he wasn't going to question right now, not with Dimi looking at him with a little heat of her own in her eyes. Heat and curiosity and lingering embarrassment. "We could just get it out of the way, you know," he suggested, stepping toward her.

"Get what out of the way?" But she licked her lips and glanced at his mouth, giving herself away.

"You know what."

"I don't even know why you're here, in my kitchen, getting yourself sexually harassed by my sister, much less anything else."

"I'm here to pick you up."

"Ah." She nodded in sudden understanding. "You thought after your little shenanigans yesterday that I wouldn't show up for work. Good. That means I'm not fired. That you need me."

"Oh, I need you," he murmured, a bit surprised at how much.

At that, she took a step back, so that she was caged between the dishwasher and the oven.

He followed.

"Sexually aggressive men annoy me," she said.

Sliding his hands to her hips, he turned them around so *he* was the one caged in. "Okay. You be the sexually aggressive one, then. I'm an equal opportunist when it comes to—"

She put a finger on his lips. "Don't say the word sex."

"Why not?"

"Because when you say it, it does something funny to my knees."

"Yeah?" He liked that. She was close, her mouth softly parted, her eyes slumberous. He liked that, too. "Kiss me, Dimi."

"Uh." She swallowed, hard. "That would be extremely unwise."

"Why?"

"Why?" She looked lost for a moment, as if she couldn't quite remember why.

"We both want it," he said.

"Do you give yourself everything you want?"

"Absolutely. That's the bonus of being all grown up. I can break curfew, not eat my spinach…and kiss whomever I want, even if it's extremely unwise."

She stared at him, actually considering.

"Think of all the fire it will give the show today," he coaxed, but that was where he made his mistake. He knew it as soon as her eyes cooled and her mouth hardened.

"That's right," she said, straightening away from him. "The show. This is all for the show." She gave him a tight smile. "Let's just save it for the camera, then, shall we?"

Grabbing her purse off the counter, she walked out the door without another look at him, back to the serious, quiet, original Dimi, not a cooking sex kitten in sight.

"Note to self," he muttered. "Next time you get Dimi in your arms, don't open your idiotic mouth."

# 5

DIMI HAD JUST applied her lipstick when the knock came to her dressing room.

"Costume!" Leo's voice called.

There were no costumes on this show, and Leo knew it. She wore her own clothes. In fact, she'd been given a budget for a new wardrobe but hadn't as yet spent time figuring out what that new wardrobe should be. Prepared for one of the cast's usual jokes, she cautiously opened the door.

Leo stood there holding a hanger. Swinging from it was a little black push-up bra beneath a gauzy, completely sheer long-sleeved chartreuse blouse and a pair of black...pants. She used the word loosely, since they were cut so low she doubted they'd ever cover any normal woman's hips, of which hers were more *normal* than most. Hanging from Leo's fingers were a pair of high-heeled, open-toed sandals, designed to torture some poor woman's feet.

"Made just for you," Leo informed her. "Look."

Indeed, when she leaned forward and squinted at the see-through top, she could see the words *Food Time* engraved in black letters high on the left side.

"Good one," Dimi said, laughing. "Now take it back to whatever poor delusional teeny-bopper you got it from and tell everyone I appreciated the joke."

Leo shifted on his feet, a look of hesitation on his face.

"Leo?"

"Um…it's not a joke. Mitch had this sent over for you to wear on the show today."

"Funny."

But Leo didn't so much as smile, and a sinking feeling began in Dimi's stomach. "Leo, you're not laughing."

"That's because I like it. The outfit, that is." He shot her an apologetic smile. "It's cool, it's hip, and you'll be able to move more freely than you can with those wide skirts you prefer."

"But…"

"The new image, remember? Fun and sexy."

"But—"

Leo thrust out the clothes.

But she *so* wasn't this person that Mitch apparently thought she could be. She wasn't! Didn't he know that by now? Hadn't everyone told him? Hadn't she shown him over and over? She was serious. Intense.

Not sexy.

And anyway, even if she wanted to be, she didn't know *how*.

"Dimi, believe me. You're young enough to pull it off, and after seeing the response from our viewers with Mitch, you're also hot enough."

"Oh, no." She backed up, laughing in horror. "I'm not...*hot*." Though she'd felt it, she really had, for that one little flicker of a moment in Mitch's arms.

Hot to the core.

"It wasn't an insult, Dimi. Demographics show we can pick up more men if you keep on doing what you're doing."

"But my apron has more material than that shirt!"

"Um, yeah, about the apron." Leo looked at his shoes. "Mitch said to lose it."

*"What?"*

"Actually, what he said was burn it so that you couldn't use it to hide behind, because a sex goddess in the kitchen would never wear a full apron. And with the new direction of the show— that being you as a sex goddess in training, and him being the trainer—you needed to have your clothing selected for you.''

"Sex goddess in training," she repeated carefully. "And him being the trainer. He said that.''

Leo winced. "Oh, jeez. Look, I'm pretty sure I wasn't supposed to repeat that part, so if you could not tell him—''

"Oh, okay." She nodded agreeably. "I'll just let him take over my show, pick out my clothes and run my life. Does that work for you, Leo?''

Leo rolled his eyes. "Now, Dimi—''

"No argument, no fight. In fact, I'll just roll over like a puppy. Is that the right response? Is that what you meant by not telling him—''

"Cool clothes," Suzie said, coming around the corner and snagging the hanger from Leo. "Love the material on this blouse. Oh, man. Feel it, Dimi. It's so soft—" She finally caught the expression on Dimi's face. "What? Did someone die?''

"She doesn't like the outfit," Leo said.

"But it's fabulous. Those pants must have cost a fortune.''

"Mitch picked them out," Leo said meaningfully.

"Oh." Suzie fingered the material of the pants. "Which of course makes them cheap, ugly and unwearable, right?"

Dimi just glared at her, making Suzie sigh. "Hon, look. Hate the man if you must, but he's got great taste. This is exactly what the young, gorgeous, amazingly talented chef and host of a cooking show should wear."

"They won't fit," Dimi assured them both, but Suzie set Leo free and pressed Dimi into her dressing room.

"Show me."

"Gladly." Dimi stripped. Muttered about the temperature in the room. Swore at the new clothes. Beamed at Suzie when she could barely get the pants up.

Then stopped in defeat when she looked in the mirror.

Because it fit, all of it. Like a second skin, but it fit. The pants didn't cover her belly button, but they did cover her hips, just barely. The bra fit, too, and gave her generous breasts more…generousness. "Holy smokes," she muttered, staring at her reflection.

Suzie handed her the blouse, which covered exactly nothing and had only one button.

"One button!" Dimi wailed, closing it between her shoved-up-and-out breasts. "I need more buttons, Suzie."

"It drapes closed perfectly."

"Yeah, because what does it matter when you can see everything right through the shirt!"

"It's not *that* see-through, Dimi. You're perfectly covered."

"I can't show my belly button on the air."

Suzie laughed good and long over that. "You do realize this is the twenty-first century, right?"

"Said by the woman who's five foot two and one hundred pounds. You could get away with this, but not me."

"Have you seen a Brittney Spears video lately?"

"A little sympathy would be nice."

"Okay," Suzie agreed. "I'm sorry you're so tall and curvy and gorgeous. What a curse."

Dimi rolled her eyes. But after she applied her makeup and took a brush to her already curled hair, she had to admit, she looked...well, pretty damn fine.

"Whoa, baby, who knew you were hiding such a great set of breasts," Suzie marveled.

"And that tush. Good Lord, girlfriend, you should have been wearing pants all along. Good thing no one can see that you prefer plain white cotton panties."

"I like cotton."

"You know they make it in colors now, right?"

"Everybody's turned into a comic." Dimi tried pulling the pants up a little more, to no avail. "This is crazy. If I so much as bend over, I'm going to expose my butt like a damn contractor."

"So don't bend over. Dimi, can't you feel it?" Suzie's eyes were lit with excitement. "The new direction of the show. We're going to go big. We're all going to make it." She hopped off the chair she'd plopped into and twirled around. "No more unemployment threat looming, no more scanning the classified section in the newspaper."

Her earnestness had Dimi biting back her disgruntled reply. She wasn't *that* selfish as to take away Suzie's hope and joy, and she knew it wasn't just Suzie. In fact, she knew exactly how many people depended on the success of this show.

Dammit.

"Look, I almost forgot," Suzie said. "I came to tell you, Mitch wants to see you before the show. He wants to go over today's dialogue."

"We're going to plan our dialogue?"

"Apparently." Suzie grinned. "Make it as hot as yesterday, and we're all on easy street for the season."

Dimi thought of yesterday, and how she'd nearly melted watching Mitch handle the food, the cooking, *everything,* with a masculine flair that had left her...hungry.

And not for food. "I can't do this," she muttered, but Suzie was already gone, so she took herself down the hall to tell Mitch that very thing herself. She wouldn't follow his dictates. She would dress and walk and talk however she wanted.

Only as she went, no less than six male crew members dramatically fell to the floor when she passed.

"Very funny," she told them, getting more and more righteous and worked up, until finally she stood right outside Mitch's office door with damp palms and a racing heart.

What if he gave her that look again, the one that scrambled her brain and made her want things she couldn't even think about without getting all hot and itchy from the inside out?

Just as she lifted her hand to knock, Mitch opened the door, startling her into a very unrighteous squeak. "Do you have radar or something?" she demanded.

His gaze traveled the length of her, heating up from a mere smoldering to full-blown sizzle by the time it met hers again. "The outfit is good."

"Tell me again, exactly what does being a sex goddess have to do with cooking?"

He grimaced at her loud voice, took her arm and pulled her inside his office. She had to stalk the length of the room a few times because it was hard to gather her temper again after that brain-cell-crunching look he'd just given her, but not impossible.

"I didn't say sex goddess," he said.

"Leo said—"

"I said sex kitten." He grinned when she whipped around, practically snarling.

At least he wasn't wearing black leather or those dark, dark sunglasses today. At least they weren't outside where his nearly black hair gleamed and so did his smile, not to mention the motorcycle that had given her quite the interesting fantasy the past few nights.

But the truth was, he didn't need any of that to be dangerous, because it was all in his eyes, in his smile and most definitely in the way he looked at her.

"What I said was, you needed to be coached from serious queen to sex kitten."

She crossed her arms. "And that *you* were going to be the coach."

"Yes."

Just the single word caused a ripple of awareness. She ruthlessly stomped on it. "What does that coaching entail?"

"We've already covered this. The walk, the clothes, the smile."

"That's it?"

"You're not quite ready for the rest yet."

Well, darn if that didn't send another little thrill rippling through her body. But that couldn't be right, she couldn't be...*excited* about this, could she? "I think I'd at least like a hint," she decided.

"No."

There was something incredibly intoxicating about how close his mouth was, about being able to—if she so chose—slip her arms around his neck and lose herself in him.

If she so chose.

Which, of course, she wouldn't.

His eyes were shining with approval and a good amount of heat. "You're going to knock 'em dead today, Dimi. Do you have any idea how incredible you look?"

"For a sex kitten, you mean."

Running a finger over the gauzy material covering her shoulder, he slowly shook his head. "You look like a woman full of life, confident and all too happy to show the world what she can do." His gaze met hers. "So, what can you do, Dimi?"

Anything. That's how she felt when he looked at her like that. She could do anything. "I want to pick the recipes we use," she managed to say. "If I have to walk, talk and dress like this, you can give me that."

"Okay, what direction do you see yourself and the show going in?"

She'd done this before, pitched her vision. No one had ever wanted to believe in her, and as a result, she'd been stuck with tried, true and *boring* recipes. "I want to try new things across the board," she said. "For instance, I'd like to show quick-and-easy low-fat foods that promote good health but that are also innovative and fun."

Mitch nodded.

Buoyed, she spoke faster. "I want to do themes, like specializing in California cuisine for a week. Maybe highlight regions."

"That sounds good."

"Really?"

"Really."

Hope surged. As did an almost unrecognizable joy. This was becoming a bit overwhelming, all these emotions for a man she wanted to resent with all her heart.

"You walk the walk and talk the talk," he said. "And you can cook whatever you want."

"Thank you."

"Don't thank me. Because Dimi? The outfit..." He tugged on the gauze. "It stays."

"Did you know I can't even bend over in this?" she asked in frustration.

His eyes glimmered. "Yep."

BY THE END of the week the entire town was abuzz with talk about the new and improved *Food Time*.

The change was unbelievable, including the ratings, which made Mitch's job all the easier. If it kept up, he'd be out of here in no time and back on his home turf with some new project. Just what he wanted.

So what was that strange pang he felt deep down in the pit of his stomach? It couldn't be regret. He didn't belong in a place this small. There wasn't enough room for him in a town like this. He stuck out like a sore thumb.

And he missed... Hell. He missed exactly nothing.

But that didn't mean he'd miss this place, either.

"Check it out," Suzie said as everyone gathered for their early morning staff meeting. She lifted the local paper and read. "*Food Time* modernizes. Hip hosts, great chemistry, not to mention fabulous new recipes. Don't miss it."

Mitch noted the date at the top of the paper. "That's from last week."

"Yeah." Suzie gave him a sheepish smile. "I just worked my way through my stack of mail last night."

"So what do they say about us *this* week?"

"I don't know. It hasn't come out yet."

Mitch came from a town where one could get the *Los Angeles Times,* the *New York Times* and just about every other major paper on any street corner. Daily. "You're kidding me."

"It won't come out until tomorrow."

Exactly his point about this place, Mitch

thought as everyone smiled with fondness for their little town with only one newspaper once a week.

Dimi rushed into the conference room, a suspicious, mysterious mass in her arms covered with a black towel. "Sorry I'm late."

"What do you have there?" Leo asked.

Dimi shot a look at Mitch. "Nothing." She shoved the thing under the table, sat and folded her arms. The picture of calm.

Unless one looked deep enough, which of course Mitch did. She looked ruffled, unnerved and damned distracting while doing it.

"Thirty minutes to air," Gracie announced, checking her watch.

"Okay, anyone have anything else before we disperse?" Mitch asked, keeping his eyes on Dimi, but no big surprise, she wouldn't look at him.

"Just maintain the status quo," Suzie said, consulting her clipboard. "Yesterday's calls topped our record. They're loving it all."

"The new recipes?" Dimi asked, coming to life.

"Well, yes. Among other things."

"Such as?" Mitch asked.

"Such as you and Dimi and your chemistry. They *loved* yesterday's bread-making show."

"The recipe," Dimi said, shining with pleasure. "I knew it. It was a fabulous one, from Romania—"

"Uh, no." Suzie shook her head and laughed. "What they really enjoyed was watching you and Mitch and how you kneaded the dough together, remember?"

Mitch remembered. Their hands had gotten entangled in the gooey, sticky mess Dimi had so expertly created, and at the touch, the two of them had nearly gone up in flames. Startled, they'd stared at each other like two star-crossed, unsatisfied lovers, and the camera hadn't missed it.

Not that, and not later, when every time they accidentally touched—which he perversely made sure was as often as possible—it had only upped the heat. They'd shaped the dough, stroking and stretching and pulling, and every motion had become a sensual sort of dance.

Indeed, as he already knew, the phones had rung off the hook, people wanting more. Hell, *he* wanted more. And no, he had no idea where his this-was-just-a-job mentality had gone.

"People are definitely really into this new

look for Dimi," Leo agreed. "They keep tuning in to make sure she doesn't revert to her earlier dowdiness— Er, um, I mean…"

"Thanks," Dimi said dryly. She rose. "Thanks a lot."

"Well, look at the time," Suzie said, glancing at her watch and rescuing a miserable Leo. "Dimi, you need costume and makeup, pronto."

A perfect mix of fear and reluctant thrill crossed Dimi's face. "How bad is the costume today?"

Suzie looked at Mitch and managed to keep a bland face. But both of them knew today's costume was the best yet. "Not bad at all."

A squeal startled them all. Dimi jumped, blushed and tried to look innocent.

But Mitch knew that squeal. Frowning, he looked at her, suddenly recognizing the lump beneath the towel. "You brought Brownie to work?"

"I had to. Tanner's painting my kitchen, and she hates the fumes."

"We've got to get rolling, gang," Suzie said, tapping her watch.

"I'll take Brownie," Mitch offered. "She can hang out in my office."

Dimi looked concerned. "But—"

"But what? Do you think I'd terrorize your hamster?"

"She won't strut and smile and dress on command."

"But will she be nice to me?"

Dimi smirked. "No, she's shy. And very serious about her food. Don't put your finger in the cage. She doesn't know you, she might bite."

"Got it." Mitch shook his head when Dimi was gone and pulled Brownie out from beneath the table. "Hey, girl," he said softly. "Remember me?"

Brownie rushed out of her little hideaway and wrinkled her nose, eyes bright.

"You do, don't you?"

She waited patiently, a serious look on her face.

Mitch had to laugh. "Look at that, she's even got you mimicking her expressions. Want something to eat?"

She wriggled her nose solemnly.

He bought a granola bar from the vending machine and fed a corner of it to the hamster, making her stand up on her hind legs for it, which she did willingly. "I'll be back later to teach you more tricks," he told her. "Just to annoy Dimi."

Making sure Brownie was comfy, he headed to the set, ready to face another show that would leave him sweating, frustrated and trembling like a baby.

Not to mention as hard as a rock.

# 6

"YOU HAVE TO wash them first." Demonstrating for both the camera and the enraptured crew, Dimi ignored Mitch and turned on the faucet.

Mitch said nothing, which made her nervous. He always had something to say. In fact, he'd had plenty to say just before they'd started, reminding her to smile once in awhile, reminding her to banter with him—as if she needed reminding!—and also to wear her new clothes, not let them wear her.

*Yeah, yeah,* she'd responded. *Sex kitten. I know.*

God, she knew. He didn't need to say it, she *felt* it. It wasn't the sexy clothes, either, or her new smiles, or the way she walked.

It was him. *He* made her feel it, and everything she did in the kitchen became languid, sensual. By the end of every day she was one big trembling, frustrated mass.

But she was on the air now, live, and she

couldn't lose her concentration, not when they'd been doing so well.

She dumped the vegetables in the sink. Luckily her sleeves wouldn't get in the way. How could they when she was wearing a cropped sweater with short sleeves and not nearly enough material to suit her?

And let's not get into the skirt she had on. It had to be illegal to show this much leg during the family hour.

She reached for the zucchini, running her fingers over the long, thick length to clean it. Mitch made a low, unintelligible sound, too quiet for the camera but not too quiet for her ears.

Her heart picked up speed. Her breathing quickened.

Hands still running over the zucchini, she looked up and found her gaze locked with hot, hot, hot eyes.

"You have a way with that thing," he murmured.

She froze, instantly realizing her mistake, but it was too late. Mitch had found his humor and was daring her with a lifted brow to continue.

So she lifted her chin, set the zucchini aside and reached for...a yellow squash. A deformed yellow squash that looked even more like a phallic symbol than the zucchini had. She stared at it, wondering how on earth she'd chosen these pieces just that morning without realizing how…naughty they looked.

Mitch let out a laugh. "You going to stare at that all day, or cook with it?"

"Cook with it," she said between her teeth. "It's got terrific flavor this time of year, sliced a certain way and set over the open flame of a barbecue."

"I was thinking," Mitch said conversationally.

"Oh, really?"

Mitch grinned.

The camera ate them up. Dimi knew it and tried not to think about it because it had been so much easier when it had been just her, alone on the set, doing as she pleased without this big, confident hulk of testosterone standing around making her lose her train of thought every time he so much as looked at her.

Which he did disconcertingly often.

"I was thinking," he repeated, still amused. "That the show should be called 'Now We're Cooking…With Heat.'"

She was absolutely not going to let him bait her on the air. "That sounds a little—"

"Risqué?" His grin widened. Under the bright lights, his eyes glittered and his earring sparkled. Every inch of him oozed a sexiness that left her with little or no ability to resist him. "Honey, what you're doing with those vegetables should be R-rated."

She couldn't help it, she blushed. Her body tightened in a funny way that made her want to rub her thighs together. "Why is it a man has to make everything dirty?"

"It's a male genetic flaw."

She made a sound of disgust and grabbed the next vegetable. A red pepper. A round red pepper that in no way could be construed as anything sexual. Her eyes dared him, waiting for some comment.

He was at her side, his dark hair falling over his forehead as he leaned forward and seriously examined what she was doing. Silently, thank God.

She used the opportunity to describe her tried and true method for slicing the vegetables in order to get the most flavor out of them. When she'd finished, and Mitch was handing her a bowl of oil and the paintbrush she used to coat the veggies over the flame, she gave him a sidelong look and went for broke. "I can't tell you how much I've appreciated your help the past few weeks.''

Mitch looked at her.

"But I think I could take it from here.'' When he merely raised a brow, she said, "You know, handle the show by myself. The way I used to. Without an assistant.''

"Is that right?'' He poured more oil into her bowl, making sure that their fingers touched.

"Yes.'' She hated the little spark of awareness that stunned her even now. Why hadn't she gotten used to him and all his blatant sexuality? Why hadn't he realized she was pathetic, that she wasn't suited for this hot sexy siren stuff? "Tomorrow we're cooking shrimp and littleneck oysters with wild rice. A one-person job, really.''

"Oysters. Hmm.''

She supposed that secret little grin he shot her would be considered irresistible. Not to her. "What does *hmm* mean?''

"Nothing.''

She relaxed and kept slicing.

"It's just that you said oysters.''

"Yes.''

"You having problems with your libido, Dimi?''

Too late she remembered the myth following the poor oyster. Dammit.

He merely grinned. "Hey, are the veggies supposed to be on fire like that, do you think?"

She tore her gaze away from his and wanted to groan. Live television didn't make that possible, so she held an even expression while quickly turning down the barbecue. The flames leapt until she grabbed the water spritzer hanging from the side of the barbecue and sprayed water over the coals.

Smoke filled the kitchen set. Managing not to cough, she smiled into the camera and said, "Whatever you do, watch the oil." She watched as Mitch rescued her vegetables before they got charred. "As you can see, it can easily get out of control if you let it."

"And whatever you do," Mitch added, leaning close to Dimi in a familiar way, also smiling into the camera, "don't get sidetracked by your partner."

"I did not get sidetracked by you."

"Ah, so you admit it. We're partners."

They were close enough to kiss, she realized inanely. "I admit no such thing."

"Sure? Cuz it would appear I've saved your veggies. Sure would be a shame to lose me, wouldn't it?'' He blinked innocently into the camera. ''Seeing how much she needs me and all, right?'' His smile was cozy, easy and entirely addictive.

''Break!'' the director called. ''Commercial, everyone. Three minutes.''

Dimi hightailed it off the set, leaving Gracie and Leo leaping up to clear the smoke. She assumed Mitch stayed to help, as well, but she had a whole three minutes to herself, and she desperately needed it. Racing to her dressing room to take one deep breath in peace, she opened the door.

As she entered, Cami jerked away from her closet and looked guilty.

''What are you doing here?'' Dimi knew she sounded petulant, but darn it, she wanted to be alone to clear her head of the lusty haze Mitch always managed to put her in.

Cami shoved her hands, full of something chartreuse and gauzy, behind her back. ''Nothing. I'm not doing anything.''

''You're stealing my clothes.''

''Okay, I'm stealing your clothes. But God, Sis, you have an amazing set of designer stuff now. Not a Kmart item in the bunch. You don't mind, do you? After all, you always steal my food.''

''But you sew all your own clothes.'' Dimi rubbed her temples. ''Never mind. Take what you want. I've got to get back out there.''

''Hmm.'' Cami looked her over. ''Your headache wouldn't be Mitch-induced by any chance, now, would it?''

''Of course not.''

Cami shook her head. ''If you let him go, especially after I humiliated myself to help you catch him, I'll be mad at you.''

''You're always mad at me.''

''Okay, I'll sic Mom on you.''

Dimi shuddered. ''Not that.''

''Remember all my blind date disasters?''

''How could I forget?''

''If you let him go,'' Cami vowed, ''that's what'll happen to you.''

''If I let him go…'' Dimi shook her head. ''What are you talking about? I don't *have* him.''

''By the crook of your little finger, Sis. You've got him by the crook of your little finger.''

That was when Dimi realized her sister had truly lost it. She was so in love with Tanner her brain had turned to mush.

Running to the set just in time to get her nose fluffed and to repin her mike to her shirt, Dimi caught Mitch's dark, questing gaze.

*By the crook of your little finger, Sis. You've got him.*

Yeah, right! She'd never caught anything—by the crook of her little finger or otherwise. And even if by some miracle it could be true, did she even want him?

Suzie adjusted Dimi's mike, caught the strange connection between host and producer and smiled knowingly. "By the way, Dimi, you can't lose your assistant."

"What? Why?"

"Only seconds after you suggested it on the air, the phones went crazy."

Mitch's mouth curved, but wisely, he kept it shut.

Suzie said it all for him. "People are freaking out that maybe you'll get rid of him. They're begging you to reconsider."

"Fifteen seconds, people!"

Suzie backed off the set, leaving only Dimi and Mitch, and given Mitch's superior, triumphant glow, there was nothing left to say.

She was stuck with him.

BY THE END of Mitch's second week, *Food Time*'s dramatic turn into a rating and critical success had been cemented. In the eyes of everyone around him, all of whom had thanked him repeatedly, he was a hero.

In everyone's eyes except Dimi's, that is, and as it so happened, she was the only one he worried about, which concerned him for various reasons. One, that he cared for her at all, when she was an entire world away from what he'd always gone for. Hell, make that a galaxy.

And two, that she didn't care for him back, not even a little.

Oh, she lusted after him, he'd made sure of that. Lusted even while she fought it. But getting her there had been work, and work only.

Which brought him to troubling fact number three. He never mixed business and pleasure, so this entire train of thought was moot.

Completely moot.

Yet here he was, heading out on his bike toward some small pizza joint in the middle of nowhere to join everyone for a staff dinner to celebrate their success.

Chilly wind froze his face. The smell of the mountain air assaulted his senses as he rode through the streets. The majestic Sierra peaks all around him were tall, dark. Huge. Nothing like the bright, noisy streets of Los Angeles, but for some reason, he suddenly couldn't think of any-place he'd rather be.

Power drummed between his legs, the power of his Harley. It was a release to drive through the black night with only the stars and one lone headlight guiding his way, but not the kind of release he needed after so many weeks of hot and heavy sexual innuendo and teasing.

No, what he needed now was a woman be-neath him. Or over him. He wasn't picky and would take either, but it wasn't going to happen.

Expecting to be the last to arrive, he pulled into the parking lot, but there was a lone woman getting out of a car. At the sound of his bike, she whipped around, blond hair flying around her face.

Dimi. The only member of *Food Time* who hadn't yet thanked him for saving their careers.

His heart took off like crazy as he imagined her taking the time to thank him tonight. At just the thought, his body tightened.

The thrill of the ride, he told himself, and swung his leg off the bike. He pulled the rolled-up newspaper out of his back pocket and strolled toward her.

"What do you have?" she asked, her voice sounding suspiciously breathless.

Great, so they were both frustrated no end. Well, as that was his own doing, he had no one to blame but himself. "Nothing," he said, strangely not willing to give her something else to get upset about. Not yet, anyway, because he knew she'd find out soon enough.

Putting his hand on the small of her back, he nudged her inside the noisy, musical, smoky pizza joint, feeling oddly reluctant to remove it as they came to the staff's table.

Everyone was there. Gracie with her husband. Leo with a date. Ted and his wife. Suzie, single and on the prowl. And all the others. Even Cami had come, she had Tanner with her, and a dopey grin on her face that announced to the world she'd very recently had wild, satisfying sex.

"Hey, did anyone catch today's headlines?" Leo called.

Mitch shook his head in warning, but the man was egged on by too many pre-pizza beers and the need to impress his date. With great ceremony, Leo stood on his chair, wobbling enough to make Mitch worry about the man's hard head.

Leo then cleared his throat, smoothed out the wrinkled newspaper he held and waggled his eyebrows. "We've all been talking about how we've made it," he announced. "And while we've thanked Mitch, I think most of us have forgotten to thank the other party responsible for our success." He pointed to Dimi. "This is for you, baby." With great ceremony, he shook the paper and read the headline out loud. "Sex Kitty Can Really Cook!"

# 7

THERE WAS one second of stunned silence before everyone broke out in cheers and laughter, all directed toward Dimi.

Mitch winced, then looked at her, and yep, no big surprise, she wasn't cheering. Or laughing. In fact, it was safe to assume, given the daggers she was at this very moment silently sending him, that she was nothing short of furious.

Sighing, he moved close. Amid the hooting and hollering of their boisterous crew, he bent and spoke into her ear. "You know it was meant in a complimentary way."

"Really?" With mock sweetness, she nodded. "So I'm assuming, as the coach of said sex kitty, you're proud."

Turning his head to look into her fiery gaze, he realized what he'd really done was perfectly line up their mouths.

Her eyes widened as she realized the same thing. Her lips parted. It was far too noisy to hear anything except his own racing heart, but he imagined she let out an involuntary little sound that conveyed her own wanting. "As your coach, I haven't taught you anything you didn't already know," he said, turned on by the shiver she couldn't seem to contain.

"And why is that?" This was murmured into his ear, which made him let out his own helpless shiver at the feel of her lips against his skin. "You've threatened to coach me," she said. "I know it. You know it. Everyone else knows it, too, and yet you've done nothing other than pick out a few clothes and asked me to smile. No...special lessons."

How well he knew it. The thought of what he'd like to teach her had kept him up at night for weeks now.

"Know what I think?" she asked. "I think you're all talk, Mr. Hotshot Producer. All show. Yeah, you're big and tough and unfortunately gorgeous—" She broke off at his choked laugh and frowned. "You must know that you are. But I'm left assuming you don't know any more than I do about..."

He was still digesting the fact she thought him gorgeous. "About?"

She licked her lips, then bit her lower one

before leaning close. Whether it was because she didn't want anyone to hear her words or because she didn't want to look him directly in the eyes, he hadn't a clue. "About…sexual stuff," she whispered, sending more delicious shivers down every nerve in his body and making him instantly hard.

A common reaction around her, he'd noticed. "That sounded like a dare," he managed to say.

She lifted one brow, and he had to laugh, because damn if she hadn't learned far more than she thought, the little tease. "Are you hungry for pizza?" he asked.

She didn't take her eyes off him. "No."

Okay, then. "So now's as good a time as any, right? Let's have one of those special lessons you're so worried about." He held out his hand, and she slipped hers into it with no sign of hesitation other than a hard swallow.

"Hey," Leo called, rattling the newspaper. "You can't leave yet, I haven't read you— Ouch!" he yelled, glaring at Cami, who'd reached up and pinched him.

"Let them go, you idiot," she muttered, pulling Leo off the chair and hauling him close to whisper in his ear.

Leo listened to her secret and grinned.

*"Ooh."* Enlightened, he turned to a curious Gracie and whispered in her ear.

Gracie turned to an impatient Suzie and whispered in her ear.

"And so on and so on," Mitch murmured, tugging Dimi free of the crowd around them.

"Where are we going?" she asked as he pulled her outside.

*Yeah, Mitch. Where are we going?* Even knowing that being alone with her was an incredibly stupid thing to do didn't appear to be sinking into his brain.

Not when another part of his body had taken over the thinking process. "Somewhere more suitable," he said.

"Oh, boy."

She stared at his motorcycle with a look of terrified delight. "What's it like to have all that power vibrating between your legs?"

"Pretty much exactly how you'd imagine."

Her mouth fell open. "Can I drive?"

He slid onto the bike and handed her his helmet. "Nope."

"Come on, you can make it the lesson."

"Get on, Dimi."

"You're no fun."

"You ain't seen nothing yet. Now get on."

When she did, sliding her hands around his waist and pressing the front of her glorious body to the back of his, he shuddered. "Hold on tight."

HE TOOK THEM deep into the night, along the Truckee River and up Highway 89 toward Lake Tahoe. The night was cold, but the engine beneath them kept them warm.

Or maybe it was their combined body heat, mostly hers. Dimi couldn't help it. The feel of the vibration between her thighs, matched with Mitch's big, powerful body pressed so intimately to hers...she was truly going up in smoke, in an utterly foreign way. Never in her life had she gotten aroused for no reason other than lustful thoughts and a motorcycle beneath her, but she was aroused now.

Since she'd never ridden a motorcycle before, she'd like to blame it on that, but her body was heating up from the inside out, not a usual complaint of bike riders. Mitch's hair, sleek in the wind, brushed her face. The soft leather of his jacket drew her fingers. And the scent of him—holy cow, that alone nearly pushed her over the edge.

Then she realized he'd driven her all the way

to Incline Village. "Place of sin," she said when he pulled over and cut the engine.

He tossed a look at her over his shoulder. "What better place, right?"

Oh, yeah. Her lesson. She gulped hard, most of her bravado deserting her. Then she caught sight of where they were and what they'd parked in front of and nearly choked as she leapt off the bike.

A strip club!

*Oh, my God, what have I gotten myself into, and why didn't I bring my cell phone, and how can I tell him I no longer want to—*

Mitch's soft laugh broke through her panic as he pulled the helmet off her head and studied her expression. "If you could see your face."

"Easy for you to be amused," she sputtered, pointing at the big, siren-red sign that read, All Nude, All the Time.

He tossed a look at the place, then grinned. Widely. "My God, you have an imagination on you." He wrapped a hand around her wrist, redirecting her pointing finger across the street to another sign that read, Public Beach.

"I thought we could count falling stars there on the sand," he said. "You can't see them in Los Angeles with all the lights."

"Falling stars."

"Yep."

She grimaced. "Oh."

"Now why don't you tell me what you thought I was going to make you do in that strip club?" he asked softly, leaning close with a mixture of heat and amusement in his eyes.

"Um…"

Shaking his head, still laughing in that disgustingly sexy way he had, he linked his fingers with hers and led her across the street to an incredibly beautiful beach. The water glowed from the meager moonlight, and the sand looked like silk. Above them, the trees rustled in the light wind, and the scent of the mountain air filled her senses.

And so did the man walking silently beside her. He didn't look so L.A. right now. Yes, he wore that black leather jacket and even blacker jeans that screamed sophistication and a been there, done that attitude, but she was beginning to see how much more to him there was than that. She remembered how he'd distracted her from that horrible front-page headline. She remembered how in spite of his teasing during the day on the set, he never crossed the line and made her feel anything but…well, wanted. And he'd not even once tried to make a move on her, not a real one, not even when she'd wanted him to.

An uneasy thought.

All along she'd sheltered herself from his charms by telling herself she was just a job to him. But the way he tipped his head and looked at her now made her heart tug. It also made her blood race and all sorts of other interesting things happen inside her. And suddenly, more than ever, she wanted to be the person he'd made her on television. She wanted to be that free, that sexy, and she wanted to be that way with him. "Mitch..." She stopped and turned to face him. "What are we doing here?"

"Don't you know?"

"No."

He looked a little surprised. At the water's edge, he sat on a large rock, then pulled her down beside him.

They stared at each other.

"Hell," he said after a moment. "I was really hoping you knew what this thing is all about."

"You mean the thing that makes me want to both kiss you and smack you at the same time?"

A laugh escaped him. "Yeah. That's pretty much the thing I mean."

"I haven't a clue. It scares me, you know," she admitted. "Not just because I gave up men, or that we work together. But because when it comes right down to it, I know nothing about you."

Leaning back, he tucked his hands beneath his head and studied the sky. "What do you want to know? I'm an open book."

"Yeah, right," she said with a laugh.

"No, really. Ask away."

"I don't want to be nosy." But then she decided to take him up on it because curiosity won out over being polite. "Okay, tell me this. Why is everything so casual for you?"

"Meaning I'm your opposite because you're so serious?" When she nodded, he said, "I take plenty of things seriously, Dimi."

"Such as?"

"Such as...my bike. I'm serious about my bike."

"Name something really important."

"My bike is pretty important."

"See?" she said, frustrated. "You're not taking me seriously at all."

"Okay." His smile faded. "How about life? I take that pretty damn seriously."

His jaw had tightened. His body seemed to, as well. And the part of herself she'd always held back from a man softened. Opened. "What happened, Mitch? Did you…lose someone?"

"Yeah." His voice was gruff. "My brother, Daniel. He died from an aneurysm on his twenty-ninth birthday."

"You were close."

"Close? We were both too busy working eighteen-hour days to spend any time with each other. In our family, work was everything. *Everything*. Now he's gone." He turned his head and pierced her with a look of such loss and regret, she felt her throat tighten. "Sort of takes the edge off ambition, a loss like that."

"I imagine it does," she said softly. "But you still seem pretty ambitious."

"No. I walk away from the job now when the day is done. No stress. I just happen to be good at what I do."

"I have to agree there," she said with a little smile. "I'm so sorry about your brother, Mitch."

He ran a finger over her cheek. "You look so relaxed out here, not so serious at all. What is it about work that makes you that way?"

"You." She winced. "Well, not *just* you. It's everything. The show, the people that rely on the show. It's all such a huge responsibility. I…I don't like to fail.'' She lifted a shoulder. ''And we were. Before you came along and saved us.''

''But why resist the changes so much? You're such a natural at what we're doing now. So down to earth, yet utterly, completely sexy. Why did you hide that for so long?''

''Are you kidding?'' she said with a laugh. ''It's *not* natural. You must have heard the stories, Mitch, and they're all true. I'm pathetic when it comes to…guy stuff. I mean, look at my track record of relationships.''

''I think you were looking at the wrong guys.''

She listened to the water hit the rocks for a moment. Watched the sky, which at their high altitude was more brilliant than anywhere she'd ever been, though admittedly she hadn't been very many places.

Unlike the man next to her, who'd probably seen and done it all.

A flash lit up her small corner of the night, and she straightened, excited, forgetting herself for a moment in the beauty that surrounded them. ''Did you see that falling star?'' she whispered in hushed awe, wanting him to experience her world, wanting him to know there was more to life than his city. ''Did you?''

''Yeah.'' But he was looking right at her, not

up. "You know what that means, don't you? A falling star?"

"That a sun just exploded?"

"That you have to kiss the first person you talk to after you see one."

She didn't mean to smile, darn him, but she did. "Really?"

"It's a law," he said very seriously.

"Ah." Watching his mouth, she felt the heat explode inside her just as the star had exploded, wondering if he felt a fraction of the excitement she was feeling, deciding he probably didn't and—

"Stop thinking," he commanded softly, slipping a hand beneath her hair to caress the skin at the base of her neck.

"I can't help it, I analyze everything." Her lips were so close to his she could feel his warm breath. A frisson of something electric zapped through her, making her shiver with delight. "I can't seem to help it. It's just a part of my personality. Like the fact I love chocolate." She couldn't stop talking. It was nerves, but she couldn't shut up. "They're both just there, and—"

"Dimi?"

She gulped in a deep breath. "Yeah?"

"Shut up and kiss me."

She laughed. "I've never kissed a man while I was smiling before, Mitch."

"You haven't kissed me yet." His fingers tightened in her hair, pulling her closer, and she leaned in, giving him a short, to-the-point kiss.

"How was that?" she asked calmly while the pulse pounded in her throat, in her chest, in her ears. Surely it was just the mountain air making her blood hum and body sing. Sure, she could just—

She leaned forward and kissed him again. She couldn't stop herself. More stars exploded in her eyes, bright points of pleasure at the feel of his mouth against hers. A moan of deep, dark pleasure resounded in her ears, hers, she realized with shock, locking her arms around his neck so tight he returned the deep, dark sound, but only because she was choking him.

"Sorry!" she gasped, backing up, horrified at her ineptness.

But he didn't let her go far, instead sliding a thumb over her frustrated frown. "It's okay. Breathing is optional," he assured her.

One second Dimi sat there staring at him, humiliated to the core, and the next she'd garnered her courage to try again.

*Go for the moon,* she told herself, and pressed

against him, her mouth on his. She was kissing him, kissing him as if she was starving for it.

And he was kissing her back, his mouth opening, making her let out a little whimper of need. She wanted more. She took more, losing herself in it until he let out a hissing breath. His fingers reached up and entangled with hers, making her realize she'd fisted them in his hair, tugging hard on the silky strands.

"I'm sorry," she whispered, face flaming as she pulled back. God, what had she been thinking? What had Cami been thinking? She couldn't do this! "I think," she said shakily, "I'm ready for dinner."

"Are you sure? Because I've got your hands now, so we could just try the whole thing again—"

"I'm sure."

He searched her gaze, then sighed and stood, pulling her up, as well. "Next time," he muttered, "I'm going to go bald before stopping you again." He stroked her cheek. "Remember that."

She would do little else.

# 8

"MESSAGES!" Suzie called to Mitch in a whirl-wind the next day. As she ran past him, clip-board in hand, she slapped a stack of pink mes-sage slips in his palm. "The one on top is a doozy."

She was right. It was from his home office.

Mitch, we've got another show for you to save. We'll send replacement producer for *Food Time* within two weeks.
Great job!
Now get back here as soon as you can.

Shocked, he stopped dead in the busy hallway and stared at the words. *Now get back here as soon as you can.*

Someone plowed into him from behind, nearly knocking him off his feet. "Hey!" yelled the clerk, paling when he saw who he was yell-ing at. "Oh! Sorry, sir."

Stunned, Mitch looked up from his message.

"You might want to step aside, though," the clerk said more gently. "You'll get killed standing here during rush hour like that."

Only a week ago the message he'd just received would have been cause for celebration. Now all he felt was a confusing mix of things, though a great part of that could be the way he kept getting jostled standing there like an idiot in the middle of the hustling, bustling hallway.

"Hey, boss!" Suzie came down the hallway on another mission, grabbing his arm when she saw him. "You gotta move out of the way, honey, or someone is going to plow into you."

"I know." He allowed her to pull him to the side, where the pace was more suited for an epiphany.

He was going home.

Yet he couldn't seem to work up any happiness about it, because somehow, someway, when he hadn't been paying attention, he'd started to fall for this show, this town.

The people.

One person in particular—Dimi of the serious eyes and amazingly talented mouth.

Still in a daze, he walked onto the set with three minutes to spare and found Dimi sitting on the counter in a hot little sundress, swinging those long, long legs as she read, totally absorbed in the newspaper she held.

It was yesterday's edition, the one that screamed Sex Kitten Cooks!

"Five minutes, people!" called the director.

Dimi used that as an excuse to ignore him, which she'd done fairly successfully ever since their kiss.

"You're going to have to talk to me sooner or later."

Her feet swung faster, but she didn't look at him.

"Dimi, say something."

"Okay." She looked up. "I heard you're leaving."

He sighed, not bothering to point out he'd only just gotten the message three minutes ago himself.

*Thanks, Suzie.*

Was Dimi angry that he was going? Or so happy she couldn't speak? With Dimi, he couldn't be sure. "Want to talk about it?" he asked.

She kept reading.

Okay. Well, she *had* to do the show with him,

he thought with evil satisfaction. She couldn't ignore him there.

"I understand we're preparing leg of lamb today," he said conversationally, hooking his mike to the front of his shirt.

"Hmm," she said noncommittally. An assistant handed her a mike. She held it in one hand, obviously at a loss as to where to pin it.

His mood lightened considerably.

"Looks like you have a problem there, finding a place for that thing." Before she could protest, he took it and stepped close, as if he was going to pin it on her collar, but as they both knew, her dress had no collar.

He let out a slow smile. "This is going to be tricky."

"I can do it," she said through her teeth, the serious queen once again, making him want to laugh.

"No, I've got it." He studied the spaghetti straps that held up the bodice of the sundress, which dipped low between her very appealing breasts. "Nope," he said, gliding the backs of his fingers across her collarbone. "Not here."

At his touch, she sucked in a breath.

"Maybe..." He slid his first finger along the edging of the dress just above the curves of her breasts, touching her creamy skin. He actually trembled like a damn baby at that, but he took heart in the fact that she did, as well. "Here," he decided, slipping his fingers beneath the strap where it connected with the bodice near her armpit, just above her left breast.

She sucked in another breath at the intimate touch. "Are you getting your kicks out of this?"

"Oh, yeah." He wiggled his fingers. Her nipples hardened, strained against the material of the dress, making him let out a soft groan. "Definitely getting my kicks out of this. Cold, Dimi?"

"No, I—" She slammed her mouth closed and glared at him when he laughed softly, triumphant that he'd made her admit to being turned on.

He bent his head to the task, his back to the various crew members milling around so that no one could see what he was doing. If anyone looked over, they saw a producer helping out his host with her mike, that was all. Innocent stuff.

They were in their own little world.

Which was how he found himself concentrating, not on the job in front of him, but on the sweet scent of her, the mind-blowing feel of her soft, warm flesh.

He made sure to take his time.

The pulse at the base of her neck throbbed, and he nearly moaned again. "I have to taste you," he whispered, and closed the rest of the distance, putting his open mouth against her neck, sucking.

It was her turn to let out a low moan. She lifted her hands, probably to push him away, but he quickly soothed the spot he'd bitten, using his tongue, and she ended up fisting her hands on his shirt instead.

"Twenty seconds!"

Dimi wrenched free and stared at him, wide- and wild-eyed, chest heaving as if she'd just run a mile.

He was breathing like that, too, and starting to sweat to go along with it. "Wow," he whispered, which made her let out an agreeing noise as she turned away to stand on her mark. She tossed back her hair, rubbed her glossed lips together and took a deep breath, obviously desperately struggling for composure.

She probably had no idea that her hair was tousled and gorgeous, her face was flushed and gorgeous, and her mouth... Lord, her mouth. Wet, luscious and gorgeous. She'd never looked the part of kitchen goddess more convincingly.

"Ten seconds!"

"Is it true?" she whispered. "You're almost done here? You're leaving?"

"Yeah." Regret roughened his voice. "I've been called back."

She nodded and looked away.

Mitch found his mark, but he was off balance, and knew it would be impossible to gain it back in time. The line between this show and the pleasure he found in Dimi was blurring badly. He was starting to have the sinking feeling that the heart he'd frozen after Daniel's death was defrosting.

Hell of a time for it.

"Five, four..."

It was also a hell of a time to realize what was *really* bothering him about going back to Los Angeles.

The fact that he didn't want to go.

"THREE, TWO..."

Dimi dragged in a deep breath, but it didn't clear her head. Nothing could clear her head after having Mitch's hot, open mouth on her.

"And...you're on!"

She smiled for the camera and prayed it was a good one. At least it wasn't cold and forced, but then again, nothing about her had been cold and forced since the day Mitch Knight set foot in Truckee.

But soon he'd be gone, and she'd be free to go back to being herself—only somewhere along the way she'd lost that woman.

"Welcome to *Food Time*," she said with as much enthusiasm as she could muster. "We have some great recipes coming up. Tomorrow we'll do *borlenghe* with pancetta and rosemary."

Beside her, Mitch looked totally blank. "Bore what?"

She imagined another hundred viewers falling for that helplessly confused expression on his innocent face. Only she knew he was no innocent! "Crispy crêpes from Modena," she translated. "But for today, we're cooking roasted leg of lamb."

Somehow she finished her intro, but she was painfully, vibrantly aware of the tall, powerful, far too magnificent man standing next to her, unusually quiet and speculative.

She should have known *that* wouldn't last.

"We're also introducing a new element to the show today." He broke in, surprising her.

His gaze was deep and fathomless and full of

heat—for her—and every complaint flew right out of her head.

"We're going to take call-ins on the air," he said, and when that sank in, Dimi nearly fell off her high heels.

"What?"

"Later," he said, going to the refrigerator and taking out a tray of meat.

But that was *her* move, so she stalked right up to him and reached for the tray.

"Just trying to give you a hand," he said with an innocent smile. "Don't want you to catch cold in that itty-bitty dress here in front of this blast of cold air."

That she already had goose bumps all over her body was his fault, but she didn't point it out. "Thanks, Mitch. You're going to make someone a very considerate wife some day." Smiling for the camera, she pulled the tray in front of her, which she hoped would hide the fact that her nipples were still at urgent attention.

Mitch followed her to the counter and watched with interest as she handled the meat. When she lifted a tenderizing mallet he leaned back in horror. "What are you going to do with that?"

"Tenderize the meat."

He shuddered. "Remind me never to make you mad."

"Too late," she said sweetly, wielding the mallet and making Mitch wince. One strap fell down her shoulder, and with a sideways disgruntled look at the man who'd picked the dress out, she shoved it back up. She concentrated on her task, on talking to the camera and on keeping her dress up all at the same time, until the lamb was ready for the oven.

Dimi carried the tray to the opened appliance and stood there, rooted by sudden indecision.

How was she supposed to bend over to put the food in without flashing her panties to every single viewer?

"What's the matter?" Mitch asked, lightly of course, since *he* didn't have a care in the world.

She shot him a look of panic and saw laughter swimming in his eyes. He knew exactly what the matter was. In fact, given his sick, twisted sense of humor, he'd probably planned it! "I've decided to let you be chivalrous today," she said, thrusting the tray at him, yanking on the hem of her dress as casually as she could.

Mitch put the meat into the oven and then took their first phone call. "Hello," he said into the camera. "You're on the air with *Food Time*."

"Oh! Oh, how exciting! This is Millie from Fernley!"

"Hello Millie from Fernley!" Mitch said, speaking in exclamations, as she had. He smiled sweetly. "How can we help you today?"

Though the woman sounded as if she'd been smoking for sixty years, and had maybe driven a truck for much of that time, she giggled. "I was wondering. Do you and Dimi date?"

Mitch tucked his tongue in his cheek and deferred the question to Dimi with a lifted hand.

"Um…that would be negative," Dimi said quickly.

"What a shame! You do know how handsome he is, right, dear?"

Dimi did not look at Mitch. "Did you have a cooking question, Millie?"

"Well, sort of. I was wondering, if you don't date Mitch, and you gave up all other men, who've you been cooking with, girl?"

Dimi's eyes widened. "Excuse me?"

"Well, you've been kissing someone."

Dimi let out a little laugh. "Millie, maybe you have the wrong channel. This is a cooking show. You know that, right?"

"Yes, and my question stands. Who've you been cooking with, because lordie, that hickey on your neck is making me weak in the knees. I want one of them. Did Mitch put that there?"

Dimi looked at Mitch. And mercifully, they cut to commercial.

Suzie ran up to Dimi, wisely keeping her laughter to herself as she handed her a little mirror. Doing contortions, Dimi was just able to catch a glimpse of said hickey at the base of her throat.

"Oh. My. God."

Suzie's cell phone rang. She answered it and looked at Dimi as she said, "Yeah, she's here, and she only has sixty seconds, so make it fast." Then she handed Dimi the phone.

It was Cami, and she got right to the point. "Holy cow, that hickey is amazing! Please, oh, please tell me you finally did the deed with that man."

"Cami!"

"Tell me you did it right there on your darkened set against the refrigerator, so hot and needy for each other you didn't even care that anyone could walk in on you at any moment."

Dimi looked skyward, then made the mistake of looking at Mitch again. He was studying a spreadsheet his assistant had shoved in his hands, but as if he sensed her gaze, he looked up. Right at her. *Through* her, to the inside, where she was wondering if he really *might* have taken her against the refrigerator.

His gaze heated.

Oh, yeah, he would have, and her thighs clenched at the thought. Her tummy tightened, too. "Cami, I gotta go."

"You did! Against the refrig! Oh, my God, Sis. That's so cool."

"We didn't. It's just that..." She lowered her voice to a hushed whisper. "He's driving me crazy, Cam."

"You mean he's making you hot?"

"Yes!" she cried miserably.

"Well then, beat him at his own game, would ya? Stop letting him get the better of you. Make him hot right back!"

"But..."

"But nothing, just do it."

Once again she looked at the tall, dark, mesmerizing man getting the best of her and admitted the truth. "I don't know if I can."

"What? Are you kidding? Have you looked in the mirror lately? We're hot, babe. We've got it going on, so for God's sake, use it. You've already got the new wardrobe. Now all you have to do is turn the tables on him.''

Sounded easy enough. Dimi kept looking at Mitch, at all that amazing, edgy gorgeousness, and shivered. Yeah, he'd definitely made *her* want *him.*

And she thought maybe he wanted her back, but he'd managed so far to control himself. Could she make him lose that control? It would certainly help take her mind off the fact that she could never really have him, since he already had one foot out the door.

''Do it,'' Cami said in her ear.

Could she? Testing, Dimi looked right at him and slowly licked her lips.

Mitch's mouth fell open.

Testing some more, still holding his gaze, Dimi winked.

He dropped the papers he was holding.

It couldn't be that easy. Could it?

To be sure, she ran her fingers through her hair and licked her lips again.

Mitch, ignoring the papers scattered at his feet, blinked and swallowed hard.

''Dimi?'' Cami sounded worried. ''You still there?''

"Yeah, Cam, I'm still here." Dimi let out a slow smile and felt the power of being a woman blossom through her. "I'm here and ready to rock and roll."

## 9

MITCH HAD BEEN hot for two days now, and it had nothing to do with the unexpected warm front that had blown in from Mexico.

He stalked his office, pacing back and forth, going over details for the show that had nothing to do with what was really bothering him.

"Mitch?" Accompanying that low, soft voice on the other side of his closed office door came a light knock.

Dimi. The root of all his problems in one hot little package.

"I'm not here," he said testily, and when he heard her laugh, he ground his teeth.

What had gotten into her? Suddenly it wasn't him coaxing her to be funny and sexy, she just *was* those things.

Effortlessly.

Suddenly he was the one having trouble, and it all centered on how she'd started looking at him—as if he was a twelve-course meal and she was starving.

She opened his door and danced in, wearing—

"Oh, my God." He clapped a hand over his eyes, making her laugh again.

"Oh, good," she said. "You like it."

*It*, of course, referred to her outfit, which he peeked through his fingers to see. It consisted of two spaghetti-strapped tank tops layered over each other, one bright white, the other bright red. Her denim skirt was a short, snug wraparound, which meant that as she walked toward him, one smooth, long, glorious leg after another was bared.

The camera was going to eat her up, and so would he if she came any closer.

Which she did.

She'd been doing that for two days, invading his space, smiling at him as if she knew some huge secret and generally making his life—and his body—a living hell.

"They wanted me to tell you," she said, almost purring. "Fifteen minutes until air time. You're needed on the set pronto."

He removed his hand from his eyes, and they promptly attached themselves to her body. "You have to wear a bra on television."

"I am."

He stared at her full, round, perfect breasts, both of which hardened under his scrutiny. "You are not."

She reached up and peeled down the two straps of her tanks from her right shoulder, revealing the top of her right breast.

"What are you doing?" he demanded, covering his eyes again.

"Showing you I'm wearing a bra. Suzie sewed the cups in so I wouldn't be bouncing all over the place. See?"

He squinted one eye open to realize she wasn't uncovering any more of herself, only enough so he could see the white of the sewed-in bra cup. But that's not where he looked. No, he looked at the curve that the bra barely restrained, at the tantalizing creamy flesh making his mouth water.

"We've got to run," she said, and as if he were a child, she grabbed his hand and led him from the room. He followed, his gaze drawn to her hips, which wriggled enticingly in the heels she'd adopted.

Had he ever really imagined her in need of sprucing up? Not sexy? Ha!

She had him hot, horny and hard, and he'd

been in that state for so long his mind had gone fuzzy from lack of blood.

Peeking at him over her shoulder, she shot him a smile designed to heat his blood even more, so he didn't even try to talk, try to tell her he knew the way to the damn set, that he could get there under his own steam. He just stupidly followed her, conserving what little brain matter he had left for the show.

At the set, he sank to a chair and rubbed his temples, wondering if a man could die of an ignored erection.

''What's the matter?'' Dimi asked, her voice silky. ''You have a headache?''

Before he could respond, she was standing behind him, her hands stroking his neck, urging his head back, pillowing it against her incredible breasts. Then her hands skimmed upward, sank into his hair and started massaging his head.

His entire body quivered.

And he actually forgot. Why was he resisting her? Exactly why didn't he grab her, pull her around and into his lap, and give them what they both wanted with a terrifying desperation?

Oh, yeah.

Because he was leaving.

Because he wasn't the type to want a woman to such distraction.

Because he hadn't opened up his heart in two long years, and it hurt to think about letting someone in, someone who could mean as much to him as Daniel had.

Just when he thought he had a handle on that and could resist her, she bent and put her mouth to his ear, breathing into it as she whispered, "Better?"

Any better and he'd embarrass himself right then and there. He was spared having to answer by the call to their marks.

His most pressing problem was how to remain behind the counter for the rest of the show so as to not exhibit the fact that the front of his pants was a permanent tent.

DIMI WAS well aware that she was playing with fire. And skating on thin ice. All at the same time.

It was part of her plan. Make Mitch want her while not giving him a chance to actually *get* her.

But she was weakening on that resolve. She'd created a monster. This...*thing* between the two of them was out of control.

It was just a game, she kept reminding herself. She was getting even with him for turning her into the cooking sex kitten.

Only problem with that theory...she liked what he'd done to her. She liked the clothes that made her feel sexy, liked the freedom it gave her to loosen up a bit and enjoy herself. She smiled more, and not just because he'd asked her to.

She felt happier.

Not happy enough to sleep with him, though. That would be a colossal mistake, because then there'd be no avoiding involving her heart.

And there was the teeny tiny little detail of his impending departure.

So she avoided being alone with Mitch at all costs.

But one day she found herself alone at a table in the lunchroom with him, because the two grips sitting between them finished eating and left.

"I'll eat later," Dimi said, rising, grabbing her plate of veggies—she'd given up her beloved junk food to better fit into her costumes—but Mitch stopped her with a hand on her wrist.

"Scared of me?"

She saw the dare in his gaze and slowly sank

down, because no way was she going to let him think that. She even laughed. "Hardly."

"Uh-huh." His teeth sank into his peanut butter and jelly sandwich, and he watched her with an endearing mixture of wariness and good humor as he chewed. "You've been avoiding being alone with me," he noted, downing some milk. She could hear him swallow, and darn it, his lunch looked a whole heck of a lot more appealing than hers.

"And vice versa." Daintily she bit into a carrot stick while begrudging the fact it didn't smell nearly as good as the peanut butter.

"You always eat rabbit food?"

For about the millionth time she cursed her curvy, fat-loving body, especially when he dug into a big bag of chips. Barbecue. "You're going to plug your arteries."

"I think you're jealous." He lifted the bag, offering, shrugging when she shook her head. "Suit yourself." He put a big chip in his mouth, closed his eyes and licked his fingers.

Dimi stared at her pathetic little rabbit lunch of carrot sticks and celery and wanted to smack him. "Okay, maybe just one."

"Nope," he said, pulling the bag to his chest. "Too late."

"Give me a chip."

He smiled. "What will you do for it?"

She could already smell and taste it. She *had* to have one and would have done anything, anything at all for it, until she saw the gleam of triumph in his dark gaze.

"Come on," he taunted. "Surely you can think of something you're willing to do for a chip. Why don't you...oh, I don't know. Why don't you tell me why you're all of a sudden trying to drive me crazy with that incredible body of yours. Not that I mind, you understand. I'm just wondering."

"Maybe there's no reason." She reached for a chip, but he withheld them with a shake of his head.

"There's a reason," he stated flatly.

"Okay." She lifted a shoulder. "You got me. It's because you're easy. *Now give me a chip.*"

He offered her the bag, watching her dig in. "I'm not always easy," he muttered.

"Yeah, right."

"It's true."

"Uh-huh."

"Just for you."

Her gaze jerked up from the precious chips, and she studied him, uncertain if he was kidding, but she decided he had to be. "Sure. I believe that one."

Did she imagine the flash of hurt that crossed his face?

Definitely.

But when she found herself alone at lunch with him the next day, as well, and then the next, too, and each time he was nothing but funny, sharp-witted and all around enjoyable, if not too damn sexy for her mental health, she had to wonder.

"Lunch tomorrow," he said on the fourth day. "At a restaurant this time. With food someone else prepares."

She went still. "Just you and me?"

"Yep."

"As in...a date?"

"Yep."

"But we're not dating."

He looked at her.

"We're not!"

"I'm not asking you to grow old with me, Dimi. Just have lunch. It won't be something you haven't done before."

So why did she feel like a trembling virgin? "Um..."

"Yes or no."

"I, uh...okay. Yes." And all she could think was, she'd live to regret this, big time.

But she didn't. They had lunch.

They had dinner—three nights running.

"This wasn't a date," she told him on the fourth night.

Again, he looked at her.

"This isn't a relationship," she told him on the seventh night when he walked her to her door.

And he just smiled.

THE WRAPAROUND DRESS was Suzie's idea. It took Dimi forever to figure out all the various little places to tuck and wrap so she was finally completely covered in a light but vibrantly colored Indian silk.

"Gorgeous," Suzie declared, backing up, studying her with a critical eye. "Just double knot that tie," she said, pointing to the one at Dimi's right hip, which by some miracle kept the entire ensemble together and her body decently covered.

"If I double tie it, I'll never get out of it."

They both studied Dimi's reflection in the mirror. It was an earthy, sexy, fun look that definitely worked. It was relatively conservative, if one discounted the wicked hint of a length of leg and the low dipping neckline.

"Just be careful," Suzie said, frowning at the knot on Dimi's hip.

Famous last words.

On the set only half an hour later, while explaining to both the camera and Mitch the complicated process of layering the ingredients for her special enchilada mix, Dimi skimmed around the counter, hands full, mouth going a mile a minute, and caught herself on one of the loose tiles on the corner.

Right at hip level. Which meant that delicate Indian silk, and the knot that had so worried Suzie, loosened.

Then gave completely.

Later Dimi would console herself with the fact that most people had a phobia of losing their clothes in front of their peers. It was why so many had nightmares of going to school without their clothes on. Dimi had had this nightmare herself, plenty of times.

As it was, standing there in front of a live camera, hands full, mouth open in shock, looking at herself as her dress fell away from her body, Dimi felt nothing but the horror of what tomorrow's headlines would be.

Sex Kitten Corrupts Innocent Viewers During Family Hour.

Whirling her back to the camera, Dimi dropped the dish in her hand to the counter and grabbed the material, wrapping it around herself as she heard Mitch order a cut to commercial break.

Good. Commercial. That was really good.

"Trouble?"

She wasn't ready to turn and look at the face that went along with that extraordinary voice. She just wasn't. But when she continued to fumble with the new knot—which she'd double and triple tie, dammit—a set of big, warm hands firmly turned her around.

"If you laugh at me, I swear," she said in a warning tone, "I'll—"

"I'm not going to laugh," Mitch assured her grimly as he shoved her hands away and took care of the knot himself. "I might beg, but I won't laugh."

"What would *you* beg for? You're not the one who flashed her plain white cotton underwear to the entire world."

"Maybe not. But baby, there's nothing plain about that underwear you're wearing, trust me on this."

His face was tight in a grimace she would have thought was pain, only he hadn't hurt himself. So that pain must be...yep, definitely she'd gotten to him, and good. Enough to make a grown man want to beg.

It made her public humiliation only slightly bearable.

"No one saw anything," Leo called, his eyes glued to the repeat of the take he was watching on the monitor as he spoke. "Thank my quick trigger finger for that, sweet cakes."

"Really? Oh, Leo, I could kiss you!" Dimi declared.

Leo looked thrilled until he caught Mitch's glare. "Um...you have a minute left of commercial time." He scrambled out of sight.

Mitch's fingers were still working the dress, quickly and efficiently figuring out the complicated mess in a quarter of the time it had taken her. He lifted his head and pierced her with a look of such unadulterated heat she went weak. "Thank you," she said.

"I'm coming over tonight."

At his near growl, a shiver of a thrill shot through her. "I'm busy."

"Doing what? Devising new ways to torture me?"

"No. I...have to wash my hair."

Slowly he shook his head. "We need to talk."

"Talk?" Okay, she could do that. Maybe. Probably. "That would be okay, I guess. Just talking."

"Yeah. Among other things." And then he walked away, leaving her clinging to the counter for balance in a world where there was no balance to be had.

# 10

WHAT HAD HAPPENED to casual? Everything was supposed to be casual! But Mitch had no illusions as he drove to Dimi's town house that night and sat on his bike, staring at the lights, staring past the place to the lake and the dancing of the moonlight across the whitecaps.

He'd come for sex.

Talking not required.

He wasn't sure exactly when he'd changed his mind and decided he had to have her, but it was a foregone conclusion now.

Even though he'd be leaving for Los Angeles in less than a week. He was ready to go.

After this, that is. After he went inside and hauled Dimi into his arms and gave them both what they'd been panting after for weeks.

Yeah, then he'd feel better.

Sure of it, he got off the bike and headed up the path. He faltered twice, but then figured with any luck Dimi would come to her senses, remember her asinine no-men rule and not let him within ten feet of her, anyway.

DIMI STOOD inside her kitchen, cooking with a frenzy she knew to be sheer panic mingled with wild hope. She set a Hershey's kiss on top of a sugar cookie, gluing it there with frosting, taking the extra time to lick the knife.

She set the useless knife on the growing stack of other useless knives and grabbed a clean one out of the drawer.

Her last one. How had that happened?

She refused to admit or dwell on the fact that she'd taken twenty-three licks of frosting or exactly how many fat grams that might equal.

She also refused to allow herself to look at the clock again, as she'd been looking every ten seconds or so, driving herself crazy. But she peeked, anyway, pretending to be checking on Brownie, who was fast asleep in her hut.

Seven o'clock.

Surely if Mitch had meant it, he'd have been here by now.

But what if he showed up, looking all rough and tough, wanting to talk, among other things?

Just remembering the kiss they'd shared was enough to have her sucking in a shaky breath.

She couldn't remember the last time she'd been kissed that way, so intimately it had been like making love. And if he kissed that good, she could only imagine how good he'd be at all the other stuff, the stuff that most guys were in a hurry to get past just to get to the end.

She had a feeling Mitch wouldn't be in a hurry to get past anything.

She pressed a hand to her racing heart and spread chocolate frosting all over her blouse. But that's what she got for creating cookies and thinking of Mitch at the same time.

Shaking her head, she bent to her task once again, carefully spreading frosting over the next cookie. A knock came at her back door.

She dropped the knife and went very still.

Knock, knock.

She nearly jumped out of her skin. She went to the back door and put a hand on the knob. No need for this heart-pounding anticipation, not when it was probably just Cami wanting some cookies.

"Dimi." The voice coming through the wood was deep and husky and almost unbearably familiar.

Not Cami.

She jerked her hand from the knob, then reached for it again. Then stood there frozen.

"Dimi? Can I come in?"

Yes. No. Yes. "I don't know."

He made a small sound, one of understanding, amusement. Desire.

It was the last that had her fisting the knob again. Shaking, she opened the door. "I thought maybe you were Cami. You know, for food. And then I thought, no, Cami wouldn't be showing up this late, not when she has Tanner, and so all these cookies are going to go to waste. Or into my stomach, neither of which really appeals, and—"

Mercifully, he shut her up by stepping inside, sweeping her into his arms and covering her mouth with his. His lips were as firm as his body, which was pressed so satisfyingly to hers. As he'd turned her world on its axis, she had to clutch at his shirt for support, but still, thankfully, he kissed her.

And kissed her.

When he finally pulled back, he looked down and smiled. "You taste like chocolate."

Dazed, she could only nod.

"Cookies, huh?" As if he hadn't just kissed her stupid, he grabbed one off the counter and popped it into his mouth. "Mmm, good." His eyes darkened when they lit on her again. "Not as good as you, though. Come here, Dimi."

*Oh, boy.* "I'm...sticky." She backed up. "I've got to go wash up."

"I don't mind a little sticky."

"Good, because your shirt is a mess. I'm sorry about that. I'll be right back."

When he looked at himself, at the shirt she'd personally smeared with frosting, she took the chance to bail. Down the hall she ran, like a chicken, shutting herself in the bathroom.

She'd been in a hurry that morning, so it was a mess. Makeup was scattered across the countertop. A box of tampons, not in use at the moment, was precariously perched by the sink. So was her shower cap, for those miracle mornings when washing her hair wasn't a necessity. She'd left the toilet lid up and the cap off the toothpaste, reminding her what Cami had always claimed.

She'd make a better husband than a wife.

Which was convenient, really, because no one wanted her as a wife.

The mirror above the sink reflected a rosy-cheeked, glassy-eyed, wet-mouthed, incredibly ravaged-looking woman she hardly recognized. "What are you doing?" she asked that woman.

"What we've been heading toward since that very first day."

Mitch. He'd pushed open the door she hadn't locked and come up behind her, meeting her gaze in the mirror.

"I'm...very busy," she said.

"I can see that."

His chest brushed her back. Her heart beat even faster, and was joined by a tightening from deep within. Lust to the tenth degree, she figured. Then he touched her hair, ran his fingers through the long strands in a way that made her want to stretch and purr like a cat. He eased the heavy mass aside and bent, putting his mouth to the incredibly sensitive spot beneath her ear.

Her knees wobbled, and she grabbed the porcelain sink for all it was worth. "Mitch—"

His hands found her hips, eased them to the juncture between his so that she could feel exactly what was happening inside him, as well.

She was still trying to catch her breath over that when he slid his hands up, up, up, splaying with characteristic bluntness past the chocolate stains and over her breasts. His mouth was busy nibbling her neck, and his fingers occupied themselves, as well, unbuttoning her blouse and slipping inside to unclasp her front-hook bra.

"I'm sticky," she said inanely, watching with utter fascination in the mirror as he slipped her blouse down her shoulders. Then her bra, too, until she was standing there nude from the waist up with nothing to say except a little squeak when he cupped the weight of her breasts, his fingers stroking her nipples to two hard, begging peaks. "Really sticky," she murmured weakly, shamelessly pressing her hips against his.

"I happen to like sticky. You're so beautiful, Dimi," he said, shocking her, not because of his words, but because of the look in his eyes, as if he really, truly meant them, and not just as a line to get her into bed.

"Watch me touch you," he said, dragging hot, wet, openmouthed kisses along her shoulder while his fingers continued to drive her to the very edge.

"I need to wash up," she said on a low moan.

"I'll help you. In a minute." The rasp of a zipper came next, hers, and then her skirt pooled on the floor, leaving her in nothing but her plain white serviceable panties, which naturally made him smile.

She covered them with her hands, which he

gently but firmly moved away. "You're the sexiest woman I've ever met, and I love your underwear." His eyes gleamed with affection and a hunger that took her breath. "Now let's take them off."

"I—" But nothing else came out, except for maybe another squeak as he skimmed them down her thighs to puddle around her ankles on top of her lonely skirt, blouse and bra.

Which pretty much left her entirely naked, facing a mirror, in the embrace of a fully clothed, fully aroused man, whose hands were driving her directly to heaven and beyond.

He danced those very clever, very talented fingers down her quivering belly, his mouth on her neck, her shoulders, everywhere, and then suddenly his fingers were between her thighs, softly stroking exactly where she needed them, starting a rhythm that made her cry out helplessly. She grabbed for support, and in the process knocked the box of tampons over, scattering them into the sink, onto the floor, on top of her clothes at their feet.

Staring at the paper-covered columns did one thing—it allowed some sanity to return. Along with a good amount of humility.

Mitch let out a soft laugh and lifted her face.

"So you use tampons. More than half the female population uses tampons."

At the word coming out of his mouth, *tampon*, such a feminine word, she groaned.

And he just laughed. Then kissed her, kissed her until she managed to topple some of her makeup to join the tampons.

"And so you're a slob," he added, lifting his head and looking around at the havoc. "And yeah, okay, you do own a dorky shower cap. I just don't care, Dimi." He turned her to face him, cupping her jaw in his big, warm hands, waiting with barely restrained patience until she opened her eyes to look at him. "I don't care about any of it except sinking into you, hearing you cry out my name, feeling your legs wrap around my hips and knowing I can't tell where you end and I start."

A tremor started at the region of her heart.

"I just want you," he whispered. "All of you." His hands skimmed down her body, renewing the flame as he eased her onto the counter, stepping between her legs so she had no choice but to wrap herself around him.

"Want me back," he murmured, sinking his fingers into her hair, placing his mouth over her jaw, her lips, her throat, renewing the heat and need in less than two seconds flat. "Say it."

Not a problem, since every inch of her shook with the need. "I want you back." And because she did, because she wanted him with everything she had, she tugged at his black leather jacket, which he shrugged off to join her discarded things. "Why are you wearing so many clothes?" she demanded, going to work on the buttons of his shirt.

Grinning, he added his hands to the mix, and then he was as wonderfully, gloriously naked as she.

She couldn't take her eyes off him. "Wow." She ran her hands over his leanly muscled chest, his flat belly, his amazingly strong shoulders, anywhere and everywhere except the one place on his body that was currently nudging her in the belly because...well, quite frankly, *that* made her very nervous.

He wasn't nearly as shy, and in less than a minute he had her hot and shaking and desperately whimpering, but when he brought out a condom from the pants he'd shucked to the floor, she once again came to her senses, because for all her man hunting, for all her whining, it had been awhile since the actual act, and even then it hadn't been anything to write home about.

And here was Mitch, standing in all his very naked splendor, and...he was huge.

"I know what you're thinking," he said, tearing open the little packet.

She couldn't take her eyes off him as he donned the condom. "I doubt it," she said, thinking there was something inherently wicked about watching a man touch himself.

Lifting her chin with his finger, he kissed her, soft and sweet and somehow unbearably sexy. "I'm going to fit."

She swallowed hard, nodded and prepared herself, but Mitch ran his hand down her body, over her breasts, her belly, to the throbbing flesh between her legs, teasing, stroking, until she couldn't remember what she'd been hesitant about...until he removed his hand, wrapped her legs around his waist, grabbed her bottom in his big, warm hands and sank into her.

It was so utterly delicious, and she was so utterly close, she could do nothing but clutch him and squeeze her eyes shut, waiting for him to move, waiting to be dropped off the cliff into ecstasy.

But he didn't do anything except hold himself really, really still.

"Dimi."

*Please,* was her only coherent thought.

"Dimi?"

With some effort she opened her eyes.

"Okay?" he whispered.

Okay? Couldn't he see she wouldn't be okay until he gave her that orgasm? The one she needed above all else including air? Darn it, she didn't want to talk, she wanted action!

"Baby, am I hurting you?"

"Oh, for heaven's sake," she said, the words bursting out, thrusting her hips up to meet his. "Don't talk, just do me!"

Startled, he stared at her for one heartbeat, then let out a rough laugh. "Absolutely." And bowing his back, he began a deep pumping with just the right rhythm, so that it was as natural as breathing to cry out his name, to toss her head back and explode right out of herself.

Registered blind, deaf and dumb as she was, she hardly heard his cry. She certainly couldn't respond, couldn't do anything, until finally her senses returned and she realized Mitch was leaning over her, muscles quaking, breathing every bit as harshly as she.

She was just giddy enough to open her mouth and let her first thought fly. "I'm definitely revoking my no-man rule for you."

He jerked, then stared at her. "What?"

The horror in his gaze definitely brought her the rest of the way to earth. *Crashing* to earth.

Without an air bag, no less.

"Nothing," she said stiffly. Because she wouldn't repeat it, not even at the threat of death, not with him looking at her like that, as if she'd started speaking in tongues. "Nothing at all."

She shoved him away, opened the bathroom door and kicked out their pile of clothes, perfectly aware half of them were hers, but she was having a moment here. "I'd like for you to go now." *Go fall off a cliff, damn you.*

"Dimi—" He reached for her, but she backed up and grabbed the only weapon available to her, a tampon. Still, she wielded it with honor. "Out."

He very wisely did not comment on the tampon in his face. "We're going to have to discuss this."

"Over my dead body."

Then, unladylike as it was, she pushed the

beautifully naked man over the threshold of the bathroom and slammed the door.

This time she locked it.

Her only regret was not having a freezer in the bathroom. She sank to the edge of the tub and thought about that. With a freezer, she'd at least be able to have ice cream at her own pity party.

# 11

"CAMI." Dimi gripped her cell phone tightly. "I know it's the crack of dawn, I'm sorry."

"What's the matter?" Cami croaked, obviously half asleep. "It must be bad. This is way too early for anything but very bad."

"I terrified a man in my bathroom last night."

"What did you do, threaten him with perfumed shampoo?"

"Funny." Dimi blew out a breath, merged into traffic and headed toward the studio with what felt like bricks in her stomach. "I told Mitch I was revoking my no-man rule. You should have seen him. He turned green, like he needed to puke. Flattering, huh?"

"Dimi, did you do this before or after you knocked it out?"

"Who said anything about knocking it out?"

"In the bathroom...*please*. What else would you guys do in there together? So...did you? In the shower?"

"On the counter," she muttered, swiping a hand down her face as her sister cackled with wicked delight. "Listen, you're missing the point here."

"No, I'm not. You revoked your no-man rule in a moment of passion. Understandable. There's not a woman on the planet who wouldn't get it. A man, however—they're a different breed. They don't want to hear such things while they're still breathing like a racehorse. They need to process their emotions, and honey, it takes them awhile. They are men, after all."

"Great. In the meantime I'm left feeling like an idiot."

"Oh, no. You can still turn this around," Cami promised. "All you have to do is stick to your plan to drive him crazy, remember? Don't lose focus here, Sis. Sidetrack him with your body, and he'll forget that you terrified him in the bathroom with all that after talk he's not ready for."

"Well, dammit, that's just embarrassing."

"Trust me on this one, Sis. You're still in the driver's seat."

BY THE TIME Dimi arrived at the studio, she'd come around to Cami's way of thinking. Mostly because she could only wallow in humiliation for so long. She had to do something, and it might as well be to continue to drive Mitch as crazy as he'd driven her.

If he thought she'd let loose of her passion before for the show's sake, watch out! She'd learned her powers well. After all, she'd had the best teacher—him. Tease for tease, she was going to give it back. Starting today.

She was woman, hear her roar.

A good amount of the wind went out of her sails when she got to the set and heard the latest rumor. Mitch was leaving in just two days.

Two days.

Okay. Good. No more being on edge throughout the day, wondering if he was going to look at her, touch her, make her crazy with wanting.

No more fretting over their future, because obviously there was nothing between the two of them except for a slightly out of the ordinary heat they couldn't control to save their lives.

No problem.

She got ready for the day's show, and when Mitch came in with only two moments to spare, without his usual time to talk to her, she smiled grimly. *He's just one big chicken,* she decided, which really worked in her favor and gave her even more courage.

She waited until the countdown. At the fifteen-second mark she sidled in close to him, missing her own mark to stand nearly on his toes. Sliding her hands up his body, she cupped his face and brought his ear down to her mouth, all on the guise of whispering some last-minute direction. "I'm not wearing plain white cotton panties today," she whispered. "I'm not wearing panties at all."

Whipping his head to face her, his eyes wide, he opened his mouth, but she put a finger to his lips. "Our little secret."

*"Five seconds!"*

Their lower bodies were hidden from the camera by the counter they stood behind, which gave her the courage to slide her hand down his spine as she stepped away. Down his back to his butt, which she squeezed.

He jumped and looked at her as if she were an alien.

She winked, and when she noticed his very unmistakable erection beneath his nicely fitted slacks, she grinned, satisfied.

"You're on!" shouted the director, pointing at them.

"Welcome to *Food Time*." Dimi stepped around the counter and reached a hand for Mitch to do the same.

He pulled his hand back and shook his head. It was the first time she'd seen him not quite in control.

She knew perfectly well why he didn't want to step around the corner and show off his erection, but it still made her want to giggle. "Shy today, Mitch?" she teased. "A bit silly after all we've been through together on the show, don't you think?"

For once completely speechless, he studied the ingredients she had scattered on the countertop and refused to speak.

She bit back her laughter and faced the camera. "Today we're creating sauerkraut balls, but first we need to whip up the frosting for our dessert so it can sit and thicken." Ignoring Mitch completely, she curved one hand around a large bowl, with the other whipping the contents of her frosting. "I chose to do this by hand because there's a slim chance I can work off some of the calories before I even eat the thing," she said, smiling as she worked the whisk, and in the process shaking her tush wildly from side to side. "What do you think, Mitch?" she asked over her shoulder, turning her head to smile at him sweetly, knowing that by standing behind the counter, as he was, he was getting quite the show.

All shocking intensity, he just looked at her, his dark, dark eyes promising passion, mutual pleasure…and retribution.

Somehow she managed to break eye contact. She worked diligently preparing the sauerkraut balls, though she was very aware of Mitch's gaze on her.

*He's leaving,* she reminded herself ruthlessly. *Remember that.* "Don't forget to preheat the fryer for the balls," she told the camera.

Mitch stirred and lifted a brow.

*Do not blush,* she instructed herself. *This is all about revenge.* "Roll each ball in flour." She demonstrated, and had never in her life been so painfully aware of being watched as she was with Mitch there, tall, dark, silent and simmering with tension. "Then dip your balls into the egg sauce, letting them drain slowly into your bowl."

"Pretty hard on those poor guys, aren't you?" Mitch murmured, wincing when she pinched the ball into shape.

"Roll it into the bread crumbs," she said, trying to ignore him.

He leaned over her shoulder, once again grimacing. "Hey, treat those things with more care, would you?"

"After the bread crumbs, drop it into the hot oil."

"Ouch."

"Fry for two to three minutes until golden brown."

"Whatever happened to tender?"

She refused to look at him. "Serve immediately, or they'll wither."

Mitch broke into laughter.

When they cut to commercial break, Dimi whirled on him. "I don't appreciate the comments."

"I don't appreciate the choice of today's menu. Frying balls, Dimi? Gee, is there a message in there somewhere? And what was that with the frosting, huh? Are you *trying* to drive me crazy?"

"It's a short drive," she told him, sounding superior.

"Oh, yeah?"

"*Yeah.*"

"What's your problem, anyway?"

"What's *my* problem?" They were nose to nose, and nearly yelling. "Nothing. I have no problem."

"Could have fooled me."

"Okay, how about this? When exactly were you going to tell me you were leaving in two days? Maybe after tonight's trip to my house to see what you could...*cook* up?"

That took him aback. His voice was much quieter. "I meant to tell you last night, but you sidetracked me."

"Because I forced you into the bathroom and had my way with you?"

"Well, you didn't exactly kick me out! Not until you were finished, anyway."

Most of the crew had given them a wide berth, though they were watching every move from just off the stage in utter fascination.

"That's what this is about, right?" Mitch said. "Last night."

"Oh, you're quick, Mr. Ace Producer, I'll give you that."

His eyes were fire, his jaw tight. His entire body was tense and practically shimmering with barely restrained...something.

God, she hoped it was lust. She so wanted

them to be even in this amazing, overwhelming frustration.

"Dammit, Dimi..." He shoved his hands through his hair and finally seemed to realize they had an audience. Grabbing her arm, he pulled her into a relatively private corner of the set. "Last night you kicked me out when you were done with me like unwanted garbage."

"What was I supposed to do? When I said I was revoking my no-man rule, you nearly fainted."

"Yes, because you've been so adamant about that damn rule. I'd grown to count on it to keep us sane, because we both know how this is going to end, Dimi. I'm going back to Los Angeles." He stopped, frustration and heat pouring off him. "Now is a hell of a time to tell me about the rule thing not being valid."

"Maybe I just decided. Did you ever think of that?" She stopped and looked at him. "Mitch, why didn't you tell me how soon you were leaving? You should have told me."

He looked at her with such...longing, it stole her breath. "It's not that easy."

"So last night was a goodbye?" The word hurt, and her voice caught.

His gaze softened, and so did his voice. "Last night was a necessity, and you know it."

"Yes, because you thought you were safe from the clutches of anything serious."

"Okay. Yes. Yes, I thought I was safe from anything serious."

Stunned, she stared at him. God, the truth hurt. She was hugely sorry she'd asked for that truth. "You're a jerk."

"Oh, fine. Now I'm a jerk." He tossed up his hands. "I can't keep up with you!"

"It's not that hard!"

"Are you kidding?" He ticked off his complaints on his fingers. "You *don't* want a man, you *do* want a man. You like being the serious queen, yet you like being the sexy chef. Look at you. Today you're—" He waved a hand down her very snug, very chic, very sexy pantsuit. "Looking like that, and licking your lips at me, talking in my ear about not wearing any underwear—I'd like to know how a man is supposed to concentrate on anything knowing that! And you even grabbed my butt!"

"I didn't mean to."

"But you did!"

"I know," she said miserably.

"I can't take it, Dimi. I just can't."

She'd wanted him every bit as teased and tormented as she was, and it appeared she'd been successful.

What now?

She hadn't a clue. But she couldn't leave it like this. There was only one thing left to do.

Call Cami, of course. "Hold on," she said to Mitch. "I need a second."

"Now?"

"It's important." Turning her back, she pulled out her cell phone and dialed. Thankfully Cami picked up.

"Okay, I'm in a bit of a bind," Dimi whispered, plugging her other ear with a finger. "So think quick. I've done what we discussed and I have him as frustrated as I am." She glanced at Mitch over her shoulder, then whipped around because he was watching her with a growing intensity she didn't know how to face. "Now what?" she pleaded. "Help me."

Before Cami could answer, Mitch grabbed the phone, pulled out the battery and tossed it over his shoulder. "You're on your own in this, baby. Look at me." He turned her around. "Look at me and tell me what you want from me, because I'm confused as hell and need a clue."

Dimi looked into his glimmering eyes and

knew the truth. She knew what she wanted from him. She wanted him to love her.

As much as she'd come to love him.

Talk about screw-ups.

''You're on the air in two seconds!''

Mitch was staring at her, his breathing erratic, his expression charged. Lord, he was magnificent, but he was leaving, and he didn't want her to want him for anything other than what they'd already had.

Saved by her own show, Dimi went to her mark, intending to go on with life.

# *12*

---

It was very male of him, he knew this, but all Mitch could concentrate on was Dimi's lack of underwear.

And that had been nearly two days ago.

He was dying to ask her if she'd spoken the truth about not wearing panties, or better yet, to find out for himself, but given the dark expression on her face whenever he caught a glimpse of her, he figured it was a bad idea.

In fact, everything about her was a bad idea. Coaxing her out of her seriousness. The new and wild clothes. Showing her the passion that simmered just beneath her surface.

Now everything she did made him want her all the more. Every look, every touch, every word. He'd been reduced to nothing more than one big, aching hormone.

Hell of a spot to be in for a man who'd been there, done that and figured there were no surprises left to be had.

He'd told himself all he wanted from Dimi had been sex, but really, it was far more complicated than that. He wanted in her head. He wanted to share her hopes and dreams. And dammit, he wanted another chance to have her naked in his arms, to make more wild, passionate love.

*Love.*

How was that for terror?

Because it was what she seemed to want, and because he had no idea what the hell *he* wanted, once the show had been taped he stayed as far away from Dimi as he could.

She obliged him by returning the favor.

It should have made him happy as a clam, knowing he could leave Truckee, that he'd not broken any promises or left behind unfinished business.

So why then did his business feel extremely unfinished? It shouldn't have. He'd had his last day at *Food Time* today. The staff had given him a pizza party, which was where he stood now, saying goodbye to each and every one of them.

He'd hugged Gracie.

He'd shaken Ted's hand.

He'd smiled until his jaw ached, and now Leo came up.

Mitch thrust out his hand, but Leo threw his arms around Mitch's neck. "It was a wild ride," Leo said tearfully. "We'll never forget you."

Mitch wondered if he was going to have to stand there all night patting Leo's back but Suzie tugged him free. Then she gave him her most direct stare. "You're really going," she said, shaking her head, hugging him tight. "Thanks for saving my job. Thanks for saving the show. Thanks for everything. Especially for putting all the life and spunk into Dimi's eyes."

He closed his for a moment. "I didn't do that. She did."

Suzie's smile went sad as she pulled back. "Denial is a sad thing in a man, Mitch." Squeezing his hand, she went to the food table and grabbed another slice of pizza.

Which pretty much left Dimi. No one had gone home, which meant they had quite the audience, as per the norm. No one felt the need to give them any privacy at all. In fact, as Dimi finally acknowledged him and drifted toward him, everyone seemed to shift closer in anticipation.

She smiled at him, a very nice smile, really, but he could see right through it to all the stuff beneath, and suddenly he didn't care who was watching. Reaching out, he took her two hands in his. "Hey," he said softly.

"So this is it," she murmured. "Goodbye."

"Yeah."

"Goodbye, Mitch."

"I'll miss you, Dimi."

She nodded. "You'll be missed here, too."

"By you?"

Their audience seemed to hold their collective breath, but Dimi didn't waver. She looked him right in the eyes and nodded. "Yes." Then she leaned close, kissed him softly, right on the lips. But before he could so much as taste her, she was gone.

Like a fool, he raced to the door, but she'd vanished. Tempting as it was to chase after her, he didn't. Mostly because he didn't know what to say or how to say it.

"Fool."

Startled, he looked around and found Suzie at his side, but she snorted in disgust and left, too.

Unsettled, and feeling as if he'd forgotten to do something really important, he went to the cabin the show had rented for him during his stay and packed up his stuff. It wasn't difficult, and it all fit into one duffel bag.

A sad commentary on his life.

A knock on his door surprised him. It was late, and he'd already said goodbye to everyone. He wasn't feeling friendly.

But when he opened the door he got an even bigger surprise.

"Just me," Dimi said with a shaky smile.

She stood beneath the faint glow of the porch light, wearing jeans and a sweater, looking lovely and vulnerable and sexy all at the same time. So much that he just stared at her stupidly. "Hi."

"Did you teach my hamster to beg for food?"

So much for her being here to claim her undying devotion. "Yes."

"I've had her for two years, and she's never done anything but stare at me."

"I guess it takes the right touch to coax someone out of her seriousness."

"Yeah." She looked at her shoes, then into his face. "Can I come in?"

He stepped aside, and when she brushed past him, her hair catching on him, her scent filling his senses, he nearly forgot to shut the door behind her.

"I just wanted to clear some stuff up," she said, walking into his living room, turning to face him. "You know, before you leave. First of all, I'm sorry."

"For what?"

"For seeking revenge on you for making me, um—" She blushed. "Hot for you. I know you were just doing your job, bringing out the sexiness of the show and teaching me how to do it, and I'm sorry I turned on you like that. I wanted to make you hot back and…well, it was juvenile. I can see that now."

Suddenly he felt very friendly. And very happy she'd come to see him. "I don't want your apology." He stepped toward her, so relieved at having this last chance at seeing her again he felt weak.

"You…don't?" When he took another step toward her, her eyes darkened. "What do you want?"

"Isn't that just the million-dollar question?" He tipped his head back and pretended to ponder. "What do I want? Hmm… How about I want to know if you're as scared as me that this is over?"

"I—"

He put his hands on her hips and tugged her close. "How about I want to know if you really came here to apologize or to satisfy this unquenchable need we have for each other?"

"Um…"

"And how about I want to know if you meant

it the other day when you told me you weren't wearing any damn panties, and are you wearing any now?''

Her eyes flashed, and she slid her arms around his neck, putting her mouth on his before he could ask her the rest, before he could tell her he'd discovered the L word for the first time in far too many years and that he wanted to know if she could possibly feel the same.

He wanted to tell her he didn't want to leave—what a joke that was—but he really didn't want to go, he wanted to stay forever and become a small-town man who put his nose in everyone else's business.

But he couldn't say a word because she'd opened her mouth on his, deepening the kiss, and every single thought flew right out the window.

Then she wriggled and wriggled until she had enough room to yank his shirt out of his pants and over his head. Before he could so much as blink, she'd sunk to her knees before him and was working on his belt, which she promptly tossed over her shoulder.

Her fingers danced over his raging erection as she looked at him coyly. ''I'd better be careful with the zipper.''

''Yeah, you'd—'' His words were choked off

because she tugged down the rest of his clothing, leaving him with no blood left in his brain with which to formulate a sentence, much less a thought.

"There," she said cheerfully, sitting back on her heels and looking at him with sleepy, sexy eyes. "You're the first one naked this time. I think I like that. A lot."

With a growl, he lunged at her, sprawling them across the carpet. It didn't take him long to unbutton her sweater and tackle her jeans off, where he learned she had indeed gone commando. Rolling, wrestling, laughing, he finally caught her beneath him, grinning at her like the love-struck fool he was.

"You got anything more for me than that smile, Mitch?"

"Are you kidding?" In case she hadn't noticed his erection to beat all erections, he nudged her with it.

She sucked in a sharp breath. "What do you plan to do with that?"

"You'll see."

"Might I suggest you hurry?"

"Suggestion considered." And finally, finally, he sunk into her glorious body.

Her smile faded, and so did his. Her quiet moan echoed his. And they clutched at each other, his favorite part, feeling her nails bite into him, seeing her dazed, just-as-gone gaze meet his.

Mitch was damn glad it wasn't just him feeling this way. He was so glad it was almost enough to make him weep, but then she arched up and took him even deeper within her and he was lost.

Completely lost.

"Hurry," she whispered again, and he was all too happy to oblige.

HE LAY on his back, staring at the ceiling, a contented, warm, sated Dimi curled at his side. "Okay," he said. "We're definitely even."

With a groan, she came up on an elbow to look at him. Her hair fell into his face, and though he blew it out, it hit him again.

He thought that just maybe he'd be content to have her hair in his face for the rest of his life. He should tell her that. Wanted to tell her that.

But she was looking at him with a good amount of wariness, and he sighed.

"What do you mean," she said, "we're even?"

"I played low and dirty to get you to change your persona for the show. Remember?"

"Definitely. You teased and tormented me and basically made my life a living hell."

"Uh-huh. Your show became wildly popular, you got a new contract and a great raise and you found you loved this wilder side of yourself, you poor, poor abused baby. Having me...what was it you said? Tease and torment you. Kiss and touch you. And you hated every minute of it, I know."

She glared at him, making him laugh. "Don't give me that look," he said. "Because in return you played low and dirty to drive me crazy with lust, and you know it. So we're even. And now..." He stroked a hand down her slim back, loving the feel of her against him. "And now it's time for a compromise so we don't kill each other."

"Why?" Her eyes went a little flat. "You're leaving, remember?"

"Yeah, about that." He sat, slid his hands up her arms and tried not to get distracted by the sight she made sitting there tousled and naked and annoyed. "That's the compromise part."

# 13

DIMI LEAPT UP. She knew what was coming. A man's idea of compromise meant he got to go back to Los Angeles and send for her whenever he needed his itch scratched.

Or maybe he'd show up here every once in awhile, all dark and beautiful and ready to melt her with just one wicked smile.

And she would melt, she had no doubt. All he had to do was crook one little finger and she'd drop to the floor in a boneless puddle of Jell-O.

Pathetic, that was her. Feeling very naked, she searched for her clothes and came up with Mitch's shirt. Good enough.

Mitch stood, too, and reached out to touch her cheek. "It's on inside out."

So was her heart. Darn it, how had this happened? How had she fallen for a guy who could never take her seriously?

"Dimi..." He took her hands in his and

stilled her movements. "Did I scare you when I said it was time for a compromise?"

"Of course not." Scoffing, she broke away and went searching for her panties.

"You didn't wear any, remember?" Mitch sighed when she hauled on her jeans. He reached for his pants. "You going to answer me, Dimi?"

"You don't scare me."

"The word compromise sure did." He put his hands on her shoulders and made her look at him. "What did you think I meant, I wonder?" He searched her gaze and shook his head. "It was a doozy, whatever you came up with."

"I need to get going."

"Uh-huh." He nodded companionably. "I understand. I know the feeling all too well. Things take a wrong turn or something tugs on your heart, just run like hell. It's been my escape choice for two years, as well."

"I'm not running away."

"Liar," he chided softly, holding her still when she would have torn away. "Why don't you just listen then, since you won't talk to me? Can you do that, I wonder?"

No. God, no. "You're the one who's leaving," she said desperately.

A sad smile tugged at the corners of his

mouth. "Yeah. Which brings me back to the whole compromise thing." He brought her to his couch and sank down on it, tugging her down, as well, so they faced each other.

Only he wasn't wearing a shirt, and his hair looked as if someone had run their fingers through it—which of course she had—and her poor overwhelmed senses could only imagine how it would be to still be on the floor all tangled up with him.

Bottom line, she wanted him, darn it, and her heart felt as if it was going to burst, and she couldn't believe she'd shown up at his house like this. She should have left it alone after their pizza goodbye, but no, she'd had to see him one more time.

"I don't know what's going on inside that head of yours," he said, gently tapping her temple. "But you look as if your puppy just got run over by a Mack truck."

The lump in her throat grew to enormous proportions. How was she supposed to do this, say goodbye and not let him know how much it hurt?

She couldn't, she just couldn't, so she simply sat there, tears welling in her eyes, unable to speak a word without falling apart.

"Oh, Dimi." He closed his eyes tight and then opened them. They were suspiciously bright. "I'm not good at this serious stuff. But I don't want to leave. Crazy as it sounds, I like this too-damn-small town, and I like the show, and all the people involved in it, but most of all, Dimi, this is about you."

She blinked in surprise, and a tear fell. Scrubbing at it impatiently, she gaped at him. "Me?"

"Yeah. I was hoping you'd agree to meet me halfway on this thing."

"Thing?"

"You know, what we have between us. Look, I thought maybe you could teach me how to get a little serious once in awhile. And maybe I could teach you to let your hair down, so to speak, and not just for work. We could meet halfway."

Her heart leapt straight into her throat, but she was afraid to put seed to the wild hope. "Halfway," she whispered. "As in once in awhile you come up from southern California, or I come down from northern California?"

"As in I never leave."

"That's not much of a compromise," she told him, nearly giddy. Was it possible? Could this work?

"No, I realize that." He reached for her hand. "But that's me being selfish because I can't see us in Los Angeles. I can't see us anywhere but here."

*Us,* she thought. *My God, he's using the us word.*

"The compromise part comes next," he said, looking directly into her eyes with a touching, endearing uncertainty. "It's where I tell you I am wildly, madly, helplessly in love with you, and you agree to try to feel that way back for me."

"You mean…"

"I love you, Dimi. I want to be with you forever, through white serviceable underwear and oysters and tampons and everything. I want it all." He let out a slow, purposeful breath. "Now say something back. Please. You're killing me, just looking at me all wild-eyed and repeating everything I say but saying nothing I want to hear."

"Well, I have to repeat one more thing."

He looked destroyed. "Okay."

"I love you." She smiled through her tears. "I want to be with you forever, through white serviceable underwear and oysters and tampons and everything."

The brilliance in his smile dazzled her. So did the bone-crushing hug he gave her.

"And for the record," she said, still holding him tight, "you've already taught me to loosen up quite a bit, if you'll recall. So that means really it's just teaching you to be a tad more serious. We can start with lovemaking."

Pulling back, he looked at her in surprise. "There's something wrong with my lovemaking?"

"Only that we haven't made it to a bed yet."

"Easily remedied," he said, standing and scooping her into his arms. "In fact, let's work on that immediately." He gave her a particularly naughty smile. "It might take awhile, though."

"I hope so." She loved being against him like this and snuggled closer, her imagination already off and running. "Maybe all night long?" she asked hopefully.

He laughed, then bent and kissed her. "Try for the rest of our lives, Dimi."

Her heart tipped. "Yes," she sighed, setting her head on his shoulder. "For the rest of our lives."

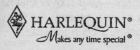

## *Harlequin invites you to walk down the aisle...*

To honor our year long celebration of weddings, we are offering an exciting opportunity for you to own the Harlequin Bride Doll. Handcrafted in fine bisque porcelain, the wedding doll is dressed for her wedding day in a cream satin gown accented by lace trim. She carries an exquisite traditional bridal bouquet and wears a cathedral-length dotted Swiss veil. Embroidered flowers cascade down her lace overskirt to the scalloped hemline; underneath all is a multi-layered crinoline.

Join us in our celebration of weddings by sending away for your own Harlequin Bride Doll. This doll regularly retails for $74.95 U.S./approx. $108.68 CDN. One doll per household. Requests must be received no later than December 31, 2001. Offer good while quantities of gifts last. Please allow 6-8 weeks for delivery. Offer good in the U.S. and Canada only. Become part of this exciting offer!

**Simply complete the order form and mail to:**
**"A Walk Down the Aisle"**

IN U.S.A
P.O. Box 9057
3010 Walden Ave.
Buffalo, NY 14269-9057

IN CANADA
P.O. Box 622
Fort Erie, Ontario
L2A 5X3

Enclosed are eight (8) proofs of purchase found in the last pages of every specially marked Harlequin series book and $3.75 check or money order (for postage and handling). Please send my Harlequin Bride Doll to:

_____
Name (PLEASE PRINT)

_____
Address                                    Apt. #

_____
City            State/Prov.            Zip/Postal Code

_____
Account # (if applicable)                **097 KIK DAEW**

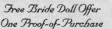

◆ **HARLEQUIN**®
*Makes any time special*®

Visit us at www.eHarlequin.com

PHWDAPOPR2

*Three sizzling love stories
by today's hottest writers
can be found in...*

# Midnight Fantasies....

## *Feel the heat!*

*Available July 2001*

### *MYSTERY LOVER—Vicki Lewis Thompson*

When an unexpected storm hits, rancher Jonas Garfield
takes cover in a nearby cave...and finds himself seduced
senseless by an enigmatic temptress who refuses to tell him
her name. All he knows is that this sexy woman wants him.
And for Jonas, that's enough—for now....

### *AFTER HOURS—Stephanie Bond*

Michael Pierce has always considered costume shop
owner Rebecca Valentine no more than an associate—
until he drops by her shop one night and witnesses the
mousy wallflower's transformation into a seductive siren.
Suddenly he's desperate to know her much better.
But which woman is the real Rebecca?

### *SHOW AND TELL—Kimberly Raye*

A naughty lingerie party. A forbidden fantasy. When Texas
bad boy Dallas Jericho finds a slip of paper left over from
the party, he is surprised—and aroused—to discover that he
is good girl Laney Merriweather's wildest fantasy. So what
can he do but show the lady what she's been missing....

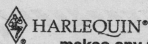

If you enjoyed what you just read,
then we've got an offer you can't resist!

# Take 2 bestselling
# love stories FREE!
# Plus get a FREE surprise gift!

**Clip this page and mail it to Harlequin Reader Service®**

**IN U.S.A.**
3010 Walden Ave.
P.O. Box 1867
Buffalo, N.Y. 14240-1867

**IN CANADA**
P.O. Box 609
Fort Erie, Ontario
L2A 5X3

**YES!** Please send me 2 free Harlequin Duets™ novels and my free surprise gift. After receiving them, if I don't wish to receive anymore, I can return the shipping statement marked cancel. If I don't cancel, I will receive 2 brand-new novels every month, before they're available in stores! In the U.S.A., bill me at the bargain price of $5.14 plus 50¢ shipping & handling per book and applicable sales tax, if any*. In Canada, bill me at the bargain price of $6.14 plus 50¢ shipping & handling per book and applicable taxes**. That's the complete price—what a great deal! I understand that accepting the 2 free books and gift places me under no obligation ever to buy any books. I can always return a shipment and cancel at any time. Even if I never buy another book from Harlequin, the 2 free books and gift are mine to keep forever.

111 HEN DC7M
311 HEN DC7N

| Name | (PLEASE PRINT) | |
| --- | --- | --- |
| Address | Apt.# | |
| City | State/Prov. | Zip/Postal Code |

\* Terms and prices subject to change without notice. Sales tax applicable in N.Y.
\*\* Canadian residents will be charged applicable provincial taxes and GST.
  All orders subject to approval. Offer limited to one per household and not valid to
  current Harlequin Duets™ subscribers.
  ® and ™ are registered trademarks of Harlequin Enterprises Limited.      DUETS01